SHADOW'S
protection

HURRICANE HEAT MC BOOK 1

I0602854

www.chellebliss.com

CHELLE BLISS

USA TODAY BESTSELLING AUTHOR

Publisher © Bliss Ink September 1st 2025
Edited by Silently Correcting Your Grammar
Proofread by Read By Rose & Shelley Charlton
Cover Design © Chelle Bliss

ONE
SHADOW

TROUBLE AIN'T the only thing blowing into town tonight.

When I roll into the parking lot of the Shady Lane Motel, the place isn't just full—there ain't a free spot to be found. I cruise right up to the glass lobby doors and park my bike in front, blocking the walkway in.

The owner of this one-star establishment, Malcolm, has got a debt payment due, and I don't give a rat's ass if it's rain or shine out there. I'm here to collect, and I'm not leaving unless I have a wad of cash in my pocket or blood on my hands. I'm ready for whatever the night brings.

I get off my bike and head inside, ignoring the security bell that chimes to alert everyone in the lobby to my arrival. A few heads turn, mostly panicked-looking tourists carrying overstuffed suitcases.

A storm has been threatening our county for the last two days. The winds picked up this afternoon, and now the news is calling for voluntary evacuations before this tropical storm turns into a full-blown hurricane. That means a shitload of traffic on the roads and a lot of people in my way.

Although I don't have time to waste, if I want Malcolm to pay back what he owes my club, I need to let him at least check in the low-rent guests who've decided Shady Lane Motel is a better option for riding out the storm than wherever it is they're coming from.

I saunter through the lobby and pretend to scan the dusty pamphlets on the decades-old rack of brochures until everyone's taken their room keys and left. The keys are the old-fashioned kind, real metal keys on cheap plastic rings with paint chipping out of the room numbers. Shady Lane ain't a place people with money—or any better options—come to stay. And I'm anxious to get what I came for and get the fuck out.

Once Malcolm and I are alone, I crack my knuckles loudly and wander over to the front counter.

"Shadow." His voice is overly enthusiastic, but there's fear underneath the fake warmth. Guys like Malcolm think if they act like we're friends, what's about to go down will happen in a friendly way.

I've got the scars on my face and knuckles to prove I won't hesitate to get a little *un*-friendly if that's what it takes to collect on a debt. I nod at him and tap two tattooed fingers on the ancient counter where a paper cup of coffee is leaking a watery brown liquid onto the already stained Formica.

"Business is booming," I say in a low voice, lifting a brow. "That's good for you."

Malcolm shrugs, and a slight sweat breaks out on his upper lip. I notice him look up at the wall, where grainy gray images from the security cameras show hallways full of customers unlocking rooms, stockpiling ice, and shoving loose change into the vending machines.

Most of the local stores closed hours ago. If Malcolm's smart, he'll lock the front doors and hunker down. But I know Malcolm. He's anything but smart.

"You believe this shit?" He motions toward the windows as if I'm here to talk about the fucking weather. "You need a place to stay, Shadow?" he asks. "I'm all sold out of rooms, but maybe we can work something—"

I silence him by slamming a fist down on the counter. "The only thing I need from you, Malcolm, is three grand. In cash. Every dollar of it. Now."

I watch the same screens Malcolm was staring at just a minute ago. Doing the math in my head fast, I know that a shithole like this selling out for the night—assuming he didn't jack up the rate just to squeeze the people trying to escape the storm—means he's definitely got what he owes me and then some.

Now the question is whether he's gonna hand it over easy. It's been a minute since I had to collect the hard way, and I roll my neck to loosen it just in case.

"Yeah, I... Right. Sure thing. I know. I got it." Malcolm's flustered and stalling for time.

I draw in a deep breath, and the stale stench of Malcolm's body odor, coffee breath, and something that reminds me of damp carpet fills my lungs. Thunder cracks outside, and all of a sudden, the rain is coming down hard. Sheets of it blur the windows and coat the glass doors behind me.

Fuck.

Searing-hot anger, fast and powerful, floods my chest. I knew I should've driven my truck today and not the bike. Riding back to the compound through this is gonna be a pain in my ass. A bigger pain in the ass than getting Malcolm to hurry up and pay me.

Before I can reach across the front counter and grab this asshole by the throat, the front door opens, that tinkling of the chimes breaking my attention. A woman, her long, drenched hair plastered against her face and back, crosses her arms over her chest and makes a beeline toward the front counter.

She looks at me and gives me one of those polite, I-didn't-mean-to-cut-in-line smiles. "Um, hi, hello." She glances from me to Malcolm like she's not sure who she should talk to. "Sorry, are you busy? I can wait. I just *had* to get inside. This storm is like something out of a nightmare."

Malcolm looks at her like he's drowning and she's just come by driving a rescue boat. "No problem at all," he says, way too fucking cheerfully. "What can I do for you, miss?"

I almost interrupt him. Keeping me waiting *is* a problem. Not having my money ready for me is also a problem. The storm is nothing compared to the destruction I'm going to lay on this guy's face if he doesn't have what I came here for.

But the money Malcolm owes me—the debt I'm here to settle—ain't because I'm running a legitimate business. Neither one of us needs a witness when he hands over an envelope filled with cash, so I cool my temper enough to step back from the counter and wait.

God, I fucking hate waiting.

Unless Malcolm was lying to me just now, Shady Lane's sold out too. Yet Malcolm's making a big show of tap-tap-tapping into his goddamn keyboard, looking for a room for this chick. I don't even think they have a computerized guest-management system. For all I know, he's banging away nonsense into nothing.

I should throw him a glare that would shred through this bullshit, but I can't help sizing up the woman while Malcolm stalls for time.

Her back is to me, but she's wearing a short yellow sundress. It's drenched with rain and clings to her ass and thighs. As she listens to Malcolm, she's shivering and bouncing up and down on her heels, making every muscle in her bare, toned calves flex. Her thighs aren't defined by tight muscles, but they look soft and thick—perfect handholds.

"Please tell me you have something," she says, a shiver raising the tiny hairs on her crossed arms. Her auburn hair is dripping onto the floor around her. Just the thought of peeling every wet layer off her has my cock waking up in my jeans.

Malcolm continues to spew some kind of bullshit while he's banging away at the keyboard. "Let me see here…"

"Oh God," she sighs, leaning over the counter to peek at Malcolm's screen. "I'll take anything. Even if it's just for one night. I'm desperate. I'm new to town, and my condo won't be ready for a couple of days. Well, it was supposed to be ready, but…"

She's talking fast. I can't tell if it's nerves or the cold or what, but the corner of my mouth lifts in amusement.

"New to town?" Malcolm asks, sounding a little too interested. He's still tapping away at nothing as far as I can see, and I look away from the little mermaid to glare at him. He pretends not to notice.

Well, maybe his distraction is real. As I return to lean against the front counter, I can see that the girl washed in by the storm is pulling out her phone and her wallet from her purse. She's gorgeous in a way most of the women in my world could never be. Green eyes, full lips, face free of makeup. Her skin is lightly tanned, and her green eyes look up at Malcolm with an innocence, a natural sweetness that I don't think I've ever seen before. And yet her body is the opposite of sweet. She was built for fucking. The dress she's wearing cuts low across her chest, a pair of incredible tits straining against the soaked yellow fabric.

I swallow hard, and my fists clench at Malcolm eyeballing this woman.

"You got a fucking room or not?" I bark out before I can stop myself.

Malcolm pales. "Um, no." He throws me a nervous look before finally shaking his head. "I'm afraid not," he says, dragging the words out way too slow for my liking. "We're fully booked."

"Oh no. Are you sure?" The woman bites her lower lip, and her full-body shiver sends an electric pulse straight through me. "I stopped at two other motels, but seems like I'm out of luck. Do you know of any place else nearby that might have something? I literally have nowhere to go."

Her voice cracks, and something breaks open in my chest. She's out of options. Desperate. Just like Malcolm. But a woman with a killer body in distress brings out a very different reaction in me.

"Let me call a few people I know." Malcolm reaches behind the counter for a battered-looking cell phone that's gotta be at least ten years old. I hate technology, and even I have a newer phone than that piece of shit.

I shake my head and face a nearly impossible choice. I can send this girl on her way and get back to my business here. Or this might just be a miracle Malcolm's shady ass doesn't deserve.

I point to the woman. "Your luck may have just changed," I tell her. I turn and gesture to the bike parked in front of the entrance. "I picked a bad night to ride. I was out all day and didn't plan for the storm to turn so fast. You give me a lift, and I'll hook you up with a place to stay."

She searches my face with distrusting green eyes framed by long, dark lashes. Her face immediately falls, and she looks between Malcolm and me, frowning.

"I, uh…I…"

I hold up a hand. "I'm no psycho," I tell her. "I've got a room in a huge place. Storm shutters, generator. Twenty guys live there, and with this weather, we'll have probably a dozen women crashing, too."

She bites the corner of her lip even harder, and her full-body shudder reminds me that she's cold.

"I, uh, couldn't," she says, shaking her head. "I couldn't impose."

I cross my arms over my chest and look her over. "You wouldn't be imposing." I raise one brow and cock my chin toward my bike. "I won't make it home on that if this gets much worse. You'll be helping me out of a jam. The least I can do is return the favor."

She seems to consider this, looking between Malcolm and me. As if sensing his opportunity, Malcolm leans onto the counter.

"This is a good guy here," he says, a little too quickly. "If he's offering a place, I'd take him up on it. You new to Florida?"

She swivels her neck again, those green eyes wider now. "Florida, no. But Tampa, yeah. I've never actually been in a hurricane before. It's seriously terrifying." She looks at me as if she's not sure which is worse—giving a stranger a ride or being stuck with no place to stay in a tropical storm.

"Shit can get rough real fast," Malcolm says. He's trying to be helpful, but I flare my nostrils and glare at him again.

I don't need any assistance from this asshat. I just need my money. But since that doesn't seem to be happening tonight...

Just then, the wind picks up and blows a large dead palm frond into the glass doors with such force, all three of us startle. The glass doesn't break, but the woman's mouth falls open in surprise. Debris blows past the glass doors—plastic water bottles, papers, and trash—and the items smack against the windows with so much force, it sounds like any one of them could shatter the glass.

The sudden turn in the wind has the woman looking even more nervous. I have to get my bike inside, or I gotta get going. The weather is getting worse, and it's only gonna *keep* getting worse before this thing is done.

I stare at the woman, who's looking terrified. "Probably not safe to be on the road. We should head out. You drop me off," I tell her. "And if you don't like the looks of the place, you keep right on going. No harm done. Maybe by then, the rain and wind will ease up and you can hit the road." I know the weather is gonna get a lot worse before it gets any better.

She presses her lips together and considers my offer. Then she looks at Malcolm, who just so happens to be staring at the woman's tits. He does a not-at-all-subtle double take, looking from her chest to her eyes and back, before she seems to decide on the lesser of two evils.

"Can I have the address?" she asks, her voice tight.

She's holding up her phone, and she sounds exasperated but resigned. "I'd like to map it before we go."

She hands me the unlocked device, and I add my name, phone number, and address into her contacts, then I hand her the phone back.

She squints, reading what I wrote. "Your name is Shadow?" she asks.

I extend a hand to her, and she takes it. "Feel free to text your mom, your friends, whoever you want, so they know where you'll be."

"My sister," she mutters softly, shaking my hand, "…and my boyfriend."

Her fingers are ice-cold, and I almost wrap my hands around hers to warm them up. Instead, I lean forward. "If you've got a boyfriend, you'd better dump his ass right now. Only a worthless piece of shit would let a woman like you get stuck in this storm alone."

Her mouth falls open, and she looks down at our hands. "I'm Violet," she says quietly. "And thanks, I guess."

I release her hand and point at Malcolm. "You're responsible for my bike," I tell him. "I'm moving it inside."

Malcolm doesn't say anything as I move my bike into the lobby. I tell him to get me some towels, and I use half of the ratty, shitty things to dry off the bike as best I can. I give one towel to Violet, and she blots her dripping hair. I tuck the rest of the towels under my leather vest and jerk a thumb toward the door.

"Let's go. These are for your seats," I tell her. We turn to leave, and I pull open the door and hold it for Violet. "I'll be back tomorrow," I warn Malcolm, glaring at him. "Be ready for me."

His face drains of color. He knows what I mean. We

don't give extensions with time. We don't do favors. This is a one-time-only consideration. Since he's gonna be responsible for keeping my bike safe, I can give him overnight to pull together the cash.

I yank open the door, holding tight to the metal handle so the damn wind doesn't blow it out of my hands. Violet grabs the edges of her skirt with both hands, trying to hold the fabric down, but there's no avoiding a Marilyn Monroe moment. The wind pummels us, physically pushing her dress from her hands and nearly sweeping her body through the lot.

"Where did you park?" I shout against the noise of the wind.

She releases one side of her skirt, apparently resigned to the fact that she picked the wrong day to wear a minidress, and points toward the street. "Over there. No spots," she calls out.

I duck my head and put my hand on the small of her back. "Take my arm," I call out.

The wind is so fierce, I can feel grit blowing into my eyes. Violet's hair is whipping wildly around her shoulders. There's no way she's going make it to her car if she can't see past her hair.

I hold up my elbow, and she slides a hand into the crook of my arm and uses her frigid fingers to hold on tight. We lower our heads, and she stands close to me, using my mass to block some of the wind from pushing her across the slick pavement.

"What do you drive?" I shout.

"There." She points to a white sedan and fumbles in her purse with her free hand for her key fob.

She disarms the locks, and I put my hand over hers.

She's just as cold and wet as before, but she looks up at me with fear in her eyes.

"Hey." I stop her there on the street and put a hand on her shoulder. "I've got a safe place. You're gonna be just fine. You want me to drive? This ain't my first storm."

She hesitates, those full lips parting as she considers, but then the wind whips some litter, a potato chip bag or something, against the back of her legs, and she jumps like she's been cut. Then she straightens her shoulders and hands me the keys.

"I told my sister where we're going," she assures me in a loud voice. "She's expecting me to check in every fifteen minutes."

I yank open the passenger door and keep hold of it while she climbs in so it doesn't blow off the hinge.

"All the more reason for me to drive," I tell her. I hand her the towels I took from Shady Lane and slam the door shut once she's safely inside. Then I run around to the driver's side. I have to move the seat all the way back, but I manage to get in, fire up the car, and flip on the heat while only getting half beat to shit by the wind.

Violet has wrapped herself in towels like they are blankets, and she peers up at me with unblinking green eyes. "So, uh, where do you live with twenty other guys?" she asks softly. "A halfway house?"

I bark out my first real laugh in what feels like weeks. "Nah." I adjust the mirrors, turn on the wipers, and pull away from the curb. "I live in a compound," I explain. "With my brothers."

"Brothers?" She cocks her chin to the side and seems to study me. "Your poor mom."

"No, sweetheart. We aren't blood." I'm watching the rain,

the traffic, and I'm not loving the way this sedan is getting tossed by the wind. "I'll explain later," I tell her. "Now, sit back, warm up, and try to relax. The worst is over."

She sniffles and shivers beside me, crossing one leg over the other and smoothing her soaked dress over her thighs. I let myself look just once, and then I fix my stare ahead at the road.

I knew trouble wasn't the only thing blowing into town tonight, and turns out I was right. I have no idea yet if this Violet woman is trouble—but I have a feeling I'm gonna have a good time finding out.

TWO
VIOLET

I'M MORE THAN A RULE-FOLLOWER.

I'm a rule-follower's rule-follower.

I've never had a parking ticket. Never shoplifted or even been tempted to steal. I've never cheated on a test, and I'm pretty darned sure that the closest I've come to telling a lie was telling this terrifyingly huge, bearded man that I have a boyfriend.

Well, I did have one—so it's not a complete lie. I just don't anymore. But since this guy is driving me to places unknown so I can spend the night with him… I think I can be forgiven for stretching the truth a bit.

Once we're inside the car, the reality of the situation hits me. It's pouring down buckets of rain, and unless this guy decides to pull over and live out a serial killer's fantasy, he's gonna have to use all of his attention to navigate the roads safely. My little sedan's in decent shape, but between the wind and the roads starting to flood, the car fishtails, and I swear I'm gripping the towel he gave me with all my strength just to calm my racing heart.

I squeeze my eyes shut when an empty plastic water

bottle tossed by a sudden gust of wind strikes the windshield. I jump so hard that the man I've somehow trusted with my life looks away from the road to glance at me.

"We got this," he says, his voice even and oddly reassuring. "We're almost there."

"What's your name?" I ask, nervous energy making me feel fidgety. I know I probably shouldn't trust this guy, but I don't get any weird vibes from him. In fact, he seems oddly distant, like he doesn't want to put up with me any more than I want to be stuck with no better options than accepting his charity.

"Told ya," he mutters. "Shadow." He doesn't tear his eyes from the windshield when he answers my question.

My sister's not going to like that one bit. "Your real name?" I press. "If I'm murdered, it will be a lot easier for them to find you by your legal name."

He flicks a fast look at me, and a slight grin peeks through his dark brown beard. "Johnny." He looks vicious and tough, but he's got a voice as smooth as honey. The sound of it calms me, oddly. "Johnny Butcher," he finishes.

Well, darn. I can't exactly convince my sister that a guy named Butcher isn't a serial killer about to make me his next victim. "You couldn't have been John Smith, could you?" I grumble.

"What?" We stop at a red light, even though there are no other cars at this intersection, and Johnny turns to look at me. His eyes are a surprisingly light shade of green, and when he lowers his brows, he looks dangerously sexy.

I swallow hard and start punching away at my cell phone. "You could have a slightly less sinister name if you're going to pick up women off the street," I say softly.

He chuckles and shakes his head. "You think my name

is bad, you won't wanna tell your sister about this." He pats the leather vest he's wearing.

I gasp. He's carrying a gun. I shouldn't be surprised. Florida is a concealed carry state. Half the mall-walking old ladies probably have weapons in their handbags. But he wouldn't have revealed that he had it if he intended to surprise me with it. Use it on me, even. Would he?

"Great," I mumble under my breath. "Definitely a serial killer."

He laughs, and the warm sound fills the car. I want to trust him. What option do I have at this point? "It's only for my protection—and now, yours."

The light turns green, and we lurch ahead, the wind changing direction and literally shaking the body of my car.

"There," he says, pointing ahead.

Not that it matters. The rain has picked up again, and I can't see anything through the torrents of water streaming over the windshield. I fire off a quick text to my sister, including Shadow's full name, and just hope this isn't the worst mistake of my life.

A one-story building is ahead of us, as best as I can make out, and Shadow pulls right up to a door that has a single lighted bulb overhead. He turns and faces me.

"You got an overnight bag? Change of clothes?" he asks.

I don't reply right away, definitely not sure I want to commit to staying here. But just then, the door of the building opens, and two girls stumble out into the storm.

That's a good sign. There are other women inside, and they don't seem to be here against their will.

Quite the opposite, actually. They are laughing, and they have their arms around each other's bare shoulders.

They're both wearing really revealing cutoff tops, and even in the rain, I can tell they've got more cleavage and skin showing than covered. They have wild hair, too, blown around by the rain. But they don't seem to care. One looks as if she tries and fails to light a cigarette behind a cupped hand, while the other bends over, puts her hands on her knees, and pukes a big puddle of something into the grass.

"Ugh," I mutter.

"Jesus fucking..." Shadow shakes his head. "Forget about those two. Grab your bag. You'll have a room all to yourself. Ain't nobody going to bother you."

I reach into the back seat and grab a small overnight bag that I'd hastily thrown together in a gas station parking lot a couple hours ago, right when the weather started to turn. "What about my car?" I ask.

Almost everything I own is in this car. Everything I could get away with. Everything I needed to start my new life. The last thing I need is to lose it all in one night.

Shadow heaves a deep sigh. "I'll park it out back. No room in the garage, but we have a reinforced fence. Should be okay."

I set my bag in my lap and clutch the towels around me. "So, am I coming with you?"

He looks at me. "That's your call. I ain't forcing you to stay."

I burst into nervous laughter. "Right. No. I mean, am I going with you to park the car?"

Somehow, over the last few minutes, the idea of leaving to find someplace else to stay seems even more reckless than taking shelter with this man for the night.

I can always leave if it clears up or if things get weird. He said himself I'm not being forced to stay here.

"Yeah. Might as well. I doubt we'll have to step over puddles of puke going in the back."

He rolls down the windows. "Get your asses inside!" he yells.

"Shadow? That you?" one of the women yells back. "Why don't you carry me inside, big man?"

Shadow shakes his head and grumbles under his breath.

I can't imagine riding out a storm with a bunch of people partying so hard they make themselves sick. I guess I don't know what I expected, so I try to reserve my judgment while he drives my car around the back of the building. It appears far larger than it looked from the street.

"What is this place?" I ask, squinting through the dark. "You live here?"

He pulls a small clicker from the inside pocket of his vest, and a gate opens on a very strong-looking metal fence. He steers the car inside and parks between two enormous pickup trucks.

"I live here," he confirms, but he doesn't offer more than that.

I take that as a bad sign, but my sister is blowing up my phone, the ringtone I use for her piercing through the noise of the storm. "I'm okay," I tell her, picking up after the first ring. "I'm just arriving. I'm going inside, so I'll call you when I'm settled."

She starts to say something, but Shadow has turned off the car and hands me the keys, so I end the call. He holds out his hand for my bag, and I trade him. Clutching the faded hotel towels around my shoulders like a shawl, I wait while he runs around the passenger side to open the door and let me out. He reaches out a hand to help me from the seat. My fingers brush his, and I can't believe how hot his skin is. He's warm like he's on fire from the inside, and God, for a moment, I wish I could curl up beside him and steal some of his heat.

It's a dangerous thought, not to mention inappropriate, but my knight in shining leather hasn't given me any reason to be afraid of him. At least not yet.

I shove thoughts of his heat and his light green eyes to the back of my mind and focus on stepping through the puddles of water that have started to form in the parking lot. I do not need to slip and fall on my butt. He's probably already had more than an eyeful already, between my wet dress and the wind. I don't need him picking me up off my behind too.

We make it through the parking lot, practically holding hands the entire way. When he releases my hand, my fingers immediately go cold again. I stare at his profile as he unlocks a door, flips a latch, and shoves the door open with the toe of his boot.

"Come on," he says, setting a hand lightly against my back. "It's gonna be a full house." His breath warms my ear. "Stay close to me."

He doesn't have to tell me twice.

As soon as he shuts and locks the door behind us, I turn to face a scene I don't think can even be real. I mean, I've seen things like this on TV, but in real life? I'm suddenly not sure I wouldn't feel safer braving the storm than this.

The room we've walked into is a huge open space, softly lit with dim yellow overhead lights and neon signs attached to the walls. There are two pool tables, an air hockey table, and probably a dozen or more couches, recliners, and chairs scattered everywhere. On every available surface, I see bottles, cans, and plastic cups that I assume contain the sticky-sweet substance that I can feel on the floors under my feet.

The air is thick with skunky smoke, and I wrinkle my nose and try not to cough. Is this a drug den? I shudder hard, but I feel Shadow's hand pressing lightly against my back.

"This way," he says.

The minute we fully enter the space, through the smoke and blasting loud music, I can make out all the people. There are so many bodies. And I'm not talking dancing bodies. I went to a couple house parties in college, but never a frat party because that wasn't my scene. I was always the type who'd rather spend the night curled up with a good book than a frat boy trying to get his hand down my pants or up my top.

But this is like nothing I could ever imagine. There is a huge, and I mean *huge*, muscled guy with his jeans around his ankles sitting in a massive leather recliner. His head is thrown back and his eyes are closed. One woman is on her knees in front of his lap, and she is...

Oh, sweet Lord.

She is literally giving him oral sex right here in front of everyone while another woman holds her hair back.

I feel a rush of heat flood my cheeks, and I tear my eyes away from them. But when I look the other direction, I see a woman wearing only a thong bottom, her breasts totally exposed, as she lies back on a coffee table. Two guys and a girl are snorting something off her belly.

I swallow hard, and my legs start to lock up. Where the hell am I? Shadow may not be a serial killer, but what the heck kind of a place is this? A sex dungeon?

If I'm staying here, will I be expected to participate?

Everywhere I look, people are drinking, laughing, talking loudly, seemingly oblivious to the fact that there is a freaking tropical storm raging outside. A couple of women wearing only push-up bras and underwear are playing strip poker with two fully dressed guys at a folding table. I recognize the two girls from outside because they are now making out with each other, their hair drenched from the rain, while the one who didn't vomit writhes in the lap of a heavily tattooed guy with a leather vest that matches Shadow's.

Now that I notice it, a ton of the men here are wearing leather vests. They all seem to match, and—

"Violet." He says my name so close to my ear, I nearly jump out of my skin.

Before I can reply, we're approached by a tall man with black hair and a beard—and so many tattoos, I can't find any bare skin except his face.

The man is wearing a vest like Shadow's and a glare that could melt the paint off my car. I curl my toes, and a shiver of real fear shimmies down my spine. I slide a little closer to Shadow, where I feel at least a little bit safer, as crazy as that seems. I guess it's true what they say about the devil you know...

Shadow suddenly steps forward and clasps the giant in a half hug. It's like watching tattooed polar bears prepare for a brawl. I'm not sure whether to be scared or fascinated.

"You back from work?" the new guy asks, his low voice somehow cutting through the noise.

Shadow shakes his head. "Didn't go as planned. Unexpected development got in the way."

The other man cocks his chin and narrows his eyes. He's looking at me. *Me*. I'm the unexpected development.

"This is Violet," Shadow says, jerking a thumb at me. "She'll be crashing here tonight." Then he turns to me. "Violet, this is Phantom."

I don't know if it's the terror of the storm, the strangeness of my situation, or some deranged sense of self-destruction, but I laugh. I *laugh*. And then I start rambling. "Phantom? It's so nice to meet you. Thank you for having me. I—"

The deadly glare on Phantom's face has me zipping my lips so fast I can almost feel the words stop cold in my throat.

Phantom growls, an actual growl deep in his chest, and shakes his head. "She's your problem," he tells Shadow. "Unless you've got your hands full with Malcolm. Do I need to handle one of them?"

Shadow shakes his head and grabs my arm roughly. "I've got him and her under control. Natural fucking disaster out there. Work can wait one more day."

Phantom grunts this time, definitely a very different sound, but Shadow seems to know exactly what that means.

"Let's go," Shadow says, tugging on my arm.

I follow him through the smoky room, unable to keep my eyes off the people talking, smoking, playing darts, and drinking. Oh, there is so much drinking. I see what looks like a serious bar, with refrigerators behind it and two really gorgeous women who look like they're bartending.

"Hey, sexy." A brunette with a dragon tattooed all the way up her left arm and shoulder leans forward on the bar. "Whatcha drinkin', Shadow?"

I try to ignore the incredibly inappropriate pangs of jealousy that creep through my chest as Shadow talks to the skinny woman with what look like startlingly large boobs. She's pretty, like really pretty, and when she turns her back to us to grab whatever Shadow asked for, I can't help but notice his eyes following her.

Ugh.

In my yellow sundress and cute sneakers, I feel about as out of place as a zebra in a lion's den. A sudden bubble pops inside me, that little bit of excitement about my new life bursting as I look around and realize, even at thirty-two years old, I'll never stop feeling uncool. Like I don't fit in. I've been an outsider looking in most of my life.

The more I glance around, the more I see. Posters of motorcycles and half-naked women on the walls. So many guys, each scarier than the next, all dressed in denim and leather and wearing heavy boots... Motorcycle boots.

That's when it hits me.

I'm not in a sex dungeon. These guys are bikers. This must be their...I don't know what it is. Clubhouse? Hangout? What did Shadow call it before when he talked about living with his brothers?

I rest a hand lightly on Shadow's bicep, and he turns in slow motion to look at me.

"Is this a clubhouse?" I whisper.

He lowers his brows. "What? I can't hear—"

The bartender takes two bottles and uncaps them for us. She shoots me a look. "Where'd you find her? She looks like a milk drinker." She chuckles, and I feel the blush turn my cheeks a deep red. I know I look out of place and it must be written all over my face, but there's no reason for this woman to be petty.

"Just the beers," Shadow snaps.

She pouts a little but sets the bottles on the bar, leaning over much farther than is necessary—I'm sure, so that

Shadow and I can both see much more of her cleavage than I, for one, ever wanted to.

Shadow doesn't seem at all fazed and grabs both bottles in one hand. Then he throws the arm holding both beers over my shoulder and steers me away from the smoke and the noise.

This close to him, I feel the heat radiating off his body. Even though everything else is competing for my nose's attention, I catch a whiff of musky, spicy cologne. Somehow, even with the rain and the storm, getting blown in the face by trash and walking through a sauna of smoke and body odors, Shadow smells fantastic. But, like, it's a *good* scent.

I try my best to keep my anxiety under control as we make it to a hallway, moving away from the main room. I can hear people talking behind closed doors and making other, more private kinds of sounds. There is water running, so there must be bathrooms nearby, and we don't have to walk too far before we stop in front of a closed door.

An ancient-looking plaque on the front of the door reads *Vice President*. Above it, a newer-looking nameplate simply reads *Shadow*.

"You're vice president of this club?" I ask. The corridor is quieter than the main room, so I don't have to shout for him to hear me. "Is this place a clubhouse?"

Shadow turns to face me, his expression bordering on murderous. I take a tiny step back. "This ain't no clubhouse." He unlocks the door and, with the beers still in his hand, kicks it open. The man must have something against doorknobs. "Hustle up," he says. "I want you out of sight and out of the way."

I try not to let the comment bother me. I already feel

like a burden and a lot out of place. I try not to overthink anything, and I yell at myself to get out of my head and just follow him inside, wondering if this will be my room for the night. If this is his room, where will he be staying? I look behind me, trying to get a sense of the place, but just then, the lights flicker out and the room goes dark.

"Shadow?" My voice comes out like a squeak.

I hear him curse under his breath, and then I hear the sound of the glass beer bottles being roughly set down on something. A quick flash of light from his phone beams a bright pinprick of light at the floor, and I take a nervous step toward him. I drop my overnight bag and consider throwing my arms around him, but I stiffen and think the better of it. What the heck is wrong with me? This man is a stranger.

But then I feel his hand at my lower back, and he pulls me close. "We have a generator," he explains. He turns the flashlight off and slides his phone into some pocket, but now, of course, I can't see anything. I can just hear the rustling of leather and fabric. "It takes a minute to kick on. You okay?" he asks quietly.

I feel his soft breaths against my hair and the featherlight pressure of a hand at my lower back. I can tell from his heat and his delicious scent that I'm close to him. I lower my chin, and my forehead bumps into his chest. I leave it there for just a second, my eyes closed, the sounds of the wind banging against the building and the party noises filling the dark space.

Then, in a flash, the lights power back on.

I jump back and look into Shadow's face. His expression changes from something soft and thoughtful to that angry mask again. He sniffs, then takes a step back. He points to a closed door toward the back of the room.

"Private bath," he says. "Use what you want." Then he looks away from me and points to a queen-size bed. "Sleep, watch TV, just do whatever."

He picks up one of the beers and points to the second bottle with it. "That's for you."

Then he walks to the door like he's going to leave me.

"Shadow," I call out before I can stop myself.

His hand freezes on the doorknob. "What?"

"What if the power goes out again?" I can't help myself. I'm in a strange place, and back here, the sounds of the party are quieter, but I can hear every gust of wind and band of rain blasting against the walls and roof. It's like I'm in a snow globe that someone has shaken with all their strength, but instead of fluffy snow, there's trash banging around inside.

"You'll be fine. We won't get any flooding this far inland. You're safe." He throws open the door and looks me straight in the eyes. "Violet," he says.

My tummy flips over, and I shiver at the intensity of his voice. Maybe it's the cold and the fear finally getting to me.

No, I think.

It's not the storm. It's him.

"Yes?" My voice is a whisper.

"Lock this door when I leave. And don't open it for anybody but me. Got that? I don't care what they say. Nobody but me." His green eyes go cold as he waits for my answer.

"Yes, yes, of course." I nod nervously, and he shuts the door behind him.

"Lock it," he says through the closed door. "I'll wait."

I flip the dead bolt on the door and rest my head against the cool metal. I've never been any place except a hotel that had a dead bolt on an inside door. I'm not sure if that says more about this place and the people here than I want to know. But once the door is locked, my shoulders sag, and I feel exhausted, cold, and alone.

Outside, the storm rages on, battering the roof and walls with water and wind. I gather my strength and take a look around Shadow's room. His bed is neatly made, and the comforter and pillowcases look clean. I wonder how many women from that party want to be in here tonight instead of out there. I wonder how many have been and might still come back here at some point, looking for Shadow.

He's a gorgeous man, but also scary hot. I can see all of the women wanting him. And why would he refuse? Maybe sex is part of what they expect to do when they come here to party. But there are a few pieces that don't make sense.

He has a full-sized couch against one wall that looks super comfy. Soft brown leather, the broken-in kind. That answers the "who will sleep where" question. Maybe he has an extra blanket he can loan me. I can't imagine I'll ever feel warm and dry again.

I wander through Shadow's room, lightly running my fingers over the dresser and side table, peeking around to see if there are cameras in the corners. I mean, why would he trust me, a total stranger, in his room if he has no way to watch what I do in here?

I shake my head at my own naïveté. These guys are bikers. They carry guns and have weapons and a fortified clubhouse or whatever this place is. I'm a soaking-wet school librarian wearing a sundress. What harm could I possibly do to them?

I give in to my impulse to check the place out. I badly

want to shower and change into something dry and fresh, but I'm afraid even the clothes in my overnight bag will be damp from running through the rain. I open a few of Shadow's drawers and am shocked to find socks and T-shirts all folded and organized. He has no pictures on his walls, but I do spot a nice TV and headphones, which I might just use to try to shut out some of the noise.

Maybe I can curl up on the couch and watch a movie or something. Forget where I am and how I got here.

When I reach an armoire, I open the knob, expecting shirts and jackets to be neatly hung, but I'm shocked to see shelf after shelf of books. I finger the spine of one and squint at the titles. I'm a librarian by training, and this excites me. I grab a book off the shelf and see it's been read. I open to a chapter that's been marked with handwritten scribbles in the margins. I note the case citations and quickly scan the shelf. Every volume is a legal book covering criminal procedure, trial practice for defense attorneys, the Florida statutes, or some very technical aspect of the law.

I return the book to where I found it and close the armoire fast. A gun-carrying biker with a chest full of law books. Is he studying to be a lawyer, or...

Who is this man, and what the heck am I doing here?

THREE
SHADOW

"SO, SHADOW, WHO'S THE STRAY?" One of the club bunnies has her hand around a prospect's cock, but she stops jerking him off to open her mouth to me as I walk past.

"Da fuck?" The kid's eyes are glassy, and he looks helplessly from her to me.

"You look busy," I tell her, giving her one chance to shut the fuck up and get back to her own business. I know this one. She's a club whore, through and through. I've got nothing against the women who hang around here lapping up free drinks. They keep their mouths shut when it matters and open them when it counts. But this one's always rubbed me wrong, and I hope the prospect knows where to draw the line between a hand job and a commitment.

That's what they all want. A piece of gold on their hand that gives them claim over us. And this one won't let it go.

"I got two hands," she says, trying to sound coy.

I bend low to her and snake my hand underneath her

hair. I tug hard enough to move her head but not to hurt her. "Why don't you do something with that mouth other than use it to talk to me." I grit the words against her ear, then release her.

She gives a disappointed little whimper but focuses back on the task at hand. I hear the prospect arguing with her quietly as I make my way through the crowd.

A cheer goes up so loud that for a second, I can't hear the sounds of the wind battering the storm shutters. I look over to Savage, who's wearing a white wife-beater under his leather vest, his heavily tatted arms punching the air like a high school football coach. Two prospects are playing some video game, and based on the scores on the giant screen, it looks like Savage just beat their asses.

Savage is the club's sergeant-at-arms and is the only one of us with elite professional training in guns and weaponry. He spent a decade in the military, but he won't talk about what went down or why he got out.

Savage knows this club, our dynamics, our rules, and how to stay under the radar like nobody else we've had. He's as all in as they come, and the only thing he's carried over from his military days is his love of video games. I guess hours of idle time in far-off places with a group of guys prepared him well for life in the compound. No matter how much shit I give him about playing games, it's the one thing he does to blow off steam.

I haven't made it even ten paces when one of two women peels away from Hawk, who's wearing his signature shades inside—even here, even in the middle of a fucking tropical storm.

"I saw that wet rat the storm washed in." Penny slides a hand inside the rear pocket of my jeans and cups my ass.

"Why'd you go out to the streets when you have everything you could possibly want right here?"

Fucking Penny.

I groan at the familiar touch, and for just a second, my body reacts. Penny's one of my favorite club bitches. She comes easy and often and genuinely likes to fuck. I know she's a little sweet on Blade. Since his old lady passed, she talks to him about his kid like she really cares. Maybe she does.

But she *wants* me, and that ain't ego talking.

Savage's going to replace him someday, I'm fairly fucking certain of that. And I don't give a shit. Savage has nothing but this club, just like Phantom. I'm stable where I am, and I plan on staying in the room with the brass VP plaque for a hell of a long time. And there'll have to be an ice storm in hell before I put a ring on any woman's finger. Doesn't stop Penny from trying, though.

Being the old lady of the VP would come with status, perks. Put her high in the pecking order. Give her claim to the thing they all want more than anything—to be part of us. Of what this is.

Normally, on a night like this, I'd take Penny back to my room and let her drain me dry with her mouth, her pussy, anything and everything. I'd probably let her bring a friend or two like we've done a few times in the past. But tonight, she's got jealousy written all over her face. Yet another reason I don't let any of these women get too close.

I gently tug her hand out of my pocket. "Blade looks like he's missing your company."

She gives me a little pout, a slight twist of her lips, then cocks her chin. "At least somebody around here does."

She tosses her long hair over her shoulder and sidles

right back up to Blade, who is so immersed in talking to Jackie, I don't think he even noticed Penny leave. Penny eyes me dangerously while she slides herself right up under Blade's arms, snuggles against his chest, and pulls his face down for an openmouthed kiss.

Good fucking riddance.

Penny can be a petty bitch, but that's one of the things I actually like about her. She says what she thinks, and she takes what she wants.

As she sucks Blade's face, I can't help but think of Violet.

I wonder if she's naked in my room right now. I shake off the thoughts. She's too fucking innocent. That sundress, those sweet green eyes. As much as I want to see what she looks like staring up at me, her lips wrapped around my cock, I don't go for damsels in distress. They're always way more trouble than they're worth. I shove aside any curiosity I may have. I'm done playing Boy Scout. It's time to get fucked up.

The beer in my hand is getting warm, and I need something stronger. I head over to the bar and hand the beer to a prospect who's three deep in line. "Drink that," I tell him, then cut to the front of the line and lean my elbows on the bar.

"You back for a good time, baby?" The bartender, Stella, leans on her elbows too, as if expecting me to unzip my pants at the sight of her tits.

I pinch my brows between two fingers. "Gimme a whiskey."

"Comin' right up, Shadow." The way Stella says my name makes my skin fucking crawl.

It's as if the walls are closing in. The heat, the people, the noise. I'm not in the mood for any of this tonight.

Phantom is leaning against a wall by the front door, talking to Viper, our enforcer, and glaring over the crowd.

Just then, some woman slips, twisting her heel on something sticky on the floor. She squeals so loudly, I nearly jump outta my skin. She's on the floor laughing, but a loud snap of Viper's fingers and two prospects jump from the card game they are playing to help her up.

"Clean that shit." Viper doesn't need to finish the sentence before the prospects are scrambling for a mop and bucket.

Stella comes back with a glass of whiskey, and she starts in on me again. "Shadow, if I'd known you were interested in babysitting, I'd have worn my little-girl dress too."

I grab the glass and down it in one chug, the liquor burning its way down my throat. I flare my nostrils and slam the empty glass down on the bar. "Gimme another," I say. But before Stella can turn around to refill me, I tell her, "Fuck that. Gimme the bottle."

"Hmmm, somebody's looking to have a good time tonight."

I practically wrench the bottle from her hands and turn away from her. I scan the smoky room, looking for any place to sit that doesn't have people fucking or talking or playing or generally being shitheads.

No such luck.

The lights flicker off and on again, and I think of Violet, back in the relative quiet of my room. Helpless, terrified, innocent Violet.

I make a snap decision. Grabbing the bottle of whiskey, I head down the corridor. When I reach my room, I pound on the door.

"Violet, it's me. Open up."

It takes about ten seconds before I hear the dead bolt turn. She opens the door a crack and peeks out.

"Yes? Is everything all right?" She's looking exactly the same as she did when I left her—wet, dressed, and terrified.

"That's what I'm here to find out." I hold up the bottle. "I brought something a little stronger than the beer."

She looks from me to the bottle of whiskey and doesn't say anything.

The corner of my mouth lifts. "You gonna open that door, sweetheart? I did say I'm the only one you could let in."

"Oh God. Yes, of course. I just thought..." She yanks the door open and steps out of the way. "Of course, come back in. I just thought you'd want to...that you'd be..." She waves a hand toward the door. "Out there. With your friends."

"In our clubhouse." I drop the bottle on the end table next to the couch and grin.

"I forgot what you called it." Her face is blushing hard, and I can't help thinking how different she is from my "friends."

"Compound," I tell her, kicking off my boots and dropping onto the couch.

"I have so many questions," she says quietly, a huge smile on her face. "But it seemed rude to ask."

I uncap the whiskey and take a long drink from the bottle. I hold it out and offer her a sip.

She looks at it but then motions toward the beer. "I haven't even finished that yet."

I shake my head. "Don't matter. Looks like we're gonna be here awhile. Unless this storm does something to shock the weather people, we might be locked down into tomorrow night."

A small frown plays on her lips, and it hits me like a fist to the gut. She's beautiful. Maybe a little uptight, definitely still scared. But she's fucking gorgeous. I can think of worse ways to ride out a storm.

I hold the bottle to my lips again. "The way I see it, you got two choices. You can get drunk and pass out, miss the whole damn thing. Or you can sit here and freak out every time the lights flicker." I take another sip. "I sure as hell know what I plan to do."

"Can I ask about this place?" she asks, holding out a tentative hand for the whiskey.

I hand it to her. "I'll make you a deal. You got a question, you take a shot. You do that, I'll answer anything you ask."

"And you'll tell me the truth?" She's standing in front of me, looking at me with this combination of curiosity and something that makes the blood heat in my veins.

"The whole truth and nothing but." I pat the couch beside me. Her dress looks like it's mostly dried, and her hair is in half-wet, long, soft-looking curls covering her chest. "I'm an open book."

She drops down onto the couch and crosses her legs under her. "That's literally my first question. Your books." She points to the armoire but then immediately covers her mouth with her hand. "I snooped. I'm sorry. But just a little... I—"

I tip the bottle toward her. "You got a question in there?"

Her face breaks into an easy smile, and even the flickering of lights doesn't dim it. She squares her shoulders, takes a small sip, and then closes her eyes, trying hard not to cough as the liquid goes down. I hold back a laugh as she slaps her free hand against the top of her thigh, her eyes watering.

"Okay," she gasps, trying to get the question out even though she's still clearly fighting a coughing fit. "Why do you have all those books? Are you in law school?"

I hold up two fingers. "That was two questions."

She looks down at the whiskey but doesn't hesitate. She takes another small sip, this one seeming to go down a lot easier. She wipes her mouth with the back of her hand and smiles, a victorious-looking little grin that sends a very different kind of heat through my limbs. "Two questions, two drinks. So now, I get two answers."

I settle back against the cushions and kick my feet up onto the small ottoman. "I read a lot," I say. "Not in law school. Doubt I'd get in."

She is studying my face quietly, waiting for me to say more. What the fuck. Why not?

"I hardly finished high school. Been arrested about a half dozen times for stupid shit. I was rowdy when I was young." I chuckle. That's putting it mildly. "One conviction. Served a couple months for beating up an asshole in a bar fight that went way too far."

She nods but doesn't look put off by anything I'm saying. "So, you study the law to understand it? Are you still a criminal?"

I burst out laughing at that, but I just point to the bottle. "At this rate, you're gonna pass out before I answer."

"Is that your way of avoiding the question? I think we should have been clearer on the rules of the game." She gives me a playful pout but takes another shot. "So, you study the law to, what, know what's legal?"

I shrug. "Let's just say I never have trusted authority. The best defense is a strong offense. That kind of thing." I'm not sure if she follows what I'm saying, but I have a few questions of my own. I reach for the bottle and take a swig. "My turn. What's a woman like you doing out in a storm like this?"

She presses her lips together and looks down at her hand. She's laced her fingers together in her lap, and it's clear I've touched a nerve.

"I was in a relationship," she says. "I ended it, and I needed a fresh start. New job, new city, new place to live. My big adventure isn't starting out so great, though."

I hold up the whiskey to signal I've got another question and then drink. "What's the new job?"

She beams at me, her face lighting up and her green eyes brimming with sunshine. "I'm a high school librarian," she says, and I almost choke on my whiskey.

"Coulda guessed," I wheeze, and she reaches over the middle cushion to smack me playfully on the knee.

"What is that supposed to mean?" she asks.

I raise a brow at her. "Is that a question?"

She scoots closer to me and grabs the bottle from my hands. She gives me a grin that holds a challenge and drinks in answer.

I breathe deep and roll my neck to loosen the tension. I like this girl. Violet, the school librarian.

"Librarian fits, that's all. You've got this innocence thing going on," I tell her. "The big eyes, the short sundress. All that's missing are nerdy glasses." What I don't say is that I have a feeling there's a tiger underneath all this sweetness. A big cat just waiting to eat a man like me alive.

"You make being smart and innocent sound like bad

things." She folds her arms over her chest. "Maybe I wouldn't fit in here, but geeks are cool now, in case you didn't know."

I take the bottle from her and chug. "You don't wanna fit in here," I say, and I mean it. "And that's not exactly what I meant. I'll bet you've got thousands of teenage boys hot for teacher. Or librarian, you know. Same thing."

She seems to register that I was complimenting her. "Was that a question? Or are you telling me I'm hot?"

"You just asked me two questions, but I'll give you this one for free." I lean forward and touch the underside of her chin lightly. "You, Violet the Librarian, whose last name I don't know, are fucking hot. Let's just say my education might have gone a totally different way if our school librarian had looked like you."

I can't tell if the shots are getting to her, but she leans forward. A flush travels from her cleavage, up her neck, and across her cheeks. I watch every inch as it spreads.

"I think you're hot too," she says quietly and more seriously than I expected. "A little scary, but definitely hot." Then she holds out her hand. "My turn. I have more questions."

By the time we've polished off almost the whole bottle, I can't tell who's drunk more. But I can tell who's feeling it more.

Violet sways closer to me on the couch, her hand permanently resting on my thigh. I force myself not to look down at it, because I know if I acknowledge what she's doing—wasted or not—she's gonna move away.

And that's the last thing I want.

The storm rages on outside, and the sound of the wind battering the hurricane shutters no longer makes her jump.

I've learned her last name—James—and that she's thirty-two to my thirty-seven. Neither one of us has ever been married, and while she didn't even have to waste a question on whether I have tattoos—she knew the answer with her first look at me—I did ask, and she apparently has none.

"What about piercings?" I ask. I lean forward and brush a lock of hair away from her ear. "Ears, belly, any place?"

She shakes her head, but I notice her eyes flutter closed when I move her hair. "You gonna drink for that question, or are you done playing?" Her voice is low and sensual, like she is asking me a dangerous question inside a simple one.

I curl my hand beneath her hair and lace my fingers behind her neck. Her skin is soft and warm, and she releases a little gasp at the touch. But she doesn't push me away.

I lean in, and she opens her mouth and licks her lower lip. "Depends. Are you proposing a new game, Violet James?"

"I…" She turns her head slightly, leaning so close to my face I can feel her sweet breath against my beard. "Shadow, would you…"

She moves her mouth toward mine, and I tighten my hold on the back of her neck. "What do you want, sweetheart?" I ask.

But before she can answer, she sighs, closes her eyes, and rests her head on my shoulder. "Mmm, you just… You smell so… You…"

I bite back a grin as she mumbles into my shoulder. But I'm racked with full-body disappointment as her words disappear into heavy breaths.

"Violet?" I pull away just a bit, but her body goes slack, and it's clear she's out.

I gather her in my arms and consider laying her out on the couch, but then I think better of it and slide my hands under her knees, pick her up, and carry her to my bed. She wraps her arms around my neck and murmurs against my shoulder, so she's not completely passed out.

"We were about to... Are we playing..." I can hardly make out the words, but I don't think I need to hear them all to get where she's going.

"You need some sleep, sweetheart."

She goes quiet then, her breathing steady and even. I reach down with one hand and yank back the covers, careful not to drop the passed-out woman in my arms. I set her on the bed, and she smiles, so I know she can't be too fucked up—at least, I hope not. I tuck her under the covers and grab one pillow from beside her so I won't have to use the armrest on my couch all night.

I grab a bottle of water from a mini fridge in the corner and set it on the bedside table with a small trash can, just in case.

I consider heading back out to the party. The wind is loud as fuck and the music is muted, but I can tell from the cheers and the talking that my brothers plan to ride out this storm with as much booze and sex as they can.

I look at the woman passed out under my covers. This ain't the same kind of party, but I pull off my vest and T-shirt, throw the pillow onto my couch, and flip off the lights, the taste of whiskey on my lips and the scent of a woman named Violet making the room swim.

FOUR
VIOLET

I CAN HARDLY COBBLE TOGETHER a coherent thought. My head is pounding. My mouth is dry. And… worst of all, I am in an unfamiliar bed.

Oh my God. What have I done?

It all comes back to me in a rush. I squint my eyes open and peer around the dark room. This can't be real. This can't be happening. I tell myself it's just a dream. A nightmare, really. I fell asleep in my new condo, and any minute, I'll wake up and be back where I am supposed to be right now—in my new life. A fresh start. Freedom from everything I had to leave behind.

But the tangled sheets and the darkness of an unfamiliar room have me questioning whether this is a new beginning or the worst decision I've ever made.

I drank whiskey shots. Straight from the bottle. With a man I hardly know. I'm not sure who this Violet James is. I grimace as the taste of the whiskey shots I did threatens to come right back up with a vengeance. I was never one to hold my drink, and holy crap, did I drink last night. And it was *fun.*

But right now, I'm not sure if I'm excited or a little scared.

Then a gust of wind blowing debris against the outside of the building pounds its way past my ears, and the fear picks right back up. The storm. The power failure. The flooding in the parking lot and the fact that there is literally no place else for me to go right now. I try to count my lucky stars that I am safe and dry as the sound echoes from one side of my very sensitive head to the other.

I press my fingertips to my temples and sit up, slowly accepting that this is all very, very real. I got wasted in a motorcycle compound with a man named Shadow.

I'm in his bed, wrapped in sheets that smell surprisingly clean and feel deliciously soft under my bare toes. I'm still dressed in the yellow sundress I wore yesterday—so it's not all bad news. My shoes are off, but somehow, I got into bed without actually getting *ready* for bed. What a confusing man. Hard and soft, sweet and complex. I roll over quietly, searching through the dark for any sign that he's in here with me.

Shadow's room is unbelievably dark, but I'm not sure if it's the thick curtains over the windows or the storm shutters he told me about. I had half a hope that the storm would be over today, but by the looks of it, what Shadow said last night is right. The wind and rain smashing against the building don't sound like a storm that's just passing by. This hurricane, tropical storm, whatever hellfire Mother Nature has decided to unleash on us, is nowhere close to done.

I peek around the room and see a pillow and blanket rumpled on the couch, but the bathroom door is open, and there's no sign of Shadow anywhere. I'm not sure how I feel about that. He slept on his couch and gave up his bed to me. I'm still not completely sure how I got into his bed. All the questions we asked in our game last night come rushing back. I try to remember it all. What I told him, what he shared.

But first...I need to use the bathroom. I can never process any rational thoughts when I have to pee this bad. And I've got to take a toothbrush to my mouth, like, immediately.

I drag my sorry self out of his very comfortable bed and grab my overnight bag. I put that toothbrush to work and run my brush through my hair. I consider changing my clothes, but as I lean over the sink, I realize that I'm still a little drunk. Every movement feels slow and fuzzy. As tempting as a hot shower is, I might need to get a cup of coffee or some food in me. Something to soak up the alcohol.

Cursing every shot I took last night, I walk in my bare feet from the bathroom to the bedroom door. The dead bolt is unlocked, so I wonder if that means a lot of the people who were here last night have left? I remember the sticky floors and the broken glass, and I slide on my shoes before gripping the doorknob in an unsteady hand and opening the door.

To my surprise, I hear literally no noise but the sounds of the storm raging on outside. To be honest, it's kind of soothing—in a thank God I'm in a storm-proofed compound kind of way. I blink against the weak lights that somehow feel like spotlights blaring into my eye sockets and follow the hallway back toward the main room with the bar and kitchen.

As soon as I round the corner, I see him.

Shadow.

He's perched on a stool at the bar counter with a cup of

something that I can smell from here is fresh, hot coffee. He's wearing a pair of tight dark-blue jeans, and he's... shirtless. He seems to be staring at the hallway, just waiting for me. Watching me.

I give him a quick smile and start to say good morning, but then I notice all the other people in the room, and I choke the words down. On every piece of furniture and even on the floor, there are bodies. Bikers passed out with their pants unzipped. Women in various states of undress, some completely naked. I see more naked breasts around me than I've seen in all the gym locker rooms I've been in over my whole life added up. I don't know how they aren't all freezing.

For a minute, my mind flashes back to Shadow on the couch. Our question-and-answer game.

Did I touch or kiss him?

I'm sure I didn't. I couldn't have. I don't drink that much, and I definitely don't drink often. But even when I get a tiny bit tipsy, I'm one of those people who becomes more logical. I'm the person who collects the car keys from everyone else in the party, because even after a few drinks with friends, I won't let anybody get behind the wheel.

I'm sure, I think, that I didn't do anything I'd feel embarrassed about today. At least, I hope I didn't... My stomach rolls over at the thought of what I did, didn't do, and don't fully remember. I woke up fully clothed and alone, which is more than I can say for the rest of the people who spent the night here.

Shadow pats the stool next to him, his eyes still locked on me. I carefully walk past a young guy who is asleep facedown on the floor, spread-eagled, the waistband of his jeans lowered just enough to expose the top of his butt crack.

As I step past his motorcycle boots—how on earth he is sleeping facedown on the floor with boots on, I don't know—it hits me that this is so not how I imagined riding out my first hurricane.

When I finally get to the bar, I give Shadow a grateful smile. "Good morning. I hope you slept okay on your couch. I didn't mean to take your bed." I can't help myself. My eyes rove over his tanned skin, the thick, dark hair covering his bare chest, and something—probably just the alcohol from last night—flutters inside my chest.

He purses his lips and grunts. "Coffee? You want anything in it?"

"Do you mean anything more potent?" I shake my head, the motion making me feel dizzy and definitely still a little drunk. "I think I drank enough last night for a lifetime. Just a little sugar if you have it."

He cracks a smile and goes behind the bar to pour me a cup. He grabs a sugar shaker and a spoon and sets them in front of me. Then he claims the stool beside me.

I can't stop myself from turning to face him, and I try not to stare at the muscles and tattoos, all the skin and hair and color that make his body so darned appealing. Instead, I stare down into my mug and take a deep sip.

We're quiet for a moment before the wind smashes something large and solid against the shutters. I nearly leap off the stool and into Shadow's lap, but I somehow maintain my outward composure.

I grab my coffee cup and take another sip, settling myself on the stool.

"Storm's still raging." His voice is like the shots we took last night, every word heating my senses and sending prickles up and down my bare arms.

I feel buzzy and loose, and I lock my eyes on the

intricate faded black ink that covers his arms. I set my coffee cup down and cross my arms over my chest protectively. "It sounds like the roof is going to blow off. You were right about the storm. I hope you can stand my company for a while longer."

He turns his body to face me and locks eyes with me as he sips his coffee. "I told you you'd be safe here."

I nod again, not sure what to say. Thank you doesn't seem like enough. He's given me, a stranger, shelter, protection, whiskey, and now coffee. Sitting beside him in the same clothes I slept in, his chest bare, chatting like this, feels intimate. Nothing about this feels like a stranger rescuing a damsel in distress. "You tucked me in last night," I say softly.

He doesn't look away from me. "Had no choice. That might be the first time a woman's actually passed out on me."

I lift my brows and wave a hand at a woman whose bare foot is tucked under the calf of a mostly dressed biker. They are so tightly intertwined on a small love seat a few feet away that my back hurts just looking at them.

"Are you sure?" I tease. "Hard to believe if you weren't babysitting me that you wouldn't have been out here with the rest of them, some naked hottie passed out all over you."

"If you stay another night," he continues, his voice low, "maybe I'll let you pass out on me. I don't have to tuck you in alone, Violet."

There is a promise in his words, and I grip my mug tighter. A flush creeps its way up my cheeks, and I try to hold back a smile. Is the scary, sexy biker flirting with me? And even more than that, why do I suddenly want him to?

Somebody releases an ear-shattering snore, and we

trade smiles. Then Shadow leans forward and rests his elbows on the bar. "You know you still owe me an answer."

I cock my head and rack my brain. "I do?" I can't remember much about last night...at least not the later part of the night. "What did you ask?"

He turns on the stool to face me, every muscle in his torso pivoting with the movement. His beard is thick and trimmed. It looks so soft. He must have woken early and cleaned up. His hair looks damp, like he might have showered. The thought of Shadow naked just steps away from where I was sleeping makes my nipples go hard.

Just then, another crash of thunder and wind startles the ever-loving daylights out of me. I leap off my stool and throw my arms around Shadow's neck. "What was that?" I look into his face, his full lips now just inches from mine. "Oh my God, I'm sorry. I—" The words die on my lips as Shadow's hands circle my hips.

He's sitting on the stool with his legs open. He pulls me between his legs and holds me close to him. He feels so, so good. Hot, hard, soft, and smooth. I want to touch his beard, run my fingers through his hair. I tip my head back and look into his green eyes.

Maybe I'm still drunk, and heck, maybe I'm more reckless than I realize, but I swear I don't even think about it. The heat of him under my hands, his smooth, corded muscles, even the feel of being between his legs. I'm drawn to him like a bee to a flower. As soon as I smell him, my eyelids drift closed. I want to taste him. I lean my face closer to his, and before I realize what's happening, I'm kissing him.

I'm about to pull away in horror when he grips my ass and yanks me tight against him. And oh, sweet mother, does he kiss me back. I open my mouth, thankful I brushed every last trace of whiskey from my teeth, and his tongue and mine meet like long-lost lovers reunited. Desperately, deeply. I may only have known him for a night, but my body didn't get that memo. I am falling, falling, literally weightless as I'm pulled under by bliss. All I feel are his hands, his lips, his tongue against mine. He tastes rich, like black coffee, and sweet, like the lightest trace of sugar.

His bare skin under my hands is hot, and I just want more of that, more of him. I want to be closer, to tangle myself against the furnace of his chest and lose myself in the pleasure.

I dig my fingers through his hair, scratching, writhing, pressing myself as close to him as I can get. He cups my butt cheeks, and while it should be too much, too soon, it's not close enough.

He feels so unbelievably good. It's like everything else fades away. The storm. The bikers. The women. I pause to catch my breath, but I wrap my arms tighter around his neck. I whimper, a needy, hungry sound, and press my chest toward him, my nipples suddenly hard and aching for contact.

"*Fuuuuuuuck meeeeee.*"

That was definitely not his voice.

A low moan from one of the passed-out people behind us breaks the moment. Someone must be waking up. I hear movement, bodies rolling, furniture being pushed around.

Shadow pulls his lips from mine, holds my face in his hands for a second before releasing me. His breathing is ragged, his eyes wild. I am breathless, unsteady—and, worse, disappointed. My knees feel weak and my legs are wobbly. I'm still drunk, yes, but not on whiskey. On him. I'm like a thirsty woman who finally took a sip of water. And now, I want to finish the whole bottle.

I've never, ever been kissed like that by anybody before. The kiss that made the storm outside look like a light summer mist.

I must be standing there looking as shocked as I feel because Shadow wordlessly grabs both of our mugs by the handle in one hand and takes my hand in the other. He gets up off his stool and drags me past people in various stages of waking up.

One guy groans and runs for a trash bin before puking loudly into it. A few women stumble around, fumbling for their tops or shoes.

But no one else matters. Shadow moves with the determination of a soldier, marching me in the opposite direction of the hallway that leads to the bedrooms.

"Where are we going?" I ask.

He doesn't reply, just releases my hand and ticks his head for me to follow.

I suppose now would be the time when a rational woman would excuse herself. Go back to Shadow's bedroom, lock that dead bolt, and keep him and all these other people as far away as possible.

Yesterday, I would have called myself a rational woman.

Today, I'm not sure. I've done whiskey shots with him. Searched his closets. Tasted his lips.

I have a split second of indecision before I take the uncharted path and follow him wherever it is he plans to lead me.

When he reaches a locked door, he pulls a set of keys

from the back pocket of his jeans and unlocks it. He waves me through and locks the door behind us.

The lights are off, so I assume either the generator isn't connected here or he's chosen to save the power. As my eyes adjust to the dim daylight, I'm stunned by what I see.

"Reinforced metal doors, no windows," he explains. "Safest room in the compound."

Shadow sets our coffee mugs down on a stainless-steel table that looks like something out of a professional kitchen. He takes my hand and walks me past row after row of gorgeous cars and motorcycles. These are not just everyday bikes and trucks like the ones outside in the lot where he left my car. These are vintage, rare, and collectible. Valuable vehicles treasured by those who own them. Antique, restored works of beauty.

We walk past a pristine black GTO that is as glossy and perfect as it must have been the day it rolled off the assembly line in the early seventies. I hover my free hand over the gleaming paint without touching it and hum appreciatively.

"This is gorgeous," I tell him. I'm not even much of a car person, but wow. It's hard not to be impressed by something this beautiful.

"I'm not looking at the car right now," he tells me.

Even in the low light, I can see exactly where his eyes are. He's devouring me, his lips parted, his gaze moving from my chest to my lips until, finally, our eyes meet.

It's like an instinct now, the way I just throw myself at him. My mouth crashes against his, and we're kissing again, his mouth open, his tongue doing scandalous things to mine, while his hands grip my bottom.

Suddenly, he picks me up and sets me on the hood of the GTO.

"I'm too heavy," I say nervously, not wanting to dent the hood. Echoes of angry voices—my ex's voice—cause me to draw my shoulders down and sink deep into myself.

I don't want to think about him right now. Don't want to hear his rage in my ears, his cruelty, his judgment. Even though it's been six months since I ended things, I just can't help it. It's like he left a trace of himself in my ears, the small, angry voice relentless in its criticism of everything I do.

"Sweetheart, this shit is old-school. It can handle a man my size. You're fine." Shadow practically growls the word at me, planting two huge palms on either side of my legs. He pats a beat against the metal hood, as if to prove the frame can hold my weight. He tips my chin toward him and claims my lips in a hungry kiss. "Unless you tell me to stop, I'm gonna make you come until you can't see straight. I know this car can take it. But the real question is...can you?"

My shoulders release, and my body nearly falls back against the hood. Make me come?

"Shadow, I..."

He leans across the bumper and grips my face in his hands. "Yes or no, sweetheart."

I don't break his intense stare, but my mind is whirling a million miles a second. "What about the others? Can't anyone just..."

"This place is off-limits to almost everybody. I'm the VP of this club, and I locked the door. Ain't nobody gonna try to come in here." He pulls me closer to him and whispers against my ear. "This beauty is mine, and I have condoms in the glove box." He points to the door. "You're free to go back to my room and read if you'd rather, Violet James."

His words aren't sharp like Clive's, not belittling. Coming from Shadow, my name—Violet James— somehow sounds sexy.

He's given me a place to be safe from the storm, and now he's giving me an out from something that might be even more dangerous than the hurricane. He's giving me a chance to walk away. To stop whatever this is from happening while there is still time. It's not too late. A kiss can be just that.

I think about Clive, my broken proposal. The heat of Shadow's shoulder, the way he tucked me into his bed and slept on the couch like a gentleman. He doesn't look the part, and God knows he could still be dangerous. But after what I've been through, the real fear I've experienced, I want to trust again and get lost in something so good that I can't worry or think or wonder.

I don't know where the words come from, and they sound silly coming from my lips, but I force myself to say them anyway. I want another life, a new start, and whether this is a dead end or a brand-new path, I'm pushing myself.

"I want you, Shadow. I want this."

FIVE
SHADOW

VIOLET JAMES IS like no librarian I've ever met. After I've kissed her until she's breathless and panting, I grab the front of that yellow sundress and free the tits I have been hard for since I first saw her wet and dripping at the Shady Lane Motel last night.

I shove the fabric down and don't give a shit when it tears at the seam. When I see those rust-colored nipples, the tips thick and hard, just begging to be sucked, I nearly nut in my jeans.

But I take my time, sucking each peak between my lips, flicking the tips with my tongue, and squeezing the fullness of her exposed breasts until she's writhing. I drag my mouth from her soft skin and rub my beard against her flesh, the rough hairs scratching her nipples until she's moaning my name and pushing herself harder against me.

I kiss my way down her body, shoving the yellow dress up past her hips. She's wearing the most ridiculous pair of plain white panties that I almost laugh. I haven't seen anything but a thong in so long, I forgot women actually wear underwear that covers their asses. But somehow, on Violet, it fits.

I run my hands from her knees to the tops of her thighs, kneading the thickness that she barely hid under that flimsy dress. I lower my mouth and suckle her inner thighs, licking and nibbling her skin until the flesh is pink and rosy with heat. I want to bury myself inside her, lose myself in her soft sweetness. I think I've figured out the perfect way to ride out this storm—by riding Violet.

She's gripping my hair and tugging, scratching and stroking my head while I work my way from her thighs to her pussy. Her panties are dark in the middle, where my good little librarian is drenched and ready. I tear the underwear off her and toss them to the floor, ravenous to taste every fucking inch of her.

She gasps a little when I expose her pussy, but I grunt before drawing in a breath.

"Fuck," I whisper. "You're pretty everywhere," I tell her. And it's true. I've fucked a lot of women, but Violet makes me want to take my time. To mark her perfect skin with my teeth, hands, lips. She's trimmed down there but has enough hair to look like a woman.

She draws in a breath and tries to close her knees.

"No." I stand back, using every ounce of my control to remove my hands and lips from her body. "Show me, Violet. Show yourself to me."

Her eyes fly open, and she lifts her head from where it is resting on the windshield of the GTO. "Show you?" she echoes.

I cross my arms over my chest, my cock screaming for release. "Show me," I say.

She swallows, her tits exposed over the pushed-down bodice of her dress. Her nipples are hard, and her chest is heaving with heavy, slow breaths. Her lips are parted, her eyes wide. She blinks languidly then lies back against the car and opens her legs. She's spread open, and she reaches down and puts a hand to her cunt. With two fingers, she parts her pussy and drags some of the wetness to her clit. She gasps again when she touches herself, and I'm on her in a second.

"Mine," I growl, grabbing her wrist and moving her hand away. "That's my pussy, isn't it, sweetheart?"

"It's yours," she agrees, her words a breathless whisper. "Shadow, I need…"

She's silenced when I take my fingers, slide them into my mouth to wet them, and then slip two all the way inside her.

"Oh my God," she moans, her knees dropping open. She wiggles her hips against the hood of the car to force my fingers deeper.

I press my left hand against the softness of her belly and work my fingers inside her, feeling every ridge and bump until I find the spots that are going to send her to the stars. I use my thumb to stroke her clit while I finger-fuck her, deep and slow, then fast and hard.

"Shadow," she cries my name, groans, writhes against the car, but I don't stop. Don't slow down. I want to see Violet come apart for me.

From this angle, her long, dark hair is tangled over her tits, her chest rising and falling as her breaths come faster and faster.

"Come for me," I demand, lowering my face to suck her clit. While my tongue works its magic, I let my fingers find that spot deep inside until, finally, I feel a flood of wetness soak my fingers.

"I'm gonna…" Violet can't finish that sentence as her

eyes slam shut. She's working her hips hard against my hand, riding my fingers while I'm licking and sucking her. When she finally comes, she cries out so loud and so long, I can't help but crack a smile, but I don't dare move my mouth from her pussy.

She falls silent after a minute, and I slowly pull my soaked fingers from inside her. I dry my hand on my jeans and unzip, but Violet is sitting up, shaking her head. For a second, I worry that it was too much. That I was too rough. That she's regretting everything she's done since the moment she agreed to come back to the compound with me. But then, her tits proudly out, the yellow sundress dropping down to cover her swollen pussy, she locks eyes with me.

"It's your turn," she says as she slides off the hood of the car and lays her hand on top of mine. She takes over the zipper, sliding it down with gentle fingers. I help her get the denim over my hips, and she gasps when my jeans fall down around my ankles. I'm not wearing underwear, and my cock is so hard it practically pokes her in the face.

She kneels on the floor in front of me.

"Shadow." She gently explores the underside of my throbbing erection with her fingertips and touches the metal of a silver barbell. "You're pierced."

"Yep." I attempt to control myself as she strokes my cock, feeling the veins and ridges and trying to make sense of the piercing.

"Is it sensitive?" she asks, using one finger to wipe away a thick drop of precome from my opening.

I reach for the strip of condoms I grabbed from the glove box of the GTO resting against the windshield wipers and tear one off. "We can play show-and-tell when we get back to my room."

She takes the condom from me and tears it open, but before she slides it on me, she draws me into her mouth, closing the soft heat around my dick. I feel her tongue lap against the barbell, curious and gentle, and I have to suck in a breath and open my eyes to try to slow myself down. She sucks lightly at first, using her tongue to explore, but then I grab her hair and tug, lifting her face before I release every drop into her mouth.

"I wanna fuck you," I tell her, and she nods as seriously as if we're negotiating a contract.

She slides the condom over my wet dick and eases it carefully over the barbell.

"It's fine," I assure her. "It ain't gonna rip the rubber."

As soon as the condom is on me, she stands. This is fucking torture. Her nipples are still hard, and her chest is flushed. She's licking my precome from her lips, and she's so goddamn gorgeous, I don't know whether to fuck her mouth, her ass, or everything at once.

"Bend over the car," I tell her.

She does as I ask, facing the GTO then dropping her hands onto the hood. I lift her skirt and settle myself between her legs, notching the tip of my dick at her entrance. Before I fuck her brains out, I reach under her arms and cup her tits with my hands. I squeeze them, tweaking her nipples between my fingers.

She cries out and pushes her ass back against me. I drop my face to her exposed back while she leans forward, supporting her weight on the hood with her hands. Using her tits for leverage, I pull her toward me and slide inside her from behind, thrusting deep and slow until I'm so far inside her I see stars behind my eyelids.

I kiss her bare back, shove my nose into her hair, and breathe her in. All I can do is suck in the scent of her skin, her hair, her pussy, like a man who's taken a nose dive into the depths of the ocean. I clutch her close, biting her shoulder. My eyes roll back in my head, and I bang her, hard, working out my pleasure against her body as she lifts her ass and presses against me.

"Shadow, I'm gonna come again." Her voice is weak, a tiny sound moving at me through the darkness of the garage. She stiffens slightly under my hands, and I just manage to pinch her nipples before I feel her walls spasm hard around my shaft. "Oh my God!" she screams this time, a long, pleasure-racked wail so animalistic and raw, the sound alone does me in.

Matching her frenzied movement, I buck against her, coming in spurts so hard, my heart thumps against Violet's back.

She slows and quiets before I'm done, meeting my every thrust with erotic panting and whimpers.

Finally, I've given her everything I've got. I'm empty, numb, and yet, I don't want to let go. Don't want to stop. Blood thundering in my legs, I bend at the waist and crash my cheek against her back.

We're totally silent, the sounds of our breathing matched to the whipping sounds of the wind bashing against the building.

When my dick starts to shrivel, I pull out of her. She cries out softly, the surprise of our separation feeling as foreign and cold to me as it must to her. I peel off the condom and toss it in a nearby trash bin. My ass is tight, my legs coiled hard from fucking her standing up. And yet, all I want to do is climb right back on top of her, stuff my face in her hair, and breathe.

I tug my jeans back up over my legs and painfully zip up while my dick is still at half-mast. I grab the rest of the condoms and shove them into the back pocket of my jeans, and then I take Violet's arms, turning her to face me. I lift the front of her dress to cover her tits and lean forward to kiss her.

She wraps her arms around me, her eyes wide. She looks thoughtful. Scared, maybe.

"You all right?" I ask, taking a small step back. I don't know shit about this woman. Her life outside of here—none of that matters. What matters is right now. "Sweetheart?"

She sucks her lower lip into her mouth and bites down. "I'm just, like, numb. In the best ways," she says. "That was the best sex I've ever had in my life." She blinks fast. "Like, ever."

I grab her hand and leave behind our mugs of now-cold coffee. I lead her toward the door, unlock it, and motion her through. "I can do better," I tell her.

———

Back in my room, I peel that dress off Violet's body and throw my jeans on the floor. We climb under the covers in my bed, and within what feels like seconds, we're kissing again, frantic, deep kisses, as if we didn't just come within an inch of our lives.

Violet is growing bolder. She takes the lead, kissing me and climbing onto my hips, shoving me back against the bed. She grabs my face in her hands and kisses me, biting my lips between her teeth and scraping my beard against her cheeks. She's going to be raw before the storm is even over, but I don't give a fuck. It can storm until hell freezes over, as long as I've got his woman in my bed.

She pulls away from feasting on my mouth and kisses

her way down my belly. She massages my arms, laces her fingers through mine, lifts my hand to inspect the tattoos on the inside of my wrist. She licks the inside of that wrist and then drops my hand and moves her attention to a tiny mole I have just beneath my belly button. She breathes hot kisses against my skin while she reaches for my balls, cupping them, massaging their weight with her fingers. My cock springs to life, and she reaches again for the underside, fondling the barbell.

"I can't believe you're pierced," she whispers, rolling another condom over my erection. "Can I ride you?" she asks quietly. "I want to know what it feels like with me on top."

My eyes are closed, my hands fisted in the sheets. I don't say anything, just wait while this woman sheathes me in another condom and uses me in whatever way she wants.

When she lowers herself down on top of me slowly, I feel the long muscles in her thick thighs tensing under my hands with every movement. I grip her legs with my hands, thankful that I just came because I want her to ride me hard, to show me everything she needs, and to take everything I have to give.

"You like it on top?" I grunt the words out, keeping my eyes closed because I swear to fuck, if I open them, if I see Violet's tits bouncing, her hair spilled out over her shoulders, her lips parted while she lifts herself up and down on my cock, this will all be over way too fast.

She purrs, a happy sound that's half groan deep in her throat as she lowers herself, and my cock jerks in response. The noises she makes when she's fully seated are hot, but when I open my eyes, seeing her head thrown back, I'm blown to fucking bits inside. Her knees are bent and her feet planted solidly on the mattress. Her legs are spread wide, so I can watch as she bounces lightly on her heels, my dick sliding in and out of her perfect pussy.

She parts her lips and locks her eyes on mine. Then she squeezes her knees into my sides and leans forward. She braces her hands against my chest like she did on the hood of the GTO. Her hair falls forward, and the weight of her tits swings as she works her hips back and forth.

She moves slowly at first, making long, loose circles with her body on mine, rolling her hips to find just the right position and angle of my cock against her walls. She tightens her fingers against my pecs and closes her eyes, losing herself to the sensations.

I lift my hands to her tits and cup them. I squeeze hard and she gasps, and then I rake the rough pads of my fingers over the tender tips of her nipples.

She sucks in air and shudders, her entire body growing tense. She pivots from rolling her hips to grinding down, bucking back and forth once she's found the right spot. She moans my name and starts to pick up speed.

"Fuck me," I demand. "Fuck me, Violet. Come all over my cock, sweetheart."

My words have the desired effect because Violet rides me violently, shaking my bed, banging the frame against the wall behind us. I don't give a fuck what kind of noise we're making. Violet fucks like a runner who loves every mile, chasing her climax, then slowing down, dragging out her pleasure and working herself into a frenzy.

I've never felt so deliciously used.

I can't keep my hands off her, my fingers gripping her thighs hard enough that I bring her closer, deeper, until finally, she is crying out, no demure librarian whimpers, but full-throated, head-thrown-back screams of pleasure.

She shudders and shakes, grinding her hips down against mine and clawing her fingers into my chest. Watching her come is like watching a force of nature. The power of her climax taking over her body is so real, so genuine. Not like some of the club women who grate out fake noises like I'm going to be turned on by exaggerated effort.

Violet is the real deal. She's breathless and throaty, loud and raw, and I swear to fuck I could come just listening to her.

It takes everything I have to control myself while her walls clamp down on me, a flood of wetness soaking the sheet beneath us. She's done too soon. Too damn soon.

When she loosens her grip on my chest and sinks down against me, I slide my hands under her hair and breathe her in, waiting for her breathing to settle and her body to cool before I even think of moving.

The wind slams against the shutters. The room is dark because we turned off the lights, but it's like I can see everything about Violet. Her trusting green eyes. Her long hair, tangled and sweaty. I hear every shaking breath, every satisfied purr that climbs up her throat as she comes down from the high she chased on my body.

I hold her close to me until she pulls away and rolls onto her back beside me.

"Any chance you can take me again?" she asks, her words shy. "Me on my back this time?"

I don't need any more invitation than that.

After fucking for what seems like hours, Violet and I are tangled together in my bed. We've got the blankets and sheets around us, and we've been talking for probably an hour about almost everything. Where I grew up—not far from here. How long I spent in prison—just a few months, but long enough to know I never, ever wanted to go back. Why I pierced my dick—that one, I don't think she even needed to ask.

Violet's telling me about her new job as a high school librarian when her phone rings in her purse. The ringtone isn't the same one I heard last night, and she jumps out of bed, grabs the phone from her purse, and sends the call to voice mail—but not before I see the name "Clive" come up on the screen. She sets the phone on the bedside table on her side of the bed, and I notice she places the device facedown.

"Your sister checking up on you?" I ask, brushing strands of hair back from her face.

There's no fucking way her sister's name is Clive, but I have no claim on this woman. She's here for a night, maybe two. It ain't none of my business if she does have a man someplace out there. Fuck. If she were mine, I'd be blowing up her phone until I heard from her too.

Scratch that. If she were mine, I'd be with her every second of a storm like this. Doing exactly what we have been doing, until the storm passed. But it's none of my business if her man's an asshole. An asshole who can't fuck her like I can, on top of it.

The phone starts to ring again. Same ringtone. Same reaction from Violet. She silences the call and sets the phone back down.

"Uh, no. That wasn't my sister. I should probably check in with her."

I wait, assuming she's going to do it now, but the phone rings again. I practically feel Violet's body go cold as she silences the call. As soon as she does, the fucking phone rings again. And again. The calls come one after another until I swear to fuck this guy has called her at least ten times. The way Violet's reacting, I'm not sure if I'm jealous about him or pissed off for her.

"I, uh, I'm sorry. I was engaged," she explains weakly. She takes the phone in her hands and holds it like it's a bomb she's afraid will detonate right before her eyes. "I ended it six months ago," she explains quickly. "Broke up with him completely, not just ended the engagement. I'm not with anyone else right now, but Clive, he…uh… He's probably just worried about how I'm managing with the storm."

I yawn and stretch a little, my stomach rumbling. It's probably time to get my ass into the shower, soap off some of the come and pussy juice, and get us some breakfast.

"Go 'head and check in with old Clive," I tell her, trying to sound chill about it. I get out of bed, my dick sore from hours of fucking her. I turn into the bathroom. "I'll shower quick and get us something to eat."

Violet must have picked up her phone the second I got out of bed because I hear a beep, and then a voice message starts to play.

"Shoot." Violet tries talking over the voice. "I must have put it on speaker."

She fumbles with her phone in the dark bedroom, but I stop dead in my tracks as I hear the message.

"You fucking cunt." The voice is seething with anger. "Answer your goddamn phone."

I can't hear everything the man says because I start to see red as soon as he says cunt. I hear him say, "You think this is a game, Violet? You think you can toy with my feelings? Ignore me when you know goddamn well all I want is to take care of you? Make sure you're safe? Maybe I should give you something you should really be afraid of…"

And then I just go cold.

The last thing that motherfucker says into Violet's voice mail is a threat—plain and simple.

I swallow back bile and grip my hands into fists. "Violet?" I want an explanation. And I want one now.

She sits up in my bed, my sheets covering her breasts. "It's nothing," she says, huffing a sigh. "He doesn't know where I am and is mad that I wouldn't tell him. It's fine. I'm fine." She drags in a shaky breath and blows it out. After all the gasps and groans I've heard from this woman today, this is different. This sounds like fear. "And that's why he's my ex," she says, trying to sound light.

I nod, not that she can see it, and go into the bathroom. I take a hot shower while I think about the ways I could tear this Clive's face from his body.

Violet may not be mine, but she sure as fuck isn't his. And I'm going to make sure he knows it.

SIX

VIOLET

AFTER A SHOWER, I feel like a totally new person. A new person I hardly recognize in a life I never could have imagined for myself. I had sex with Shadow. Like, mind-melting, intense, amazing sex that is nothing like I've ever experienced before.

I had a couple of serious boyfriends before Clive—two, to be exact—but sex was never the highlight of those relationships. With Clive especially, it was always something I did the way he wanted it. He never helped me have an orgasm. He never seemed to care if I was doing anything other than making it good for him.

To be honest, that was not even the worst thing about my relationship with Clive. But as I pull on a pair of yoga pants and a loose, long-sleeved top with a wide-open neck that slides over one shoulder, I've never felt more alive.

Shadow is sitting on the couch, his fingers locked together while he stares off into the darkness.

"You waited?" I ask. My hair is still wet and smells like my travel-sized shampoo, vanilla and lavender and delicious. My legs are wobbly, but somehow, walking through the bedroom and seeing Shadow there feels weirdly right. I have to resist the temptation to act like this is normal and just climb into his lap and kiss him.

I don't know how to act. None of this is normal. But my gosh, I have never felt more satisfied.

When I reach the couch, Shadow rakes his eyes over my body. I can't read his expression, but he looks lost in thought. My stomach growls, a loud, long sound, and I laugh and pat my belly.

"What time is it anyway?" I ask.

He grins, then gestures toward the door. "Time to see who's still alive and kickin'."

I follow him through the door, and as we walk down the corridor back into the compound, Shadow keeps his hand on my lower back. The gesture is protective, but even more than that, it feels possessive. I'm not sure how I should feel about that.

It's not overbearing like Clive, who liked to drag me by the hand when I lingered too long at a table or got lost in a bookstore scanning the shelves. Shadow may be big and scary, but he's the thing I am least afraid of in my life right now. I'm going to cling to that feeling of safety for as long as I can.

When we reach the main room of the compound, the whole place has come back to life. There is a massive guy I recognize from last night, growling as he seems to silently direct a group of young guys who are cleaning up the place. Some of the older bikers are already drinking, beers in their hands as they recline on couches and chairs.

We head toward the bar, and Shadow pours us two fresh cups of coffee. He silently hands me one while a biker even bigger than Shadow approaches us.

"Storm won't blow past for another day." This man is

taller than Shadow, and his black hair is chin-length. He's got a thick black beard and piercing blue eyes that look cold enough to cut glass. He narrows his eyes and practically looks through me.

"Violet," Shadow says, cocking his chin toward me. "Drink your coffee. I need a minute. Then we'll get something to eat."

I meet his eyes, and I see reassurance there. I feel accepted and looked out for, so even though the room is full of strangers, people I have never met and who all look like they could eat me alive, I'm not afraid.

I smile at him, and then I look at the man with him. "Phantom, thank you again for letting me stay here."

Phantom doesn't respond, just firms his lips and turns away. Shadow follows him.

Well, okay…

I'm alone on the barstool sipping my cup of coffee—at least, as alone as I can be—when I feel the cell phone in the pocket of my yoga pants buzz. After hearing Clive's message, I thought about turning the phone off, but my sister insisted that I stay in touch, so I texted her before I jumped in the shower. I take a peek at my phone and just pray it's her checking in.

My heart swells with relief when I see a text message pop up filled with emoji hearts.

> Sis: You've got at least one more night till this thing blows past, if the weather people know what the shit they are taking about. Be safe, sis. Send me updates. Keep your phone charged. Love you.

I like the message so she knows I read it before I slip the phone back into my pocket. My sister knows I'm safe, and

Clive has settled down enough to stop blowing up my phone. I haven't responded, and I'm shocked to realize that if I weren't with Shadow, I would have. I would have told him everything. Where I was. Who I was with. How I was doing.

I left him because... Well, there are so many reasons why I left that man, that relationship. And yet, for the last six months, I haven't cut the cord completely.

When he texts, I answer.

When he calls, I pick up.

Not now.

Not today.

I left to start a new life, and the storm may have blown me onto a totally unexpected path, but there's no need for me to put Clive first now. He can't get to me. I'm safe here. And I want to soak up every bit of this experience. Tomorrow morning, when the storm has blown over, this pit stop on the road to my new adventure will be behind me. I'm going to take every moment as it comes.

I have to hold back a sad grin. Tomorrow means I'll have to say goodbye to Shadow. It's weird how a morning of intense sex can make you feel so alive and changed.

Is that what great sex does? Or is that just what I'm feeling because Shadow is a man who hasn't yet tried to hold me back? Stifle me?

"Hey, princess." An unfamiliar voice breaks me from my thoughts. "You know how to cook?"

I turn to see a woman wearing a giant T-shirt that probably doesn't belong to her and nothing else that's visible, at least. I try not to cringe at the sight of her bare feet on the sticky floor.

"I do," I tell her.

She yawns and rubs her eye, smearing remnants of last

night's glittery eye shadow across her cheek. "Come on. You're on kitchen duty."

I look back toward Shadow, who is standing with his arms crossed over his chest. He's in a quiet conversation with Phantom that looks intense. When I meet his eyes, Shadow looks at the girl, then back at me. He gives me the slightest nod, so imperceptible I'm not sure he did it.

But then the girl loops her arm through mine. "Ohhhh shit," she croons. "So, you're not just some straggler Shadow brought in from the storm? The girls are going to want details."

I have no intention of telling anyone anything about what's happened with me and Shadow, but I let this woman drag me away from the bar and into a really big, beautiful commercial kitchen.

I don't know how many people actually live in this place, but the kitchen is massive. There are two huge refrigerators, a walk-in pantry, and a gas stove that has twelve burners. A couple of women who look like they are still wearing their clothes from last night are taking turns flipping pancakes, and I smell bacon that must be baking in one of the ovens.

"For the love of Christ, tell me you can cook." One of the women I recognize from outside last night—not the puker, but the other one—points at me. "What's your name? You're..." She squints, as if trying to place me.

"I'm Violet," I tell her. I reach out a hand to shake hers. "And you are?"

A woman I almost don't recognize as the bartender from last night approaches me. Her face is free of makeup, and she's not wearing the low-cut top that shows off her very impressive cleavage. She's dressed in a comfy-looking sweatsuit in a soft red color that highlights her dark hair and eyes.

"I'm Stella," she says, nodding at me. She points to the friend of the puker. "That's Amy, and over there is Jackie." She lowers her voice and nods at a woman who is rummaging around in an open fridge door, yelling about needing more butter. "Penny," she murmurs. "She's gonna give you a real hard time about Shadow. Don't show any weakness, and you'll be fine."

I nod thankfully and immediately wonder how many of these women Shadow has fucked too. I shake the thought from my head. It doesn't matter. I'm not looking for forever. I'm not looking for anything, honestly. Shelter from a storm. I need to remember that. I'm the stranger here, and these women... They are part of this world. I'm just passing through it.

I lift my chin and set my coffee down on the counter. "So, what can I do?"

Penny slams the fridge door shut, having found an unopened package of butter. "Bitch, please tell me you cook?"

Stella leans close to me and says very loudly, "We mean bitch as a term of endearment. Not an insult." She shakes her head and sighs. "Can you chill out with the new girl, Pen?"

Penny shrugs and tosses the butter on the counter. "What's your name, new girl?"

I tell her, assuming she either didn't hear it or wasn't paying attention when I introduced myself to Stella.

Penny cocks a brow at me. "That's a real innocent name for a bitch with a body like that." She looks me over. "If Shadow gets tired of you, make sure you come talk to me."

She winks, and the other women whoop and laugh.

"Penny's an equal opportunity fuck," Stella explains with a smile. "And one of the most decent bitches you'll ever meet."

She motions for me to follow her, so I join Jackie, Penny, and Stella behind the counter.

"We got twenty hungry bikers to feed and, what, twelve girls?" Stella counts on her fingers. "Wait, where's Bailey?"

The women start talking about who slept with whom last night, who is showering, who's still sleeping off the hangover from last night's party.

"Cook like you're cooking for an army," Stella says, shaking her head. "Storm'll pass through by tomorrow and the guys will shop, so anything in here is fair game."

I can see that the pancake situation is not going well, so I offer to help.

"Fuck, please." One of the women, whose name I think is Cammy, hands me a spatula. "I'm dying for a smoke. It's all you, babe."

She leaves me with a bowl that looks like it has a gallon of pancake batter in it. I take my place in front of the stovetop, where three misshapen pancakes are burning on a massive griddle. I gently scrape off the ruined ones and set them on a paper towel that I plan to discreetly throw away as soon as they're cool.

I test the thickness of the batter, add a little more milk from the fridge to thin it, and then ladle out five perfectly round pancakes. The women all chatter and laugh as I watch for bubbles to form, and even though I have no idea who they are talking about, I don't feel excluded. I just sort of fit here.

I flip the pancakes when the bubbles on one side start

to pop, and I turn back to make sure there is a baking sheet in the oven so I can keep the finished pancakes warm while I cook another batch.

One oven has sheet after sheet of bacon in it, but the other is set to a warming temp. I add what I've cooked to the lopsided stack, and before I know it, Stella has her arm around me and she's chatting at me like she's known me forever.

"So, was that your first time with a twelve-gauge?"

I look at her, confused. "Twelve-gauge?"

The women in the kitchen burst out laughing. Stella picks up a banana from a bowl of fruit on the counter, slides her index finger underneath it, and wiggles it suggestively. I immediately realize she's referring to Shadow's penis piercing.

I flush and shake my head. "I don't know what that means..."

"The piercing." Stella hooks an arm over my shoulder. "Gauge is the size, babe. It's how thick the jewelry is." She touches the tip of her index finger to her thumb to make a circle. "Bigger hole in the body fits bigger jewelry. Shadow's got a twelve-gauge in his pants. I'm not saying I've seen it, but let's just say, I've heard about it."

The whoops and laughter from the women take over the kitchen, but it feels...I don't know...inclusive. Like they are laughing with me, not at me. I blush hard because they all seem to know—or at least assume—what happened with Shadow and me. "Okay, then I guess it is my first time with a twelve-gauge."

I know I've just admitted the truth to a room full of strange women, but I don't know. I've seen half of them naked and watched a couple of them actually being intimate with the guys in this club. Admitting I've seen Shadow's piercing feels almost modest by comparison.

"Frenum..." Cammy practically purrs yet another word I don't understand. She shivers. "I dated a dude in college who—" she takes the banana from Stella and pretends to stab her finger right through the middle of the fruit "—who had his junk itself pierced straight through." She shakes her head and makes a sour face. "He had to sit to pee for months until he figured out how to not spray piss everywhere."

"Prince Alberts freak me out." Another woman whose name I don't know sniffs and shakes her head. "Shadow's is classy."

I've never considered a piercing classy before, but then I also never considered that some of these women also went to college.

"Where did you go to school?" I ask, slipping another perfect stack of pancakes into the oven.

By the time I've cooked the entire bowl of batter, I've learned that three of the women have really great jobs. Stella isn't just the club's bartender. She's a bookkeeper who owns her own business. Cammy is a paralegal at a law firm that specializes in divorces, and one of the other women is a therapist. A couple of the girls are waitresses, and one works at a car dealership. These women are smart, interesting, and they have jobs and lives outside of the club. But they all share one thing in common.

"We like to party," Stella says. "And there's no place better than here. The guys are generous, and there is a clear pecking order. It's like being part of the popular group in high school. You know who's who and what's what. If the guys accept you, you drink and party for free. There's always somebody looking for a no-strings-attached good time, and if things get more serious…" She shrugs. "Some of us want this life for the long run. I don't think Shadow's the settle-down type, but there's nobody here who'll show you a better time."

My stomach flips over when she says settle down. Why would I even think about such a thing? It's obvious that we're opposites—although, based on everything the club girls are saying, maybe Shadow and I aren't that different after all.

"A book babe will be good for him," Stella says, giving me a genuine smile. "Shadow's into that shit. Reading, bettering himself. Unlike some of the other jokers who just wanna fight and play video games."

"Feeding time." She grabs a baking sheet covered with pancakes and motions for me to join her. "Let's eat."

I eat at the bar with Stella, Jackie, and Cammy, while Shadow is still talking to Phantom and now Savage. I've learned a little about the structure of the club and what it means that Shadow is the vice president. Stella refills my coffee and recruits a couple of the late risers to work cleanup duty.

The rest of the day goes by in a blur. After breakfast, Stella and Cammy ask for my help planning dinner. All around the compound, people are chilling out, having fun, or finding ways to pass the time. It's all starting to feel not just normal, but fun. I recognize more and more people as the day goes on, and I ask Stella anytime I have a question about who's who.

"That's a prospect," she says, nodding to a guy who has his hand on the butt of a much older woman. "Watch this." She tsks and shakes her head.

Not two seconds later, Savage, the guy who I believe is ex-military and who's got the steely eyes and massive muscles to go with the reputation, crosses his arms over his chest and clears his throat.

The kid yanks his hand away like it's on fire, and he practically falls over himself asking Savage what he should be doing. I don't hear what Savage says, but it's clear he's messing with the kid. He cracks a huge grin then uses both hands to grab the butt of the same woman the young guy was messing around with.

Savage bursts out laughing, pulls the woman close and gives her a playful kiss on the lips, and then he hands her back to the younger guy.

"Prospect?" I ask, watching the exchange curiously.

"He's not a member yet," Stella explains. "Young guys or new guys hang around for a while, prove their worth, and then sometimes they get patched in—meaning they are officially members of the club."

I have so many questions, but I'm a little embarrassed to ask. I know nothing about this world, but I want to learn. I take it all in but try not to be too nosey. "So, Savage is just messing with the younger guy?" I ask. "Or is that woman his girlfriend?"

Stella laughs. "No one says girlfriend. We're bunnies until we're locked down, and after that, we're old ladies."

I must make some kind of face because Stella leans forward and touches my arm.

"I'd rather be called a bunny or a piece of ass by someone who would kill anyone who dared to hurt me than be called baby by someone who enjoys hurting me. Maybe some women want that, but I'll take crude honesty over pain and lies every day of the week."

I look away from Stella and just nod. This bump on the path to my future is feeling more and more like destiny.

SEVEN

SHADOW

"JIZZY, GRAB ME ANOTHER BEER." Hawk, his signature sunglasses on even at the dinner table, slaps the shoulder of one of the prospects. He's laughing so hard, he can hardly get the words out. He actually has to lift the corner of his shades to wipe a tear from his eye.

One of the prospects jumps up from where he's standing in the corner, eating a burger with one hand and holding his beer in the other. The kid jams the last few bites of burger into his mouth and hustles off toward the bar. "Anyone else?" he asks.

"I'll take one, baby," Jackie calls from a cushy spot on a recliner. She's got a paper plate of food balanced in her lap.

"Fuck off, Jackie," Jizz mutters.

Hawk shakes his head and shoots Jizz a look, and the kid grabs two beers from the fridge behind the bar. He hands one to Hawk, keeping his eyes toward the floor. Hawk pops the cap off the bottle with his thumb and takes a long sip while Jizz walks over to the recliner and motions for Jackie to get up. She does, and he sits down in her seat and motions for her to sit on his lap. She leans over and gives him a long kiss on the neck, then plops her ass onto his lap and shimmies so her tits bounce. Then he hands her the beer.

"So, you wanna tell the ladies how you got your nickname, or should I?" Hawk drains half the beer in three long pulls, then sets the bottle on the table.

The corner of my mouth curls into a smile. I may be the only one who's heard this story as many times as I have, but it'll be at least a year before Hawk gets sick of telling it. Or until Jizz is patched in and has earned a more respectable name.

I'm sitting across from Violet. Twelve of us fit in the chairs that surround the large wooden table, while prospects and club bunnies are scattered on couches and chairs, using tray tables for their paper plates of food just like we're a family at a big Thanksgiving. A couple of the prospects run back and forth between the kitchen, taking orders to bring out more burgers, dogs, and buns from Penny.

It's rare that we have this many people for a meal, but with the storm and so many of us locked down together, I made sure Violet got a chair close to me.

Phantom's at the head, like a grim father looking over one very fucked-up family. He's not smiling, but he almost never does. Savage paces the perimeter of the room, always keeping his eyes on shit. Stella sits next to Violet, and I notice her making an effort to talk to the sexy librarian and explain the jokes or details about the crew that an outsider wouldn't know.

Stella's good people.

I'm not surprised she's taking Violet under her wing. What surprises me more is how at home Violet looks at the table.

Her innocent green eyes take it all in, her dark hair falling loose over her shoulders. One of them is bare where her slouchy shirt has fallen over to the side, revealing a thick bra strap. She was so scared of the storm but then so free on the hood of that GTO. She's unpredictable.

Just thinking about her tits and thighs makes my cock jerk in my jeans. She clocks me looking at her while Hawk stands over the prospect's shoulder, laughing his ass off, and her face lights up with a smile.

Hawk's got all of our attention now. He loves telling stories, especially stories that make our prospects look stupid. Lucky for him, they almost always give him more than enough material to work with. "So, this moron's dick is all rashed out, it burns when he pees, so he thinks he's caught some shit from one of the bitches he's been banging."

"Hey." Jackie is sitting in the prospect's lap, sipping from a bottle of beer. The kid is blushing red as a tomato and squirming like he's about to shit himself.

"Fuck you, Hawk," he mutters, but he knows he's gotta sit there and take it.

Hawk continues, the weak lights powered by the generator reflecting off the lenses of his sunglasses. "So, I take his ass over to urgent care. He's expecting some kind of STI test, and they give him one of those plastic cups and send him to the bathroom. But the kid's gone a long-ass time. I mean, I'm starting to get worried his fucking dick fell off or something. When he finally comes out, he says to me in a real hushed voice, 'That was weird. They don't even give you any magazines or anything. I watched some porn on my phone, but you'd think they'd have, like, something in there for you to use.'"

Hawk bends over and braces heavily tattooed hands on

his knees. "So, I go, 'You dumbass. What the fuck did you do in the bathroom? You're supposed to *piss* in that cup.'"

It takes about a second for everyone to realize what the kid did, and then the entire table bursts into laughter.

"How the fuck was I supposed to know?" Jizzy puts his hands on Jackie's hips to stop her from jumping from his lap. "I told them I had some issues down there, and the nurse hands me a fucking cup with no instructions."

Hawk is laughing so hard I can see the tears streak past his glasses. Phantom's got a smirk curling just one side of his mouth—about as much humor as that guy will ever show to anyone. Savage is shaking his head, a shit-eating grin on his face. He's an ex-SEAL or something like that. He doesn't like to talk about his past, but I'm sure he's seen a lotta stupid shit from new recruits.

"It was a serious case of fucking jock itch, okay?" Jizzy rubs his head in frustration. "No big fucking deal." He reaches a hand around to cup Jackie's shoulder. "A little cream, and my shit's as good as new. I was just relieved I didn't catch anything from you, babe."

She fakes looking offended, but she is laughing too hard to pull it off. "I wanna know what the hell you did with the cup of jizz."

Hawk fills in the rest of the story. "You've never seen a prospect move so fast. He goes up to the nurse and, in a scared little kid voice, is like, 'Ma'am, could I possibly get another cup?'"

I feel Violet's eyes on me, and I flick a look her way. Along with everybody else, she's laughing, but she never once looks away from me.

I lower my brows toward her empty plate. With one finger, I gesture at it.

She gets me, shakes her head, and mouths, "I'm good."

I grab my empty plate and walk around the table to pick up hers. Then I take her hand. "Let's get out of here before we get dragged into cleanup."

I dump our paper plates in a trash bin near the bar, then lead Violet back toward my room.

We enter without a word, and once we're inside, I grab a book of matches and light a few jar candles I have in my room.

Violet smiles. "Books and candles. What's next, Shadow? Are you going to show me your library card?"

"Ain't had one of those in a couple of decades." I chuckle. "We have a game to finish playing, and I figure with all the cooking we did, we can leave off the lights. Give the generator a break."

I grab the bottle of whiskey and drop down on the couch. Violet sits on the opposite side and faces me, crossing her legs under her.

"Same game?" she asks, holding out her hand for the bottle.

"You got a better idea?" I pass her the bottle, twisting off the cap and setting it on the side table.

She shakes her head and holds the bottle up to me. "I've got so many questions." She leans forward slightly, her tits moving against the soft fabric of her shirt. She takes a drink. "You ready?"

I grin and nod. "Lay it on me, librarian."

"What do you do for work?" She asks the question delicately, like she's not sure whether it's okay to ask.

I hold out my hand for the bottle. "The club has businesses," I say simply. The less she knows, the better. "I do whatever's needed."

She hands me the whiskey. "The club seems more like a family than I would have thought."

"Is that a question?" I lift my brows and offer the bottle back, but she shakes her head.

"An observation," she says, smiling. "I can see why people like it here. It's fun."

"Fun?" I drink because that one word is a whole-ass question. "One thing I never call this place is fun." I point the bottle at her. "You, however, are a hell of a good time."

She blushes and takes the bottle back. "Well, I can't say I could ever see myself...I don't know..." She's quiet for a moment, as if she's convincing herself it's okay to say the words. "Snorting coke off Jackie's stomach. But I had fun today."

She takes a long sip, and I notice she's not wincing as much as she did yesterday. Maybe it's the full belly, or maybe my girl is already building a tolerance to the burn. "Two-part question."

I expected questions about my dick, and she dives in headfirst, wanting to know about my frenum piercing. I explain that, no, my piercing never shreds through a condom and, no, it doesn't require any special care other than keeping it clean.

We pass the bottle back and forth and answer what feels like two hours of sexual questions that get me hot and hard. Finally, she's sitting in my lap and kissing me with every shot she takes. We're both fully dressed and enjoying this game, but just like last night, I start to see signs that she can't take much more booze.

"Shadow," she pants my name against my ear. "How the heck are you so delicious?" She trails her tongue along the side of my neck.

I clamp my fingers against her plush ass. "That's a question. You've got to drink," I tease.

She does, and I reward her with a kiss so deep and

hungry that I swear I come back a little drunker from the whiskey on her tongue.

"My turn." I've been waiting for the right moment to ask this, but if she passes out, I'll miss my chance. I drink, and then, holding her face in my hands, I ask, "So, this fucker Clive. What's his deal?"

She sobers up a little and looks down. "That's a big question, but I guess it's a fair one."

She climbs off my lap and turns away from me. She shoves her ass between my legs, and I stretch them out along the length of the couch, letting her rest her back against my chest. I lower my chin so I can smell her hair, which, despite the cigarette and weed smoke in the main room, and the cooking and cleaning she did today, still smells like *her*.

"I never really dated much," she explains, slurring her words a little. "I'm thirty-two, but I never had a serious boyfriend until after college. My second one was in grad school, a fellow librarian. But neither one of them lasted. It wasn't any big thing. I just..." She draws in a huge breath and sighs. "I never felt like I was enough for the guys I dated. I was too thick, too smart, made too much money, and that made them insecure." She laughs. "Don't get me wrong. I don't make a ton as a school librarian, but back in grad school, I had a great job when most of the other students were unemployed or doing part-time work-study jobs. I had money and a car. The car I still have, by the way."

She swallows and is quiet for a minute. "Clive was different, right from the start." She sighs. "It all happened so fast. We met about a year ago, and within six weeks, he told me he wanted to marry me. He was so intense. I think it's called love-bombing. He fell so fast and was so, I don't know, *into* me. Half the time, I didn't even know what I felt about him because I was too busy thinking about how devoted he was to me. We took weekends away, spent all our time together."

I stroke her head absently while she talks.

"He surprised me with a ring when we'd only been dating for four months." She doesn't look up at me, but I notice her stroking her left ring finger with her right hand, as if feeling for something that was once there but isn't anymore. "I had never been proposed to, and my first instinct was to say no." She turns slightly to face me. "I should have listened to my gut. It was too much, too fast, but Clive was good to me. I had no excuse to say no."

The blood freezes in my veins. "What you deserve is a reason to say yes, not an excuse to say no."

She gives me a half smile and then runs her fingertips along the tops of my thighs. "Thank you," she says quietly. "I guess I know that now."

She goes on to explain how fast everything changed. "Once I took that ring, he moved in to my townhouse. We hadn't lived together before, and I found out later he'd been evicted. Had been crashing with friends the entire time we had dated." She shakes her head sadly.

"He never told me how much trouble he was in. Financially, that is. He has a good job, but I don't know, Shadow. He had no place to live. In four months, I'd only been to his place a couple times early on. After that, we'd always go to my place. I never thought it was strange. I liked my place, and it seemed easier to have him pack a small bag than for me to live out of a huge bag with toiletries and clothes and stuff." She laughs, but it's a dry, brittle sound. "Things fell apart fast once he was under my roof."

She tells me the basics—the control over her schedule, time with her friends. Normal douchebag shit that guys like that do to feel powerful. Big.

"Did he hurt you?" It's a question, but this is no game. I can't help my hands clenching as I imagine taking a fist to this Clive asshole's face.

She nods, a slow, slight movement. "In his way. He hurt me in ways that wouldn't show. Holding on to my neck a little too hard and too long during sex. Not letting me keep anything private. He believed our relationship meant he had an all-access pass to everything about me. That's why I don't have a passcode on my phone. He never trusted me, but I never had anything to hide. I keep telling myself to put one on my phone now, but I don't know. Maybe I'm afraid he'll catch up to me one day and break my phone instead of just looking through it to see who I'm talking to."

I start to feel sick with rage, fury simmering in my gut. "What else?"

She yawns sleepily and laces her fingers through mine. She holds my hands over her soft belly and squeezes my fingers. "I ended it," she says. "That was the biggest insult of all."

I feel her shoulders rise and fall, and I'm pretty damn sure she's asleep. The storm is still raging outside, and the candles flicker, casting a dim yellow light over her sleeping body. We sit there, Violet snoozing and me just holding her, until that damn ringtone I recognize from earlier jerks me awake. I must have dozed off, but Violet is out cold.

She doesn't flinch as I reach over her to the opposite corner of the couch, where her phone blares incessantly against the leather.

I climb out from under her and settle her back against the cushions, and then I swipe the touchscreen to answer the call. I say nothing.

"Violet? Do you think this is a game I'm playing? You want to play with me, I play to win, Violet. You know this about me, you know—"

I can't stand the sound of the douchebag's voice. I cut him off. "The only thing I hear is a whiny prick of a loser. Now, shut the fuck up and listen."

There's a split second of silence in which I swear I hear him gasp. But then, he takes off. "Who the fuck is this? Where the fuck is Violet? Put her on the phone. Put that stupid bitch on the phone, asshole."

I smile. So, it's gonna be like this. "The only stupid bitch I hear is the one talking to me right now. So why don't you stop your crying and listen carefully." I pace my dark room, wishing like hell I could meet this cocksucker face-to-face. For now, this will have to be enough. "I know who you are, and I know what you did to Violet."

"Wait, wait, wait. What did that bitch say? Who the fuck is this?" He tries to talk over me, but I ignore every question.

"You're gonna wanna listen and listen good, *Clive*." I stress his shitty name so he knows that I know exactly who he is. "You're going to forget you ever knew Violet James. You're not going to call her. You're not going to see her. You're not going to bother anybody who even knows that you know her. Are we clear? I really need you to tell me you're with me on this."

I hear Clive cursing up a blue streak, calling me a bitch-ass pussy and dropping f-bombs like they have some kind of power over me.

I laugh in his ear. "I can see you're too stupid for

subtlety, so I'm gonna make this fucking easy. Stay away from Violet. No more calls, no more nothing. Forget she ever existed. Or I'll find you and make sure you stop breathing. Permanently. We clear, shit-for-brains?"

The line is silent for a second before I hear Clive, his voice shaking like this is his first big-boy fight. "I'll kill you!" he screams, his voice cracking on the threat. "You're fucking threatening me? I'll kill you."

"That's right," I say, trying to sound like I'm soothing a spoiled toddler. "We see each other, and only one of us walks away with a heartbeat. I'm betting on me, little man. So just stay the fuck away from Violet."

I end the call before he can get in another word and toss the device down on the couch. Violet's slept through the whole thing, but I'm wound up tight.

The woman passed out cold on my couch is sweet, smart. She's strong enough to weather a storm with a stranger, but trusting enough to open herself to me, a man who, for all she knew, could have been as shitty and useless as her ex.

It sickens me to think that asshole ever touched Violet —that he pretended to love her, slept beside her, gave her a goddamn ring.

I'm pacing furious circles in my room when Violet moans and rolls over onto her side.

The couch did a number on my back last night. I'm not going to sleep in my bed while she jacks up her body because she passed out on me this time.

I kneel beside her on the couch and think about picking her up. But then I realize she's wearing yoga pants, and I don't know a woman alive who can sleep in those. I skim a hand over her belly and hook my fingers under the waistband. It takes some effort, but she seems to lift her ass a little to help me while I push the snug fabric down to her ankles. Once the yoga pants are off, I slide my hands under her knees and scoop her into my arms.

I set her down on the bed, and she rolls to her side. I reach beneath her shirt, unclasp her bra, and pull both the loose top and the bra off her. Then I tuck her in and unzip my jeans. By the time I'm stripped down to my birthday suit, I realize that I've fucked this woman senseless on the hood of a car. There ain't no way she's gonna mind sharing a bed. I blow out the candles and climb in beside her.

I stick to one side of the bed so she's got room, and I tuck a pillow under my head. I close my eyes, but then I feel her soft body roll beside me. She plants her cheek against my chest and snakes her bare legs through mine. I'm naked, but she's still wearing panties. My cock is not happy about the situation. He's like a five-year-old who refuses to go to sleep. But I close my eyes and hold her close against my chest.

I breathe in the soft scent of her hair, and my breathing slows to match the steady pace of hers. Before I know it, my body wins out, and even my cock gives in to the sweetness and softness that is Violet James.

EIGHT
VIOLET

I WAKE up in the most comfortable and warm position I think I've ever been in in my entire life. Before my eyes even open, I register where I am—back in Shadow's bed. Blankets and sheets around me. The room is dark, but instead of the sounds of storms and wind, I hear the gentle thud of…*Shadow's heartbeat*.

We're woven so tightly together, I don't know how I'm going to get myself up.

I can feel the cool air on my bare toes, and I realize I'm naked except for a pair of panties. I don't remember how my clothes came off, but after everything I do remember from yesterday, I'm pretty sure I'd remember if Shadow and I had a repeat of any of the fun we had in the garage or right here in this bed.

I wiggle my toes and press my lips to his broad, hot back. I kiss him gently and realize that once I get up…if the storm is over, it'll be time to go. Time to end this small detour on the path to my new life, and that is not something I'm excited about doing.

I have to admit to myself that I have had fun. Shadow

is a surprise… Not a serial killer, thankfully. A big, beefy, complicated man whose touch makes me feel safer and more alive than I have ever felt before.

I run my hands over the tattoos that cover his back and try to remember the stories he told me about them last night during our drinking game. I must have been really smashed, because I remember some but not all of what we talked about.

Before I untangle my limbs from his, he rolls onto his side and faces me. He looks wide awake, and he smooths the hair back from my face. We lie there facing each other, maybe both taking in the fact that, at some point, I'll have to leave. Let him get back to his life, his work, whatever things he would do with his club and the club bunnies if I weren't here.

The thought makes me suddenly sad.

Shadow seems to notice. He rolls me onto my stomach and kneels over me. "Storm's passed," he says quietly. I don't want to read too much into the way he sounds. Is he regretting that it's almost time for me to leave? "Power's still out in most of the county."

"Mmm." I'm so lost in the feel of his hands as they explore my bare flesh, I can't really process what he's saying.

"Power lines are down. Roads are gonna be covered in debris, downed trees. Puddles as deep as your knees."

His hands slip under my panties and I sigh, and it's as if every weight, every worry, leaves my body and seeps into his mattress from his touch.

"You," he says gently, hooking his fingers in the waistband of my panties, "might have a hard time getting where you need to go." He slides my panties off, wanting more, and tossing them on his floor.

"Yeah," I whisper, resting my cheek against the sheets that still feel warm from our bodies.

I feel him open my legs, separating them and then lowering himself between them. I nearly cry out when I feel the hot, slick tip of his tongue flick between my thighs.

We don't talk anymore. Shadow moves his tongue from my clit to my wetness, licking and sucking with perfect pressure. I've never had an orgasm from oral sex before, but Shadow's mouth, his soft breath, the light prickles of his beard have me lifting my butt and rocking my hips greedily against his mouth.

He flips me onto my back and grabs a condom from the bedside table. I take it from him and tear it open, then I roll the rubber carefully down his head and past the large silver barbells of his piercing.

"I'm going to miss this," I say, in spite of myself.

Shadow doesn't reply. He just thrusts inside me, slow and deep. He's supporting his weight on his hands, and I lift my legs and hold myself open as wide as my muscles will go. I close my eyes and feel everything. His heat, his weight. Every powerful thrust and shuddering breath.

I circle my ankles with my hands and put my feet on the mattress, lifting my hips to meet his. The friction is perfect, the pressure intense. He breaks out in a sweat, small droplets falling from his brow onto my chest.

He clamps his lips onto my breast as he moves his hips back and forth, driving his erection deep inside me. He tightens his teeth around my sensitive nipple, and I feel a gush of wetness before my walls clamp down.

I release my ankles and scratch his back, pulling his weight closer to me. I am filled by him, crushed beneath him. Complete in the pleasure that he gives with every movement, every breath.

I climax, but I don't open my eyes. I want more. I want to come again. I don't think I can, my body so raw and full of him, but he's fucking me, shaking the bed. The power moving from him through me is so intoxicating, he makes the whiskey seem like water. I rock my hips, chasing more —more of this, more of him—until I come again, my legs crossed behind his back, my hands crushing his head to mine.

When he starts to shudder, I feel the head of his cock get bigger, fill my walls so deeply and so deliciously, I want him to come for hours, days. Being filled by him, feeling this—I don't even recognize myself. My body, my pleasure. Shadow is going to be an impossible act to follow. I only wish I didn't have to leave.

But thoughts like that are dangerous.

Falling too fast, not knowing enough about a man... I know where that ends. And I want to leave while the memories are good.

That means I have to leave today.

After Shadow is done, he kisses me everywhere. My shoulders, arms, my belly. He flops onto his back, breathless and damp with sweat, and I curl under his arm. The room is quiet.

The storm has ended. And now, so has this.

By the time I've showered and packed up my overnight bag, Shadow has brought me a cup of coffee and a couple slices of toast.

"Soaks up the alcohol," he says, but his words feel different.

The power is back on, and his room is a lot brighter

than I've seen it before. The generator must run on a lower power setting than the bulbs can handle, because the room is bright. Maybe it's also all the whiskey and all the sex.

I sip the coffee and eat the toast, then stand to grab my things. "Can I say goodbye to the girls?" I ask.

He nods, his hair slightly messy. He opens his bedroom door, and I walk down the corridor, fully aware that his hand isn't at my back. He's not guiding me. Not protecting me. I'm really on my way out. He's probably counting the seconds until I'm gone.

But I'll be okay. I can't let it get to me. This was a—

"Nerd girl." Cammy runs up to me before I even make it back to the main room and slams me in a hug. "Power is back, and I have a hankering for omelets. You're on egg duty."

I give her a fast hug. "I wish I could stay," I tell her, my voice trailing off. What is wrong with me? I'm acting like these people are my friends, when just two days ago, I was terrified they were some kind of sex slaves entrapped in a dungeon. Now, I'm wishing I could make breakfast with Stella and the girls. I wonder what more I could uncover if I had one more night to play drinking games with Shadow.

Cammy gives me a long, hard hug back, and I squeeze my eyes shut so I don't have to look at anyone as I say goodbye. She releases me and bounds back to wherever she was headed.

I continue down the corridor to the main room, which is once again a mess of half-naked sleeping bodies. Two of the prospects, including Jizzy, are already cleaning up, throwing empty bottles and cans into big plastic bags. I see Stella talking in a low voice to Phantom, whose arms seem permanently crossed over his chest.

Even the president of this club seems a lot less terrifying and imposing now. I approach them and clear my throat loudly.

"Hey, babe." Stella looks a little troubled, but she manages a smile. I wonder what she and Phantom were talking about, but his face is a solid wall of stone. Unreadable.

"Thank you for letting me stay here." I hold out a hand to Phantom, who looks at it like he doesn't have the first clue what to do with it. I wait, though, giving him a bright smile. "Uh, Phantom, thank you. I truly don't know what I would have done if you hadn't given me a place to stay."

He flicks a look at Shadow, one of his dark brows lowering. He grunts, then looks at my hand and takes it. He shakes it once, then claps me on the shoulder. He looks into my eyes but doesn't say anything else. Then he turns away from me, putting an arm over Stella's shoulder.

"I'm going to make a real pain of myself and interrupt you to give Stella a hug goodbye." I tap her on the shoulder, and she turns away from Phantom.

"Wait, you're going?" Stella opens her arms and gives me a tight, fast hug. "Girl, you were just getting started." She tosses a look at Shadow, but he just looks away. "Come back anytime to party. I'll have a drink waiting."

I smile and wave as a few more of the bikers and women wave back.

Then I feel it.

Shadow's hand against my lower back. I lean into it instinctively and can't help but wonder how many times after today I'll miss the feeling of his hand right there.

I shove the thought away.

I'm sure he's done this walk of shame with so many

women before me. And he won't give me another thought once I'm out of his hair.

We leave the compound by the back door, the same one I came in just two days ago. It feels like a lifetime, somehow.

I scan the parking lot and see all the cars are unscathed. Windows aren't broken, but there is a ton of plant debris—branches, leaves, even small shrubs that seem to have been completely uprooted and blown about—all over the lot. There is so much trash—water bottles, papers, food wrappers, even used clothes. It looks like someone dumped over a public trash bin and soaked everything in the ocean. It's distressing, and I hesitate for a moment. Maybe Shadow was right. Maybe the roads won't be drivable. As far as I know, my condo isn't ready yet, and who knows if it's suffered any storm damage.

We walk toward my car, and I unlock it with the fob. The sun is out now, but it's not really sunny. It's just bright and stiflingly hot.

After tossing the overnight bag in the back, I squint up at him. I can't make out his expression, and I lower my eyes. I have to go. There's nothing left to say.

"Violet." His low voice at my ear has me turning back. "My bedroom door is always open for you."

I flush hot and try to think of something to say to that. Thank you? Goodbye? But I have no words. The last two days have been life-changing.

"If you can't get where you're going, come back. The road crews will be working to clean up for a couple of days, but it might be bad out there."

I hear his words, but I can't stay. I don't know what it would mean for my heart, my body, my future if I did. I have to leave now or I know I won't go at all. I'll stay here and do what? This isn't real life. This is a bump in the road. A pit stop. In a few hours, Shadow will have another girl in his lap.

I yank open the car door, refusing to meet his beautiful green eyes. I can't say anything. I feel like half my body is still back in that bedroom with him. I don't do one-night stands. I don't do casual. I don't know how to do this. I don't know how to leave.

Suddenly, his hand is on my wrist, and he's pulling me from the car. He angles my hips to his and lowers his face to mine. He kisses me, softly at first, but then he opens his mouth, and I feel every ounce of his hunger.

I don't know what it means. I don't know what to do with whatever he's trying to show me, but I kiss him back. I don't want to say goodbye, but I don't belong here—no matter how much I wish I did.

I want to memorize his taste, and I swear the way that he's kissing me, it's as if he feels the same. He grips my behind, tugs me close, and feasts on my mouth for so long that I'm breathless and panting. He's so hard, I half expect him to bend me over the hood of my car and take me right here, but he doesn't. He pulls away, his eyes blazing hot.

"Johnny Butcher." I whisper his real name. I don't know why I said it. Don't know why I felt like taking away the sexy nickname, the tattoos, the scary exterior, and just whispering his name. But that's what I do as I lace my hands together behind his head.

"Violet James." He says mine, lowering his forehead to mine.

I have to go.

I *have* to go.

I can't do this.

I turn away fast, get in my car, and slam the door shut.

My fingers are shaking as I turn the key in the ignition. I don't want to leave. Don't know how to say thank you, goodbye, and what? Thank you for showing me the time of my life? For showing me fun and sex and friendship and...

No.

I have to leave.

I'll unpack this when I'm alone. When I can trust my heart won't lead me down a path I'll deeply regret.

So, I don't say anything. I just drive.

I leave the parking lot and pull onto the road, refusing to look back because I know Shadow hasn't moved. He's still standing right where I left him, looking exactly how I feel, and it doesn't make any sense.

My phone starts to ring, and I grab it on the first ring, before I even register the ringtone.

"You fucking cunt. Who the fuck is Shadow?"

I slam on the brakes. "Excuse me?" I put the phone on speaker and set it in my cupholder as I drive slowly toward the main road. I'm going to need my GPS to navigate my way away from the compound, but right now, I'm realizing that Shadow may have been right. The road is littered with debris, branches so large and sharp, I'm terrified I'll shred a tire.

This is stupid.

I'm so, so stupid.

Clive clearly agrees.

"I'm gonna kill him, Violet. Did he fucking touch you? Why the hell did another man answer your phone?"

I slow my car to a stop and rest my head on the steering wheel. I listen to Clive rant and rant, spewing hatred at me, insults at Shadow. I slowly piece together that Clive must have called last night and Shadow must have answered my phone.

Shadow talked to Clive, and he threatened him. And now, Clive is threatening me.

My mood flip-flops from lost to furious. I've spent six terrifying and stressful months carefully planting the seeds of a new life. A life that Clive shouldn't have been able to penetrate. He shouldn't know where I am. He shouldn't know anything about Shadow or the compound or where I spent the last few days. Shadow had no right to pick up my phone. He had no right to put himself between me and Clive. I was handling my ex. I was handling my own business. And now, all I hear is the rage, the threats, the shit-talking that I thought I had put behind me for good.

"I know where you are, Violet. And I'm going to make you pay."

I don't even have to end the call. Clive hangs up, and the sudden silence shocks me into action.

Clive knows where I live? He found my new address? Even if I could get there, now I can't go there. Not now when I don't know if there's power.

Two days ago, I was scared, but I wasn't helpless. Now, I'm powerless.

Vulnerable all over again.

And this time, it's not my fault.

It's Shadow's.

NINE
SHADOW

"STELLA, GIVE ME A BEER."

I straddle a barstool and take a huge sip to wash the taste of sweet Violet James off my lips. I've fucking sunk for this woman. Never have I been so whipped that I practically begged her not to leave. But she didn't want to stay, and that's for the best. Not everybody's cut out for this life; she should leave if she doesn't want to be here.

My mind starts spinning.

I need to go to Malcolm's to collect. We have business to do, shit that will all go back to normal now that the storm has passed, and yet, I don't want to think about anything but Violet James.

I chug the entire beer and slam the bottle down on the bar when Stella points at me. "Looks like your nerd girl's back."

I jerk my head up but not before I feel the vicious poke of a slim finger against my back.

"How dare you."

I turn on the stool and face the fuming woman whose ass I had in my hands just ten minutes ago. I cross my arms over my chest so I don't grab her and kiss her. My heart beats faster, and for a minute, I'm so fucking relieved she's here, I feel damn near happy. "How dare I what? Be right about the roads?" Worry takes over. "Are you all right? What happened?"

"What happened is you put your nose in my personal business." Violet's cheeks are flushed, and she's continuing to point at me with that finger.

I feel dozens of sets of eyes watching the scene unfold. Stella has the class to turn her back to us, but bunnies and brothers alike are watching this woman point in my face and accuse me of God only knows what.

"After fucking you senseless, sucking you off, and feeding you my dick, excuse the fuck out of me if I don't exactly know what *personal business* is supposed to mean."

Violet's eyes storm, and she glares at me. "Now you're going to just air our sex life in front of your whole compound?" Another poke to my chest. "I would never kiss and tell…"

"Sweetheart, we did a whole lot more than kiss back there in the garage." I can't help but have a little fun at her expense. She's making a scene, and I can't have that. It's one thing to bring my business to my brothers. It's another to have it thrown at their feet for sport.

"Shadow. I can't—"

Before she can say another damned word, I pick her up around the waist and toss her over my shoulder. I plant a firm smack on her ass. "Now, shut your damn beautiful mouth before I put something in there to keep you quiet."

I storm down the corridor toward my bedroom, leaving behind whoops and hollers and a lot of high-pitched whistles from my brothers. I kick open my door, set Violet down, then slam the door shut behind me.

"How could you?" Her nostrils flare and she glares at me. "How dare you."

I lunge for her, cupping the back of her neck and dragging her toward my chest. She lifts up on her toes and takes my face in her hands.

"You embarrassed me," she seethes.

"You left me," I spit out.

She seems startled, her green eyes wide and her lips parted. Then she yanks my face to hers, and we kiss. The kiss is enraged, violent and demanding, accusing and so goddamn greedy.

I want to take her and make her mine.

Never, ever let her walk away again.

What she's feeling, I don't know, because she's rabid. A woman unhinged with passion. She bangs her mouth into mine, kisses me until I'm breathless. She's yanking off her clothes, tugging down the same yoga pants and loose top I stripped off her last night.

"Spank me." She breathes the word as we stumble, tripping our way onto my bed.

"Fuck," I groan. "Is this about what I did out there? Sweetheart, you—"

"I liked it." She silences me with a daring look. "Now, do it like you mean it. Spank my ass, Shadow."

Violet James cursed. Violet James, my sunshine innocent librarian, asked me to spank her ass.

"Turn around." I point toward the bed. "Hands down, ass up."

She follows my instructions, turning her body to face my bed and bending over so those large, plush ass cheeks are facing me. Her long hair is spread over her back, her face looking up toward the ceiling.

"You praying to the heavens, baby? You may be an

angel, but I'm damned sure not." As I say the words, I draw back and plant a solid smack on her right butt cheek. The sound of my palm against her skin echoes, and I immediately bend to blow cool air against the red mark my hand left. "Do you like a little pain, Violet?"

I sweep two fingers between her legs, parting her trimmed curls to slide my knuckles across her wet seam.

"You do like pain." I punctuate my words by gently biting her ass right in the same spot I spanked her. Not hard enough to leave a mark but enough that she sucks air through her teeth. "You tell me when it's too much," I whisper against her ear. "I want you to want the kinda pain I give you. I want you to get off on it. You hear me? If it's too much, you tell me. And if it's not enough, you beg me for more."

She looks over her bare shoulder at me, her lips wet and parted, her eyes blazing. "Spank me harder, Shadow."

I drop my ass onto the edge of the bed and pull her down so she's lying on her belly over my lap. I spear my left hand through the back of her hair and wind the long tresses around my fist. "You like this?" I ask, tightening just enough to hear her suck in a breath.

"There," she murmurs. "That's enough. That's good."

I don't move, don't lighten the pressure of my left fist in her hair, but then with my right arm, I lift my palm and bring it down across her ass.

She whimpers, a seductive moan that sends the blood barreling through my veins.

My cock is screaming against the inside of my jeans, demanding it be set free to fuck this woman boneless, but I'm so goddamn happy she's back, I'm going to make this last. Make her feel so good, she'll think long and hard before she walks out on me again.

This may not be forever, but I know what I want. And I want Violet James more than I want my next ride, my next beer, my next breath. I want her pussy and her ass, her mouth and her mind. And tonight, I'm taking all of her.

I bring my hand down three more times until she's wriggling on my lap, fighting to keep her legs closed. I slide a hand between her thighs and coat my fingers with her pussy juices. I slide two deep inside, widening my fingers and stroking her walls as I enter her.

Violet groans, a throaty sound that sends my heart rate through the roof, and works her hips against my fingers.

"Nuh-uh," I say, withdrawing my fingers and spanking her again. "This is my pussy…ass too, and I'm taking it my way."

She clamps her legs together, and I flip her onto her back and motion for her to move to the top of the bed.

While she climbs across the blankets I didn't bother to straighten after I fucked her the last time, I strip off my pants, boots, and T-shirt. I grab the strip of condoms from my bedside table and tear one open. I kneel before her. "Suck me," I demand.

She scrambles to her knees and peers into my face. "Uh, I can't exactly reach if we're both kneeling."

One corner of my mouth lifts in a grin, and I climb back off the bed to stand beside it. Now, my erection is level with her eyes.

"Better?" I ask, stroking myself and fondling the shaft of the barbell on the underside of my dick.

"Perfect," she breathes. She swats my hand away and takes my entire cock in her hand. With the other hand, she cups my balls, and she licks long, wet strokes up the underside and along my piercing.

"*Goddamn.*" I gasp the word the minute her sweet, hot

mouth closes over me. I fist her hair with both hands. "Violet, you're fucking perfect. Perfect."

I can feel her smile around my cock at the praise. My innocent little librarian has a naughty side, and that makes her exactly what I said.

Perfect.

She grips my shaft with one hand and plunges my cock deep into her mouth. She's wet and hot and manages to keep suction on my dick so good, my knees start to go weak. I release her hair and push her shoulders back.

"How do you want to get fucked, sweetheart?" I ask her.

"Every way," she says, and I think that's the moment I start to fall in love.

As soon as I think the words, I banish them from my brain and focus on the task at hand. "I'm going to make you come so many times, you're gonna beg me to stop," I tell her. "Now, how do you want to get fucked first?"

She purses her lips and swallows, the long, beautiful column of her neck making my mouth water. I want to devour this woman. Eat her pussy. Stuff her ass. Fill her mouth and sink myself so deep inside her I'll never again see the light.

"Behind me," she says, turning her face toward the bed. She kneels with her ass in the air, her forehead resting on her arms on the mattress. "I need you so bad, Shadow." Her words are garbled against the sheet.

I slide the condom on and roll it down, thanking the gods who sent the tropical storm to Tampa for blowing her into my bed.

Once I'm sheathed, I grip Violet's thighs and thrust deep inside her pussy. She's so drenched, I slide all the way in, and she lets out a pleasure-soaked cry so loud, my cock jerks inside her.

"Fuck me," she begs. "Fuck me, please."

Her words send me into a frenzy, and I fuck her, my thighs slapping against the backs of her legs, my nuts smacking into her clit until she climaxes so hard I have to stop moving and let her grind against my cock.

She bites out her pleasure, screaming into the mattress, which thankfully muffles the sound. I don't know that I'd care if every last asshole in the compound heard her. I made her sound like that. Me. This perfect, sexy, wild, yet innocent woman...she's *mine*.

And I'm gonna make sure she knows it.

"Shadow..." A light mist of sweat dampens her back, and she sinks slowly onto the mattress, her limp legs spread wide open.

"Yeah," I grunt, tapping her ass lightly. "Up. I told you I was gonna make you come until you beg me to stop."

She moans but does as she's told, lifting herself until she's kneeling on the bed, her ass in the air. This time, I reach between her legs, steal some of the wetness from her seam, and smear it across her clit. Then I pinch the swollen bud between two fingers.

"Oh my God," Violet cries out.

I work my fingertips over her clit, stopping to spread more of her wetness over the nub until she gasps and shudders lightly, her tits shaking and a sweet moan climbing from her throat with every breath. She sounds like a cat purring, a steady sound muffled again by the bedding.

This time, though, I want to watch her come. I nudge her to roll onto her back, and she collapses, her eyes closed and her hair wild against the pillow. I lower myself onto my side and lean down to suck her nipple into my mouth. I suck her hard and then soft, puckering my lips around the sensitive bud until she's writhing against the bed.

I love learning every secret spot, the way spanking gets her wet, but sucking her nipples edges her, brings her close to the brink until I ease her back down. I tease her relentlessly, sucking her nipple, squeezing the fullness of her tit in my hand until she's bucking against the bed. Then I slow my movements until she's whimpering and begging me for more.

I suck her and flick the tip of her nipple with my tongue, nibbling lightly with my teeth until she's grabbing my head and pulling me closer.

But I'm not done torturing my sweet, sweet librarian.

"Open your legs." I kneel between her knees and watch as she opens her legs wide for me. I feel how wet she is, and fuck, I want to sink inside her and thrust until I can't see.

"Touch yourself," I demand. "Play with your pussy for me, sweetheart."

She doesn't hesitate and doesn't open her eyes. Just slides a hand down her belly and past her tightly trimmed curls. She moves her fingers around her slippery folds and holds her lips open so I can watch her touch her clit.

"Show me what you do to make yourself come," I say, fisting my still-hard cock.

I stroke myself through the condom, watching as her mouth falls open and she curls her toes into the sheet. She uses two fingers to rub fast circles across her clit, her tits bouncing with the energy of her movements.

"Don't come until I tell you." I inch my knees forward and press my hands to the insides of Violet's knees. "Keep touching yourself."

I watch her finger that sweet, swollen clit while I slide my dick all the way inside her. It's fucking bliss, feeling her, watching her, hearing her. I can't remember a time in my life when anything felt so perfect, so important, so real.

She gasps when I pull out, but I'm not going anywhere. I slide the tip in and rock my hips back and forth so I can watch her finger herself while I watch myself fucking her.

The way her pussy moves as I enter and exit her makes me so hard, I can hardly handle the pressure. I feel it coming on, a massive orgasm, but I need to hold out. I need to hold out for Violet.

"Come for me," I growl, squeezing her knees with my hands. "Come for me, goddammit."

She sucks in a breath and cries out, her fingers working her pussy until she's bucking hard against the sheets. As soon as she starts to ride the wave, I ram myself all the way inside her, slamming my cock into her while her walls convulse around me.

She's screaming, her mouth open, her eyes slammed shut, frenzied, frantic cries of pleasure marking her every shudder. I collapse then, the climax overtaking me, and I empty myself out in powerful, exhausting spurts.

When we're done, I collapse beside her, tuck her tight against my chest, and we drop exhaustedly into sleep.

TEN
VIOLET

WHEN I WAKE UP, I don't know if it's been two days or two years. My body is sore and satisfied, and my mind is happy, content, and, oddly, I feel at ease.

My eyes are sealed like they are glued shut, so I squint them open and check the clock on Shadow's bedside table. *Phew.* It's not even lunchtime.

I roll my shoulders and slide out from under Shadow's heavy limbs. He's snoring lightly, so I go into his bathroom, pee, wash my hands, and clean up a bit. Even though we used a condom, I came so many times, I feel wet and sticky everywhere.

I have to balance my hands on the sink and gather my strength. I need a big glass of water and a good meal. Shaking legs, tired-out lady bits, a smile that won't wipe itself off my face. In my entire life, I've never, ever felt this way.

I can't help the smile that crosses my face. I was so pissed off when he picked me up and tossed me over his shoulder like a rag doll. That was some impressive feat, because I am *not* a small girl. But then it was like all that anger and emotion just...I don't know, went away. We worked it out or banged it out.

The smile I can't wipe from my face gets even bigger. Me. Violet James. Banging out my emotions.

I'm drying my hands when it comes back to me.

Clive.

I pad back to bed and crawl back under the covers, trying to banish the idea of Clive from my thoughts. It doesn't work.

"Why the frown, sweetheart? You okay?"

I peer up at Shadow, who looks wide awake. I snuggle down against his chest. He pulls the covers up over me and kisses my forehead.

"Yes," I say. "I'm okay. Just sad and a bit confused, I guess."

Shadow stiffens beneath me but wraps me tighter in his arms. "Confused about what?"

"After I left Clive, some days I felt like he followed me." I trace the tattoos on Shadow's chest with my fingers. "It was the weirdest thing, and I know it's not possible. But things that unsettled me kept happening. He'd text and ask me if I had time to talk to him. I'd tell him no, that I was doing whatever I was doing. Going out, running errands. I never told him exactly what I was doing, not for real, but I always had a reason why we couldn't talk or see each other. And somehow, more often than not, he'd end up showing up wherever I was not long after I got there."

I can feel Shadow's heart thundering beneath my ear, and I turn my cheek and give his chest a light kiss before continuing.

"I just don't get it," I admit. "He knows I don't want him. He knows I'm moving on. The job I took, the new one here in Tampa, I accepted it because I wanted to get away from Clive. Move somewhere I could live, go to work, go to the store or the library and not constantly look over my shoulder and watch out for my ex. But something he said on the phone today, Shadow. It didn't sit right with me."

I think back to what he'd screamed into the phone while I was in my car. About knowing where I was and making me pay.

I look up into Shadow's face. "I honestly felt like he knew where I was," I whisper. "And he sounded pissed. A different kind of pissed. When he said he was going to make me pay, I believed he really meant it, Shadow. I never thought he'd actually go out of his way to hurt me before, but now, I'm honestly not sure. I came back because I didn't know where to go. This is the only place I can think of where he won't know how to find me."

I roll onto my stomach and prop my hands under my chin. I close my eyes. "That's why I came back at first," I say, that smile claiming my entire face again. "I really was mad that you'd talked to Clive." I sigh. "I don't want him and you mixed up together. It's not, I don't know…"

Shadow is so still for a minute, I think he's stopped breathing, but he's suddenly out of bed like a shot went off. "Get dressed," he says, pulling on his jeans and boots. "Get up, Violet. Get your clothes on."

"What?" I ask. I scramble out of bed and hurriedly put myself back together while Shadow tugs a T-shirt over his chest and opens the door. "Shadow, what is it?" I'm still sliding into my sneakers when he shouts down the corridor.

"I need all hands out back."

I follow him through the main room and out into the parking lot. Six guys have assembled in the lot. Two of the prospects, including the one they call Jizzy, Savage, Blade,

Hawk, and Viper. Shadow points to my car. "Sweep for a tracker," he tells them. "Tear that fucking thing inside out."

Immediately, they go to work, popping the hood, the trunk. Two prospects slide under the car, and two of the other guys climb inside.

"A tracker?" Stunned, I echo Shadow's words, a sick feeling stirring in my stomach. What does he mean, a tracker? "Do you really think..."

I look up into Shadow's eyes, his lips set in a deep frown. He doesn't have to respond. I know what he thinks. He thinks Clive's been tracking my movements somehow. And to do that, he needs a device. If it's not in my car, it's... I think of the phone in my yoga pants. My laptop. I have no understanding of this kind of thing. Could he have been monitoring me all this time? And if he has, maybe he knows where I am right now and just couldn't get to me because of the storm.

A full-body tremor tears through me, and I wrap my hands around my arms, shaking uncontrollably. I don't want to think that Clive is capable of that, of violating my privacy and following me. I don't want to think it, can't believe it, and yet...

"Shadow, do you think he's been following me?" My voice is a whisper.

"We'll find out for sure." Shadow sounds convinced. "But it damn sure sounds like it."

No, no, no, no.

This is too much. This isn't fair.

Shadow didn't sign up for this. He offered a woman in distress a place to crash for the night. He didn't ask to get mixed up with an ex who may or may not be a bona fide stalker. I can't involve him in this.

"No, stop." I shake my head. "Tell them to stop, Shadow. This is too much. I'm not your problem. You gave me a place to stay, but this?" I sweep my hand toward my car. "I can't make whatever this thing is with Clive your problem. He could be really dangerous."

Shadow takes my hand and lowers it, then holds it between his. He strokes the back of my hand with his thumb and leans down to meet my eyes. He lifts a brow. "Dangerous?" He squeezes my hand in both of his. "You think we're not used to a little danger?"

His words are interrupted by my phone ringing. I shake my head. I'm going to ignore it.

"The minute I laid eyes on you, I knew you were gonna be a problem, and yet I brought you here anyway," he says. "And once I stuck my dick in you, you became my problem. *Mine*, Violet."

It's not a ringtone I have programmed in, so the incessant ringing makes me panicky, edgy. "I'm sorry. Let me just make sure it's not him." I grab the phone from my pocket. When I answer the call, my voice is guarded. "Hello?"

"Violet James?" asks a woman I don't recognize.

"Yes, this is," I say.

"Oh, good. I'm glad you picked up. We were without power for a few days due to the storm, or I would have called you sooner. This is Margaret Thompson, from public school district..."

I remember the voice now. "Of course, Margaret. Hi, hello. Is everything okay?"

I passed the background check and sent in all my required employment documents weeks ago. I am scheduled to get the keys to my new condo as soon as the association can schedule the final walk-through. The storm is likely going to delay that for some time. In fact, I don't know when I'll be able to actually feel at home again, but as I listen to the woman on the phone, it's as if my entire new life flashes before my eyes.

"So, you see, Ms. James, the medical leave that our previous librarian intended to take has been postponed until summer break. Under our seniority policy, we're obligated to take the other librarian back. Unfortunately, that means we will have to rescind the job offer we made to you."

"Rescind?" I echo her word. "What do you mean, rescind? You can just take it back?"

"Yes, that's exactly what we mean. Unfortunately, we no longer have a vacancy. The librarian who intended to go on leave—"

"No, I'm sorry. I heard what you said. I just don't understand. You offered me a job. I accepted that job. I quit my old position and moved to Tampa. I rented out my townhouse. I—"

"Well, I'm very sorry, Ms. James, but there is nothing we can do about all that. If you read the offer letter, it did clearly state in the fifth paragraph that the offer was contingent upon us having a vacancy, and if at any time the vacancy was filled by a change in the proposed leave—"

I stop listening then and there. It doesn't matter what she says. What the letter I signed says.

I have no job.

That is it.

The reality.

I quit a job, and now, I have no job.

I moved away to try to leave Clive, and there might be no escaping him. I have no job.

I'm screwed.

"Wait," I say, not caring that I'm interrupting her. "So, if there's no job vacancy, there's no separation package. No severance pay? No benefits of any kind? Is that right?"

"No, Ms. James. Your offer has been rescinded, so you never had a job with this district. That means no employment date, so no compensation will be paid. And, of course, no benefits. We're terribly sorry, and if anything changes, you'll be the first to—"

I swipe the touchscreen to end the call, and I just can't help it. My hand goes weak, and my phone clatters from my fingers to the concrete.

"Violet, what the fuck?" Shadow bends down and checks the phone for damage.

Well, at least I have that much luck. My phone is just fine. I, on the other hand…

"I'm screwed," I say, shaking out my hands and starting to pace. "I'm so, so, so screwed." I walk wide, frantic circles in the lot, shaking my hands and clenching my fingers together into fists.

"I'm fired," I say, rambling to myself in long, unbroken sentences. "Not fired, but out of a job. A job I guess I technically never had because I signed a piece of paper that said there was no job if there was no vacancy, but I thought there was a vacancy because I interviewed, right? I interviewed for a job because there was a vacancy, but now there is no vacancy because there is no job—"

"Violet." Shadow grabs me by the arms and pulls me to a stop in front of him. "What the fuck happened? You're out of a job?"

I almost scream the answer. "Yes. Yes, I'm out of a job. This is not okay. I am not going to be okay." I try to pull away, to cover my face with my hands and start pacing again, when Shadow wraps a hand around my waist and nods at his biker friends.

"Keep looking, boys," he calls out. "I gotta get Violet inside."

His hand never leaves my waist as he moves me through the main room, down the corridor, and back to his room. He closes and locks the door before pulling me to his chest.

"What the fuck is happening?" he asks.

"I don't know." I wrap my hands around his back and hold on with all my strength. "I feel so helpless."

Two days ago, I had a job offer, a contract on a condo, and a new lease on life. Now, I have no job, no home, and my ex might be stalking me. I've had lots and lots of wicked sex with a total stranger. A total stranger who is a biker, by the way. That part has been amazing, wonderful. But eventually, I'm going to have to pull out of the compound parking lot, make my way through the mess that is the outside world, and live somehow.

Where will I go now?

What will I do?

I can't go back.

Clive is there.

I can't go anywhere, it seems, without Clive—and trouble—following.

How is this my life?

I try to release Shadow, to push away from his heat and the comfort of his size, but he won't let me. He holds me firmly, cupping the back of my neck and breathing kisses into my hair.

"Enough," he says. "You are not ruined."

He sits on the couch and pulls me into his lap. I curl up against him, resting my face in the crook between his shoulder and neck. I don't want to cry, but I'm overcome with sadness. I've never been taken care of by anyone—not Clive, not other exes. Yes, I have parents who love me and a sister who probably would kill or die for me, but that's family. I expect nothing less from them.

Making my way in the world has been impossible. I chose a career but never had whatever it took to find love. I thought I had love, and that turned out to be nothing more than manipulation and control. Now, the job and the future I thought I had are gone in the blink of an eye.

What's left? I start to spiral.

Maybe I can waitress or work at a bookstore.

I stop only when I feel Shadow's hands lift my face from his shoulder.

"You ever been to prison?" he asks me, holding my chin so our eyes meet.

I shake my head sadly. "No. I imagine it's pretty bad."

Shadow's body goes rigid, but he doesn't release my face. "You want to feel like the most worthless piece of shit alive?" he asks. "Get yourself locked up. In there, you got nothing. Family won't call, won't visit. The shit you did on your worst day becomes the only thing that matters. Not a thousand good days before. It all comes down to your worst choices."

He shakes his head. "You're not ruined any more than I was ruined by spending time on the inside. You're smart, you're gorgeous. You have a degree and skills. All you need to do is believe here." He taps my breastbone with a finger. "Believe that this is a detour on your path, babe. That's it. A wrong turn. A closed exit. You're still behind the wheel. It's not too late. For somebody like you? It'll never be too late."

My eyes flutter closed, and I grab the fingers he's

holding against my chest and bring them to my lips. I kiss them.

"How did you find the strength to remake yourself after you got out? What did you do?" I ask.

"I took it one day at a time. Now, come here."

He kisses my cheeks, my eyes, the tip of my nose, and then my lips. I relax into his comforting touch, grateful that my lowest moment, the detour on my path, brought me here to him.

Our kisses are soft and sweet, until I feel him harden beneath me. I can't help grinning. My God, this man. He is insatiable.

I reach down to stroke him through the denim. I'm already wet, hoping there's still time before I have to leave again to take this man. To feel his body inside mine. To touch him, lick him, love him.

I'm realizing so many things about myself through this experience.

That maybe I had to be ruined to release the purest, newest form of myself. The word "shadow" starts to take on a new meaning for me.

It's not just what's left behind, the darkness that lurks within us. Maybe it's the simplest form of what we really are.

When the bullshit is pulled away, all that's left is what's most true about us.

I can only hope that some of what I've experienced the last couple days isn't just true. I need this to be real.

ELEVEN
SHADOW

VIOLET SUCKS my dick like her mouth was made to fit me. Her tongue laps the barbell more confidently now, like she's no longer afraid she'll pull it out or hurt me. Her confidence would be sexy if I had the brain cells to think. Right now, with her hand cupping my balls and her head bobbing on my hard-on, thinking is the last thing I can do.

We're still on the couch, and when I'm good and wet, she stands before me naked. I don't care how many times I've seen this woman, every angle, every new glimpse of her, brings out something violent, primitive, and possessive in me. I want her.

I reach for her and bring her close. "Straddle me," I demand, and she centers herself over me.

She's about to sink down and lower herself when she stops, the muscles of her thighs rippling. "Condom…"

I groan. "Over there."

She practically runs over to the bedside table, yanks open the drawer, and pulls out a condom. Then she comes back and kisses me as she tears open the foil. "Someday, I want to feel that piercing without anything between us."

My heart rate slows in my chest. What is she saying? Is she saying she wants more of this? More of me? A someday beyond the short-term future in which the roads are too bad for her to leave?

I don't ask. I don't want to know. I'm not a forever guy. I break faces for a living, doing the most I can to keep my contacts in law enforcement happy—happy enough that they don't look too closely at everything else I do to make a living. There's no room for long-term in that situation. There's only room for my brothers. The next score. The next ride.

"Fuck me," I tell her, and she rolls the condom over my cock before she lowers herself onto my lap.

Bracing her hands on the back of the couch, Violet rides me violently, pounding the back of the couch against the wall, her head thrown back. Her bare toes push against the backs of my calves, and it seems like she's coming in seconds, not minutes. I watch her work out her pleasure against me—rough and needy—and I don't need more than a couple of seconds before I'm shaking beneath her, my climax chasing hers.

She is sweaty and looks stunned when there is a rough pounding against my bedroom door.

"Shadow. We found something." The voice that comes through the door is Savage, our sergeant-at-arms. His booming words sound as serious as a heart attack.

Violet's body stiffens, and we both go cold.

"Get dressed," I tell her. "I'll handle this."

She lifts herself off my cock, and I dispose of the condom in the bathroom and get back into my clothes.

Violet is already dressed, sitting on the couch, shaking.

I take her in my arms.

"Whatever we find, you're gonna have to be ready to

deal with this. I've got you. I know you've got this. You with me?"

She swallows and licks her lips, but her eyes never leave mine. "Okay. Okay."

I yank open the door to find both Savage and Viper in front of me. Savage nods at Violet, but Viper just stands there, gritting his teeth so hard a vein pops in his forehead.

"We found this." Viper is holding a small black thing shaped like a hockey puck.

"Bastard's good," Savage says, turning and immediately taking off down the corridor. We're not going into the main room, but we're heading to the opposite side of the compound—the offices.

I reach my hand behind me and take hold of Violet's while we walk toward the office I share with Blade, the treasurer. Violet's hand is weak in mine, but I keep a tight grip on her until the four of us are inside my office with the door shut.

The compound has only two designated office spaces—one that Phantom uses full time, and another with two desks and two laptops that Blade and I share. Most of our business isn't done behind a desk, but it comes in handy to have a private space to talk at times like this.

I motion for Violet to sit in a chair, and she does, looking from Viper and Savage and then back to me. Her hair is mussed from fucking, but all the glow and satisfaction are gone from her face.

She's pale.

A fist clamps around my heart, and my gut twists into a knot. I want to kill the man who's making her feel like this. This worthless piece of fucking shit who can't take no for an answer and leave well enough alone.

I'm furious, but I need to control my reactions. I'm surprised by how brutal I feel.

Any threat to Violet—even the idea that this worthless squirt won't let her go—sends my vision to a dark, dark place.

I'm not at all surprised that they found something.

Of course, that asshat Clive was tracking her movements.

What surprises me is how completely invested I am in making this right. In making him pay for what he's putting her through. How completely invested I am in freeing her and making sure Violet James never, ever feels unsafe again.

Now I just need to know what he knows, so I can be prepared.

"What do you know?" I ask, glaring at the device. "Tell me everything."

Savage rattles off stats, addressing Violet directly.

Every one of us is already familiar with this thing and what it's capable of. "This device is as cheap as they come. He's probably got two or three of them. They cost $80 or 90 bucks each and have a powerful magnet inside." He takes the device and flips it over, then attaches it to the metal desk to show us how it sticks. "With an older car like Violet's, this was really tough to find. The fucker hid it inside the front bumper. We tore that car apart. The only reason we found it…" He trails off.

He doesn't have to complete the thought. I know how he found it. We stash trackers just like this one on some of our clients. One of the best places to hide these buggers is not in the wheel well like they show on TV, but inside a bumper where it's protected from wind, rain, and pebbles.

Unless the car is in an accident and the device is damaged, it's almost impossible to find.

"Inside the bumper?" Violet looks confused. "What does that mean?"

I trade a look with Savage and then explain. "The tracker has a battery life of eighteen to twenty-four days, depending on how much driving the mark is doing."

"Wait, wait...days? Eighteen to twenty-four *days*?" Violet covers her mouth. She looks like she's gonna be sick, but there is no way I can sugarcoat this for her. She needs to know what this asshole has done.

I blow out a long, tense breath. "With the storm and how little your car was moving, who knows how much life is left."

"So, he knows I'm here? He knows exactly where I am?" Her eyes are wide, and her voice trembles. "For a couple hundred dollars, he could keep track of me for months?"

I nod. "Absolutely. These things are accurate, Violet. Very accurate. That'd explain why every time you went someplace, he'd show up not long after you got there."

She rubs her face with both hands and looks at me, those wide green eyes searching for answers. "What does that mean, Shadow? I don't understand. How accurate are these trackers?"

I take a slow, steadying breath and look at Savage. This is his area of expertise.

He lowers himself into the chair beside Violet and speaks to her gently. I can imagine the days in the past when he was a hero, on the right side of the law—or so he thought.

When he was in the military, doing special ops or

whatever he did, vital witness extractions were one thing I know he specialized in.

I can see how good he must have been at the job, and yet again, I have to wonder what brought him so far from that lifestyle. I'm just grateful he's on the club's side now.

"Violet, these trackers provide real-time data to the device owner using the cellular network. No Wi-Fi required. They are accurate to within six feet, so whoever planted this on your car would have no trouble getting this close to you." He uses an arm to gesture between himself and her. "He probably has a couple of these devices. Keeps one charged at all times. When he knows you've been on the move long enough to drain the battery, or when you're conveniently not on the move, he could park beside your car in a lot, pretend to drop something on the ground, and swap them out without you ever knowing."

I drop into the chair behind my desk and rake my hands through my hair. I know what this means. This fucker is stupid, and he wants Violet. He knows I've been with her, so he's assuming—rightly so—the worst. That I've fucked her. That she's mine now. And a dumbass like him is gonna make damn sure he gets up in my face and forces me to make good on my threat to stop him from breathing. That is, if he doesn't get to Violet first.

I can't let her leave the compound. Not until Clive makes his move. Reveals himself as the bottom-dweller he is.

"Where's this asshole live?" I interrupt. I have a lot of calls to make, and with the storm, I'm gonna need all the time I can get.

She swallows and looks from Savage to me. "Just outside of Tallahassee. A little ways north, by the Georgia border." She closes her eyes and clasps her hands tightly in her lap. "He could make it here in…"

"Three to four hours," Savage tells me. "Maybe five to six, depending on the state of the roads. That part of the state won't have the same storm damage we do, and we don't know how far away he was when the storm hit."

"What?" Violet cries out. "Wait a minute. Do you mean you think there's a chance he's been here in Tampa this whole time? He could be close right now?"

I come around the desk and pull Violet out of the chair. "How long were you on the road before the storm hit? Did you drive straight here the morning of the storm?"

Anguish coats her features. "Yes. But it's not like I was watching to see if I was followed. Why would I even suspect such a thing?"

"He was banking on you trusting him. Not believing the worst about him. For all you know, Clive could have been behind you the entire time." I hate to say it, but we all need to be braced for the truth.

She looks from me to Savage and Viper. "Where would he have stayed? Could he have gotten a hotel room when I couldn't?" She bites her trembling lip. "I listened to an audiobook the entire drive. I was so lost in the story, I didn't pay attention to the news. I literally didn't know the storm was developing the way it was until I got into Tampa. By then, it was too late. If he'd been tracking my movements and paying attention to the storm…"

She doesn't have to say the rest. Clive could be very, very close. Too close.

"Is there any way to know where he is?" she asks. "If he can track me, can we, I don't know, contact the manufacturer? Damage the device so it doesn't send my location to him?"

Savage shakes his head. "No, we can't reverse-track him just because we have the device. I wish we could. The only thing we can do is assume that he's close. And I wouldn't recommend doing anything to let him know we're onto him." He stands. "In fact, we might want to use the fact that we know about this to our advantage."

I know exactly what he's thinking. If Clive doesn't come to Violet soon, we'll put the device back on her car and draw the little fucker out.

Violet starts to tremble, and I pull her to my chest. "Call a meeting," I tell Savage. "All hands on deck. Ten minutes."

Savage and Viper head out, leaving Violet and me alone in the office. I lean back and look into her face.

"He's coming, isn't he? He's coming for me. And he's coming for you." Her words aren't a question, so I don't answer her.

I just hold her silently against my chest, and together, we cling to each other. How is it that this woman, whom I've known for two days that feel like two years, now means enough to me that I'd put my brothers on the line to protect her?

"Shadow, I should go." She pulls away, wiping her tear-streaked face and sniffling. "I should leave right now. You have the tracker. My car is clear. There's no way he can find me, right? I have to go. Now. Get away from here where I can't put you in any danger."

I shake my head and tighten my grip on her arms. "You think running is going to stop him? You think one missing tracker is going to throw him off for more than, what, a couple days? I know guys like this, Violet. He won't stop until somebody stops him."

"How?" She looks at me, lost and, now, maybe a little

angry. "How the hell do I stop a man I already told to go away? It's not fair. What do I have to do? Buy a gun?" She shudders. "I never thought I'd be the type of person to use a gun on another person, even in self-defense. I never thought I'd have any reason to find out what I would do in that kind of a situation. Who does? Who does this, Shadow?"

I can't do anything, say anything, to that. She's right. It's one thing when a client owes the club money and attempts to make a run for it. It's one thing when we keep tabs on our enemies so we can stay ten steps ahead of them—using techniques just like this. I don't want to show Violet the drawer full of devices identical to this one that we use to run our business.

But there's a big fucking difference between me and what this fucker has done.

We're not the same as Clive.

We don't victimize innocent people or stalk women who have already told us to fuck off.

We protect our investments and make sure we get what we're owed. That's it.

The people who go into business with us do so willingly, knowing the consequences of going back on their word. That's a fair exchange in my book.

But I can't risk her thinking I'm anything like this guy. I need her to trust us. Her life may depend on it.

"You know what kind of man Clive is," I tell her, layers of meaning in my words. "This is just one of the ways he won't take no for an answer. Now is the time to stop him. If you want to be free, if you want to get a job, move in to that condo of yours, and ever feel safe again, he's got to be stopped."

"Isn't this illegal, what he's doing?" she asks. "I feel so

violated. Can I take out a restraining order? Go to the police and show them what you found?"

I huff a deep sigh. I only wish it were that easy. "You think a guy like that's gonna care about a piece of paper, Violet? You told him no. You broke off your engagement, left fucking town, and got a new job, you were so serious about moving on. You think a court, a judge, or even a cop is going to convince this asshole to leave you alone?" I shake my head. "I wouldn't even try. There's only one way to deal with a guy like this. You have to trust me on this."

She drops into the chair, and I kneel on the floor beside her.

I grab one of her hands and lift her chin, so her eyes meet mine. "While you're under my roof, you're my responsibility. While you're in my bed, you're mine, Violet. And I take care of what's mine. Do you hear me?"

She looks past me, her eyes fixed on some point on the wall behind me. "I've been nothing but a problem since you met me, Shadow. I should never have gotten you mixed up in my shit."

"Wrong." I kiss her lightly. "But even if you're right, you're the best damn problem I've ever had. Now, listen to me. Clive is coming for you, and I'd be willing to bet my left nut he's coming here. It may not be today. He's got an ax to grind with me, and he may *not* be fool enough to try to fuck with me. But make no mistake about it. He's after you, and you're going to be prepared."

Another silent tear slips down her cheek. "Thank you. I just don't know what that means. Are you going to hurt him?" She flicks a look toward my chest, where I was carrying the day we met.

"I've got no plans to go back to prison," I assure her. "And if my luck runs out and I do go back for some reason, I sure as shit ain't going back over some douchebag like that." I stand and pull her to her feet. "Go relax. Watch TV, play video games. Talk to Stella. Have a drink if you want. Just don't go outside, okay? And whatever you do, don't leave."

She clasps her hands in front of her chest. "What are you going to do?"

"I'm calling a meeting. But first, I need you to tell me everything you know about this prick. I need his last name, date of birth. What he drives, where he lives. Violet, I need you to remember anything about him that might help me keep him away from you? Can you do that?"

She sighs, but then, she starts talking.

TWELVE
VIOLET

I WANDER BACK down the corridor that leads from the office space toward the main room of the compound.

Massive guys in leather and denim pass me, headed toward Shadow and whatever meeting he's called.

I get friendly looks from the bikers, but I don't respond. I keep my head down and eyes lowered.

What can I say?

Thanks for attempting to stop my loser ex from trying to find me. Thanks for letting me crash here, even though I unknowingly brought danger right to your door.

If I make it out of here in one piece, I'll thank them. But right now, I don't feel very grateful. I feel trapped.

Clive is hunting me, and while I appreciate what Shadow is trying to do, I feel like a prisoner here. I can't find it in my heart to be angry, though. All these people are willing to put themselves on the line for my safety.

As much as I hate this situation, as much as I feel stuck and scared, I have to admit, at the same time, I've never felt safer.

When I get back to the main room, I'm shocked at how quiet and empty it is.

The televisions are off. No one is playing video games. No one's making out on the couches. I'm immediately rushed by Cammy and Stella, the latter of whom throws her arms around me in a hug.

"You look like you need that drink," she says.

I shake my head. "Maybe some water. I don't think I can handle much else." My stomach flips over, and I take a seat at the bar.

"I'm craving fucking nachos." Cammy claps her hands together and heads off toward the kitchen, leaving Stella and me alone.

She grabs a cold bottle of water from the fridge behind the bar and slides it across the top to me. Cammy comes back a second later with a bag of tortilla chips in one hand and a bunch of jars and cans in the other.

"Nacho party." Jackie appears from God only knows where and gestures with grabby hands toward a can of cheese. "Ew, gross. Cammy, fuck. Did you even heat this up?" She takes the can and disappears back into the kitchen, while Cammy winks at me.

"Reverse psychology. Is that what that was?" she asks.

Stella shakes her head. "If you ever want Jackie to do anything useful, you've gotta find a way to make it seem like it's her idea."

Cammy tears open the bag of chips and pops one into her mouth. "Mmm." She makes a yummy sound then crunches the crispy chip. "No shit. The last time I asked Jackie to cook or clean something, I almost got knifed."

She rolls her eyes. "I'm almost not even kidding. Better to just act stupid and let Jackie feel smart."

Stella pops the top off a jar of hot salsa. "Eh, she's not all bad. She's just independent."

Cammy and Stella trade looks and laugh, then Stella hands me a plate.

"All done." Jackie sings as she comes back with a bowl of bubbling nacho cheese. "See, you heathens? Was that so hard?"

She sets the bowl of cheese on the table, and Stella puts out some serving spoons. We each grab a paper plate and put chips, sliced jalapeños, salsa, bean dip, and cheese on our plates.

"Goddamn, that's good." Jackie slaps the bar and talks around a mouth full of nacho. Then she turns to me. "So, what the fuck did you do to land Shadow? Spill it, nerd girl."

I have a crisp nacho in my mouth, loaded high with spicy peppers and hot salsa. My mouth waters at the flavors. It's so good, and I realize how little I've eaten the last few days I've been here. I've probably burned thousands of calories with Shadow, so it's not the healthiest snack, but I'm grateful to fill my belly with women I trust.

I shake my head. "Land him? Oh no, it's not like that."

Cammy directs a nacho dripping with hot cheese at me like a pointer. "I call bullshit. Who seconds me?"

Stella raises a hand, giving me a wink. "Come on, babe. He's gone. G-O-fucking-N-E." She spells out the word, then scoops up a load of salsa on a chip. "He's never like this. We would know."

Jackie bursts out a laugh. "You mean you would *like* to know. You've been trying to get up close to that piercing from the jump."

I look at Stella, worried that she has feelings for Shadow. Feelings that maybe I've stomped all over.

Stella waves off my worries, giving me a sincere smile. "Don't listen to Jackie. Every one of us has been sweet on these guys. That's why we stick around. Fucking around with any one of them is a guaranteed good time. But getting any of them to make an old lady out of us?" She shrugs. "I haven't seen it happen yet."

Jackie helps herself to a beer from the fridge behind the bar and swats Stella's butt. "Speak for yourself, bitch. It's only a matter of time before one of those assholes wises up and makes an honest woman out of me."

Cammy lifts a brow. "Jackie, you're about as honest as a fox in a henhouse."

Jackie doesn't get offended. To my surprise, she laughs so hard she almost spits nachos onto the bar. "Well, I'd rather be the fox than the hen, bitch."

While they tease each other and eat nachos, Stella leans her arms forward on the bar and studies my face. "You're into him, right? Shadow?"

My mouth goes suddenly dry. How am I supposed to answer that? Shadow is a biker from a world I can't even begin to understand.

At the same time, my life is about as messed up as the streets of Tampa after the tropical storm. How could a guy like him and someone like me ever work?

Stella doesn't wait for me to respond. "We've all been through shit, babe," she says quietly as she stares off into the distance. "How we got here doesn't matter. Where we go once we find each other does." She snaps out of her trance and turns to grab herself a beer. She pops the cap and lifts the bottle to me in a toast. "I've never seen any one of them look at a woman the way Shadow looks at you. Like he's claimed you. Like he'd move heaven and earth to get to you."

Stella sighs and hums a little, sounding almost jealous. "A lot of us would do a lot of things—illegal or legal—to land a man like Shadow," she says.

The thought of being claimed by anyone, especially Shadow, makes my belly do weird flips. Maybe it's the salsa or the stress. Maybe it's the fear that lurking underneath every man is a little bit of Clive.

I find myself resisting that idea. I can't believe it. I just can't imagine Shadow ever doing anything to scare me, harm me, or control me. Claiming me, though…

My heart thunders in my chest, thinking of all the ways he's claimed me. The ways I've claimed him.

Stella studies my face with a smug grin. "Thought so," she says. "And welcome to the club."

I can't say anything.

I don't want to reject the only friends I have right now, and I wouldn't reject them even if they weren't my only options. I like these women. I may not be like them, but I like being around them. I want to get to know them. I want to know Stella's story and what she whispers about when she and Phantom are alone. I'm curious about Savage and Viper, even Cammy and Jackie—whom I'll never be close to, but I can still appreciate.

"Thank you, Stella," I say, before using the spoon to drizzle a little cheese on my chip.

Before I can say anything else, the sound of heavy boots fills my ears, and the room is swarmed with bikers. All of them. Phantom, Shadow, Savage, Viper, and even the prospects.

"Let's go," Shadow says.

For a second, frustration rises in the back of my throat. I don't like being told what to do. I don't like being powerless in my own life. But I remind myself this is not like Clive. Shadow isn't trying to hold me back. He's trying to protect me. To stick his neck out when no one else would. No, scratch that. He's sticking his neck out and bringing the necks of everyone who means anything to him along with him.

If they have a plan, I am going to listen. I may not like it, but I like the idea of Clive hurting any of these people—hurting me—a heck of a lot less.

Once we're back in Shadow's room, he points to the bathroom. "I want you to stay here," he says. "Shower, clean up, nap. Do whatever you need to do. Just relax and lie low for a while."

I see that the suitcase I'd packed for the trip to Tampa is on the floor.

"Grabbed that from your car," he says. "Went through it myself, just to make sure there wasn't another tracker."

I shake my head. "I wouldn't have thought there was any way that Clive could have put something in my luggage. But now? I don't know what to believe."

"It's clean. Take it easy. I'll handle everything from here."

"Shadow." I stop him with a hand on his arm. He turns back to face me. "What are you going to do?"

He hesitates and looks like he's going to ignore me and just leave. "We found some dirt on Clive. Some very, very damaging dirt. Enough to get his ass put away for a long time. End his career, definitely. End his freedom—

possibly." Shadow pinches the bridge of his nose and sucks in a long, frustrated breath. "Violet." His voice goes deadly serious. "If the man is willing to track you down across the state after a fucking hurricane, then I'm not sure threatening his livelihood will do the trick. Much as I'm hoping we can get him to go away without resorting to violence, it may come to that."

"Would you kill him?" I squeak out the question.

Shadow snorts. "I'm not opposed to beating his ass. We'll start there and see how deep this asshat's dug his heels in. If we're lucky, he'll learn his lesson and move the fuck along."

"And if we're not lucky?" I have to ask the question. Because as safe as I feel here right now, I know I can't stay here forever, eating nachos with the girls and having sex. I have to move in to my condo. And I can't live looking over my shoulder and into the bumpers of my car for the rest of my life. I need this thing with Clive to end.

"I'd put my money on your luck, not his."

Shadow leans down and kisses me. It's soft and makes me wish we could shut the doors and just be alone.

The two of us.

But the serious look on his face lets me know that his mind is far from sexytimes right now. "I'll be back," he says, then heads out the door. He doesn't lock me in, and he doesn't remind me to lock the door behind him.

How much has changed in such a short time.

I grab the fresh towel Shadow brought me and head into the bathroom. The hot water barely lasts long enough to wash my body, so I cut the shower shorter than I would like. I towel-dry my hair and put on some comfy clothes, then head into Shadow's bedroom. I see an e-reader and the remote control for the TV on the neatly made bed with a note.

A little something to keep you entertained, "nerd girl." Power's back on, but I'm helping the guys shut down the generator and secure the storm shutters. Be back soon.

He signs the note with a single capital S.

As tired and stressed and frustrated as I am, I can't help smiling. I stretch out on the bed and turn on the e-reader. This must be Shadow's. It has all kinds of books on it. History books, books about politics and the law. Biographies. There are even magazines and a few popular novels. I smile at the gesture, but for once in my life, I'm too wired, my mind racing too fast, to even think about reading.

I flip on the TV and catch the tail end of a news report about the storm. It sounds like Shadow was right. The roads are a mess, and emergency crews are only now being dispatched to start the cleanup. Many of the roads are completely impassable, and many thousands of people are estimated to be without power for days, maybe even a week or more.

I thank my lucky stars I found Shadow. I think back to that first night, how terrified I was. How the storm practically blew my car off the road. I can't imagine Clive trailing me through that storm. Or even worse, being someplace safe while I was out there at the mercy of the weather and wherever I could find to take shelter.

My anger about Clive is rising, and I find myself wanting this fight. But I'm even more grateful that I do not have to do it alone.

My phone rings and breaks my train of thought. My heart practically leaps out of my chest, as if, for a second, I'm afraid I summoned Clive by thinking about him. But the ringtone belongs to my sister, so I pick up on the second ring.

"Violet, oh my God." My sister's voice brings a tear to my eye. "Babe, are you okay? I thought you were going to text me when you got to your new condo."

I explain that I'm still at the place I've been staying the last few days. I haven't exactly told my sister I've been staying at a motorcycle compound, and now that I know Clive had a tracker on my car, I'm glad I didn't say more. I suddenly wonder if there's any way he's been monitoring my communications too. I sigh and add "getting a new phone" to the list of things I need. Right after a job.

"I'm more than safe," I tell Ivy. "I'm great. Good. There are lots of people here, men and women. Everyone has been really welcoming, and it's actually been kind of fun."

"What kind of fun?" My sister's voice is teasing, and I know she wants details about the hot, scary, bearded guy who invited me here. I don't think I'm ready to talk about Shadow, though. Especially not now when I can't be entirely sure that our conversation is completely private.

I do decide to tell her about the tracker on my car, though.

"That's fucked up. What are you going to do?"

"I'm going to try not to worry about it right now," I tell her, purposely downplaying the situation. There is nothing my little sister can do from so far away. She's in college and, thankfully, is safe and sound, far from the storms of the state of Florida and her sister's shitty taste in men.

"Check in with Mom and Dad, will you?" Ivy asks. "They've been calling me, but I just keep telling them you have to preserve your phone charge."

I feel sick with guilt. My parents. Of course they would be worried about me.

My sister is in college in Chicago, and my parents are safe in the house where I grew up back in the suburbs of Atlanta. They have no idea about a direct hit from a hurricane, and they never even met Clive face-to-face.

My parents had me young and they both still work, so given how fast everything moved with Clive, all we'd managed were a few video chats. My engagement didn't even last long enough for them to meet my fiancé before he became my ex.

"You know Mom and Dad are gonna want to know where you are," Ivy says. "I've been able to put them off for a while, but just be prepared. They're gonna want an address."

I sigh, knowing that I'm going to have to keep my chat with my parents quick. I don't want to worry them, but the less anyone knows about where I am and what I've been doing here the last few days, the better.

Part of me feels guilty even thinking that. Am I feeling guilty because I've spent the hurricane having sex with the most gorgeous, contradictory, confusing man I've ever met? A man who's been to prison, but who welcomed me in, brought me an e-reader, and who has rallied everyone in his life to protect me at the first sign of danger?

It's strange to feel a combination of guilt and excitement just thinking about Shadow. How would I introduce him to my parents or my sister? What would I tell them he does for a living? I don't even know what he actually does for a living, so...

I tell my sister I love her and swear her to secrecy. She promises not to tell anyone my location, and she promises to be careful. She lives in the dorms in a secure campus downtown, but if Clive can't get to me, who knows.

We hang up the phone and I call my parents. My heart

aches, hearing their voices. They are both so worried about me and ask a million questions, but I just have to assure them that I'm safe and that I will call them as soon as the power is back and I don't have to ration the charge on my phone. I tell my parents I love them, and I hang up.

For the next few days, I have one priority: figuring out my next moves. What my parents and sister don't know won't worry them. And I'll catch them up once I'm safely in my new place and, hopefully, well into the next steps of my future.

I settle back against the pillows and turn on an old movie. Something classic, black-and-white, and completely soothing. I must fall asleep while watching it because, suddenly, I am imagining the GTO and the compound garage. The quiet, private space where I first felt Shadow inside me. Where we first acted on this flirtation, this attraction, making it something so, so much more.

What is it? I don't know, but in my half-dream sleep state, all I do know is that my body can't get enough of Johnny Butcher. I picture him and all the things we've done. The barbell on his private part. The way he cups my breasts and works my nipples. The throbbing between my legs is so strong, I don't know if I'm half asleep or dreaming, but I moan and feel my fingers slip between my legs under the covers.

"Shadow..." My eyes closed, I move my fingers faster, chasing the memory of the pleasure I've only ever experienced with him. "Shadow," I pant again and work my fingers faster, harder. I'm wet and my eyes are closed when I hear the sound of the bathroom door open.

Shadow stands in just a towel, his hair and beard damp from a shower.

My eyes fly open, and I realize that I am not asleep and I am not dreaming. Shadow's bare chest, muscular, hairy, and covered in tattoos, tightens as he releases the towel and tosses it over the towel bar.

"You wanna let me finish what you've started?" he asks, and then he climbs in bed beside me.

THIRTEEN
SHADOW

VIOLET LOOKS HALF ASLEEP, but her eyes fly open when I pull back the sheets. She's got one hand down the front of her pants.

"Dreaming about something?" I tease.

She yanks her hand away, but I shake my head and lift her fingers to my lips. I lick the salty sweetness from her fingertips and groan. "My baby is insatiable," I say, sucking her fingers deep into my mouth.

She whimpers and squirms against the bedding.

"Take off your pants." I watch as she lifts her hips and wiggles out of her bottoms. "Now everything else. Do it slow."

My eyes sear into her as she parts her lips, and her breathing quickens. She unfastens her bra and works her arms through the straps, then tosses the offending garment across the room. It hits a lampshade by the couch and almost knocks the thing over.

"Oh God, sorry." She tries to scramble off the bed to get it, but I shake my head.

"Leave it."

She obeys and focuses back on me, sliding the loose T-shirt over her head. I'll never get sick of this woman's body. Her hips are round and full, her belly soft and inviting.

"Lie down." I don't know how much more time I have with her, and I'm going to make every single second count.

She settles back against the pillows, and I lower my face to her stomach. I kiss the softness there and slide my hands under her hips to knead her ass cheeks. She rewards my touch with a groan, and my cock bobs between my legs, ready for the promises I know Violet's body will fulfill.

"Turn over," I tell her.

She does so without a word, and I lie over her, careful to support my own weight so I don't crush her. My cock slips against her ass crack, and I lean forward to whisper in her ear. "Tell me what you were dreaming."

"I was thinking about the garage, the car," she says.

I knew she liked it from behind. I lift off her and spread her legs wide, then settle my face as close to her pussy as I can get. "Pillow," I demand, and she hands one back to me, but I refuse it. "Under your belly."

She props the pillow under her stomach so she can lie against it, and her hips and ass are slightly elevated. Perfect. I use that angle to my advantage, spreading her legs wide and kissing long, hot paths from her inner thighs up to her pussy.

She's wet and so, so hot for me. I can smell her arousal, a heady mix of sweetness and spice, and my mouth waters in anticipation. With a feast like Violet in my bed, I could eat her forever and never notice going hungry. She's delicious and soft, and before I know it, my tongue has worked its way to her wet, wet seam.

Her legs are spread wide to give me access, and I lick her from clit to ass and back again. She tastes so sweet, so clean, I tongue her opening and slurp tiny pulsing sucks against her clit. She wails out, a cry that's part "more" and part "perfect." I don't care if she thinks this is perfect. I have so, so much more to give.

"Flip over."

She obeys slowly, taking her time to wiggle her hips and roll onto her back. Once she's got her ass on the pillow and her hips are slightly angled up, I spread her knees wide and stroke her seam with my fingertips. I go nice and slow, trailing her wetness up and down along her opening, teasing her lips by slipping just the tiniest bit of my finger between her wet folds.

She shudders and groans, moving with an aching need to get closer, but I'm in control of her pleasure now. I withdraw my fingers and taste her again, sucking every last drop off my fingers and then wetting mine so they slide up and across her clit with ease.

She's losing herself in the pleasure. I can see it in the flush across her heaving tits, the way she grabs her own nipples and squeezes the tight copper tips between her fingers.

"Good girl." I coax her to touch herself harder, more.

She pants, squeezing her tits and rolling her hips to get closer to the pressure of my fingers. I can't imagine ever getting sick of this. Ever tiring of fucking this woman's body. Of hearing her sounds and sharing her pleasure. Something I've never felt before washes over me and leaves me weak, feeling suddenly drained. I want to fuck her, hard but soft, and hold her. Everything at once.

She must notice something change in the way I'm fingering her because she lifts her head. "Shadow?"

"Sorry." I snap away the daydreams and shove all emotion aside. There will be plenty of time for feelings, whatever this is, at some other point. Later. Right now, she's here in my bed. She wants this, and I need her. God, how I need her.

"Shadow," she says, her voice sounding fragile, vulnerable. "I want to feel you. Really feel you. Just once."

I freeze, thinking about what she's suggesting. "I've been tested recently, sweetheart. You wanna go bare, you say the word."

"Maybe not fully bare," she says shyly. "Do you think you could pull out? It should be safe. I've been tested too. I got tested after Clive, and there's been no one since."

I think about what she's offering. Weigh the risks. "You think you're good?" I ask. "You sure?"

She sits up and looks me in the eye. I move the pillow out of the way so we can face each other. "I'm supposed to get my period any day now," she says. "I am pretty sure, no matter what, I can't get pregnant right now. Just pull out," she says. "But if you want to, would you...you know...come on me?"

I let out a feral growl and bring her close for a kiss. "Fuck yes. I'll come wherever you want, sweetheart."

She lies back and spreads her legs, and I dive between her knees. I lock eyes with her as I notch the head of my cock against her opening, the immediate sensation so wet and so fucking delicious, I have to remind myself I cannot come. I will not come. My woman wants to feel me bare, and I'm gonna make sure she doesn't forget the experience.

I slide inside her and hold onto her knees for support.

I'm kneeling on the bed, watching as my cock slides in and out of her pussy. I have to close my eyes because the way her pussy lips move around my cock, drawing me into her sweet heat, makes me want to blow my load. I squeeze her legs and work my hips until I feel her reach between us and gently stroke her clit.

"Touch yourself," I demand. "I wanna feel you come all over me, sweetheart."

Violet whimpers, her throaty gasps letting me know she's getting close. My God, I thought she was wet before. Without a condom to separate us, she's fucking drenched, every thrust slick and perfect. I feel her walls contract around me, tightening, and I know I have to be careful. She comes in waves, small, steady shudders with tiny, composed moans until she's screaming, grabbing her knees to hold on, her full breasts trembling with every rocking movement.

I pull out as soon as she's done and fist my cock, jerking to the familiar pace I need until I, too, sail over the edge. I spurt ribbons of hot come across her belly, her tits, and on the bed until I'm spent and empty.

I drop onto the sheet beside her, and she rolls over to the side. She uses a hand to wipe my cock clean, then gets up and trots into the bathroom to clean herself off. She comes back and cuddles behind me, spooning my bare body with hers.

I sigh, a loud, long groan of thanks. "You're fucking unreal," I tell her. "Absolutely perfect."

A million other thoughts race through my head, but I shove them away. I can't have real feelings for this woman. Not her, not now. Maybe never. This has to be enough. But God, is it good.

I let exhaustion claim me, and before I know it, we're both sound asleep.

As soon as I open my eyes, my stomach rumbles, and I think back to the last time I ate—yesterday.

"Come on." I kiss her lips and roll out of bed. "Let's get something to eat."

We dress slowly, stopping to kiss and touch each other. I'm going to have to shove our asses out of the room, because if I don't get some food in me, I'm gonna be useless.

We head back to the main room, holding hands, grinning at each other like there's nobody else in the compound. I can feel every eye on us as we walk past people on the couches making out or arguing over some shit on their phones. Phantom lowers a brow to me. Savage, as usual, is making the rounds, but his eyes follow us.

"My kitchen assistant." Stella rushes over to Violet and grabs her hand. She gives me a playful pout. "Stop hogging the nerd, Shadow. Share the love a little, will ya?"

She drags Violet off to the kitchen to cook, and I walk up to the bar to polish off what looks like the last of a plate of nachos that aren't half bad.

Savage joins me at the bar as soon as the girls are gone.

"Got through to our guy," he says in a low voice.

He means the sheriff. The one we pay big cash deposits to every single month. He splits the money with two of his buddies. I know who our "friends" are, but it helps to have fewer hands in the stew, if you know what I mean. We have friends in both high and low places. And with a shithead like Clive out there gunning for Violet and probably me, the best way I can think of to shut his ass down is to call in our "friends."

I nod. "Good."

"Looks like the roads should be clear in a day or two. Three, tops. You thinking you're gonna need backup when you head back to Shady Lane?"

I shake my head. "As long as Malcolm's good for it, I say we give him a hurricane discount. Half the regular interest for the late payment."

Savage lifts a brow. "You don't normally show your generous side," he says. If he's thinking about saying anything else, he doesn't.

I wander into the kitchen. I have no real plan. I just know Violet's in there, so I follow my gut.

She's standing with Cammy and Stella at the counter. All three of them are dicing veggies for a salad. When I walk in, Violet's eyes flick up, and a huge smile takes over her face. But she keeps chatting away with the girls like she's known them forever. I come up behind her and lace my arms around her waist.

"Ladies," I say, greeting Jackie, Penny, and the rest of them. I plant a kiss on the top of Violet's hair and breathe her in. God, she smells fucking outstanding. Clean and sweet and delicious. "What's for dinner?"

Stella's eyes are wide as she stares at me, my arms still locked around Violet's waist. "Uh, salad. Phantom said we could pull chicken out of the deep freezer, so we've got wings in the oven."

I kiss Violet's head again and then steal a carrot she's chopping from the cutting board. "Sounds good."

As I leave the kitchen, I hear Jackie's jealous whoop.

"Girl, what the fuck is that pussy made of? Shadow's got it bad."

I shake my head, relieved when the rest of the women —Violet included—break into laughter. She fits here. She fits me. In fact, now that I have her, I can't stand the thought that she's only got a few more days before the roads free up and she'll be clear to go on to whatever's next. Another job, back home to Tallahassee.

I don't have time to give it a lot of thought, though, because suddenly, a security alert blares through the compound. I'm on my phone, swiping to the security app to check the footage.

"Driveway." Phantom is steps ahead of me. He points silently to Savage and Viper. "It's go time."

"How many?" Viper asks.

I peer down at my phone. A skinny, deranged-looking motherfucker is pointing a baseball bat at the front door of the compound. He's screaming so hard, I can see the spittle flying from his mouth, but I have the app silenced so I can't hear what he's saying.

"Keep Violet in the kitchen." I point to Jizzy. "She gets out of here, and I'll separate your dick from your balls so fast, they'll start calling you Jizz *Queen*. You got me?"

His eyes wide, the prospect nods, looking terrified. "Yeah, yeah, Veep. I got you. I'll keep her inside."

"In the kitchen," I stress. I don't want her seeing or hearing what's about to go down.

I slide my phone back into my pocket and point to Savage. "Make the call."

Then I open the door and head outside.

The second I hit daylight, I can see the guy doesn't just have a baseball bat. The bat's got nails hammered around it. I hold up my hands in front of me, intentionally trying to look like I'm reasoning with him. I don't take my eyes off the man.

"Hey, man. You're on private property, and I don't know you. What's the problem here?" I ask, keeping my voice calm, hands visibly raised so he can see I don't have a weapon.

The guy is raging, seething, and ready to burst. He points the end of the bat at me like a pointer. "You're fucking hiding her. Is she here against her will? A captive?" He searches the surroundings with his eyes, as if he's going to spot Violet handcuffed to a tree. "*Violet!*" he screams. "*Violet!*"

Fucking Clive.

I shake my head and keep my hands in plain sight. "You need to take your janky-ass weapon and get the fuck outta here before I start to think you're planning on using it."

"*Violet! Violet James, you fucking whore! Come out here and talk to me!*"

Clive starts dancing around, pointing the tip of the nail-studded bat at me like it's a wand, and screaming into the air.

I keep my hands visible, but fury sears through my chest, and it takes all my self-control not to rip the bat from his hands and tear his shoulder from his socket in the process.

"Get the fuck out of here, Clive!" I shout.

"Fuck you! Fuck off! Violet!" Clive continues his screaming rampage, bobbing back and forth from one foot to the other.

I realize now that he's dressed like some punk wannabe burglar. Nasty-looking gray jeans, a dark gray hoodie, and combat boots make the skinny, furious guy look comical. Pathetic. This is the man Violet was manipulated by. I can't let myself think for a second this is a man she could have loved. He's tall and wiry, with lean muscles and a bony face. He'll put up a fight, but I won't have to break a sweat to take him down. I just have to keep control of my temper so this fight is the asshole's last.

I want to finish him for good. Make sure he'll never get close to Violet again.

I cross my arms over my chest so there can never be any question where my hands were and what I was doing with them. "You're the loser who Violet dumped, right? The skinny needledick who lost his home and had to shack up with a librarian so you weren't on the streets. Is that right?"

"She never said that. Fuck you. You're the needledick."

I laugh, a loud, mocking laugh that visibly infuriates Clive. "She didn't say anything while I had my dick in her mouth. Maybe it was after, when I fucked her in the ass."

I'm making shit up now. Baiting him. I need this asshole to make the first move. I don't have much more time.

"Stupid fucking bitch." He meets my eyes as if we're about to agree on something. "She's shit in bed. Send her out here, and I'll take her off your hands."

"I've got a better idea," I tell him. "I did some looking into you. You know, when I wasn't fucking Violet. And let me tell you, she was very, very good, so I didn't have a lot of time to dig up dirt on a shithead like you. But I did learn some interesting things about you, Clive."

I uncross my arms again and hold up my hands. "You can leave right now, and I won't bother telling you about the deal the rich lady up in Valdosta was offered by the DA. You know the one? Your client whose little fire you helped set with your intentionally faulty electrical wiring. I'm sure you thought the scheme to get a cut of the insurance money would help you win Violet back, but..." I shrug. "I don't think the district attorney believes you didn't know that rich husband of hers was asleep in bed when the fire started."

"You don't know shit about shit!" he screams, breathing so hard, I can literally see spit flying from his bared teeth again. "I'm just an electrician, man. Sometimes mistakes get made. That's what insurance is for."

"Yeah, and sometimes husbands just die in bed when a bedroom closet remodel sends the house up in flames. I get it. But I don't think Violet's interested in a guy so stupid he made a wiring error that killed a man." I lace my fingers together and hold my hands where Clive can see them. "Looks like, no matter what you do, you're on the losing side there, buddy."

My voice is mocking and cruel, and I get a zip of pleasure at the momentary lapse in the asshole's anger. He looks like it's all hitting him now. How there's no way out. His little insurance fraud scheme is going to send him to prison. Tack on a bunch of years for the suspicious death of the man in that house that went up in flames, and maybe—maybe—he won't get manslaughter or murder as an accessory.

No matter how he looks at it, he's fucked. I can only hope he realizes it and acts soon.

"Send Violet out, or I will fuck you up, man. Send Violet out now." Clive, out of options, apparently chooses to resort to Plan A—be a douchebag who somehow still thinks he's getting the girl.

I shake my head. "I'm doing you a favor. You want the last memory she has of you to be like this?" I pause to let that sink in. "You showing up here because you tracked her to a place she feels safe? And, I should add, very, very satisfied—"

At that, Clive lunges at me, bat swinging. I've been ready, waiting, so I duck out of the way. Clive rushes past me, narrowly missing me, and slips on the rough gravel of the unpaved road.

I give him one more chance. "Put the bat down," I demand. "Or I'm gonna have to hurt you."

He charges me again, swinging his bat toward my knee. I move just far enough out of the way to avoid being hit, then grab his hands, crushing his wrists together with such force, he drops the bat.

Just then, the door to the compound opens, and Viper yells, "Hey, asshole!"

Clive throws a terrified look behind him while I have his wrists pinned. I release him and throw it as far as I can. Then I grab the front of Clive's shirt, pull him toward me, and punch him in the face so hard I hear his nose crack.

He falls to the gravel, his nose painting the rocks with blood, and screams like a fucking bitch.

Viper and Phantom stroll from the door toward the scene just as a cop car, its lights off, creeps up the drive. Nobody moves, except that asshole Clive. He literally turns on his hands and knees and tries to crawl toward his bat.

Phantom, Viper, and I stand there, our hands up so the cops can see them. Clive starts screaming like a baby, yelling at the officers for help.

Two cops get out of the car, looking pissed off. They point to Phantom.

"Somebody wanna tell me what's going on?"

"Not sure what to tell you, Officer. My brothers and I

were inside making dinner when our security system went off." Phantom jerks a thumb toward Clive. "This asshole was in our driveway, waving around that bat. Seems like he wanted to see Shadow's lady friend, but the lady wasn't interested in talking to him."

The second cop walks up to Clive and asks him to stop moving, but the idiot doesn't. He keeps screaming and crawling toward his bat. The woman cop orders him to stop moving and put his hands where she can see them, but he is in a frenzy, bleeding, crying, crawling.

The next few minutes are a blur as the cops tell us not to move while they subdue Clive. By the time the bat has been bagged for evidence and Clive's in handcuffs and in the back of the squad car, Phantom and the responding officer are shaking hands.

"You happen to have any security footage that backs up your version of events?" the cop asks. "I'd love to be able to show the DA that at no time was this man threatened by you. That he had no reason to suspect you had a weapon, that he was the aggressor. That kind of thing."

Phantom nods. "I'll go download the footage to a drive right now."

The officer motions toward the car. "Email it to me. I'd like to get this fucker processed so I can get home for dinner. We finally got power, and my wife went shopping today. Sounds like she's planning on steaks."

"Will do." Phantom, Viper, and I stand in the driveway, waiting until the cops pull away. Once we hear the crunch of gravel and the lights from the car disappear onto the road, Phantom claps my hand in a high five. "I wouldn't have been able to keep my cool as long as you did."

"Let me through!"

I hear Violet shouting behind me just seconds before I hear her running down the driveway.

I turn to face the door and am greeted with flying auburn hair. Violet charges at me full speed, leaps into my arms, and wraps her legs around my waist. Tears streak her face as she kisses me, all the while cursing and asking if I'm okay.

"Shadow, oh my God. Are you hurt? Did he hurt you?" She holds my face and looks me over.

"I'm fine," I tell her. "But I can't say as much for the prospect who let you out of the compound."

I glare past her, untangling her limbs from mine and setting her on her feet. "How much did you see?"

"Don't blame him," she says in a rush. "I may have threatened him. I think he's a little afraid of me."

I lift a brow and put a pin in it. For now, everything is handled. Violet is safe. Clive is going away for a long time.

"He's not going to bother you again," I tell her.

"Did you break his nose?" she asks quietly.

"Probably. The cops will make sure he gets medical attention. If he needs it." I'm sure I did break his nose, but it's only a fraction of what that needledick deserves.

"What happens now?" Violet's eyes are wide, and she looks to Phantom and Viper. "Thank you," she says. "And I'm sorry? I don't even..."

Phantom claps me on the shoulder. "We'll leave you to talk." Then he and Viper head back into the compound.

We walk past the drops of Clive's blood staining the gravel. "The club'll press charges," I tell her. "Trespassing, assault. Since we have video and proof of him trying to track you down, you'll probably want to go make a police report about the tracker. They may be able to nail him on stalking. But that's the minor shit. Clive's in a lot of trouble, sweetheart. He's not going to be a problem for you anymore."

The death investigation was probably one of the reasons the asshat was so anxious to get back together with Violet. Maybe he did love her, but I see the need for legal expenses and a ready alibi as a hell of a lot more likely. A guy like him might want to control a woman like Violet, but I refuse to believe he truly loved her. The thought of him even touching her makes me wish I could have landed a couple more blows to his face.

I'm happy I got the one in. We planned exactly how to set him up so he couldn't claim he was jumped or threatened. Even if he was trespassing, he was outnumbered and definitely outsized by me alone—forget about my brothers if they'd come out. The security footage tells the story. My hands were up and out. I was being threatened. I did everything right. Even if I wish I'd smashed his skull in before the cops made it here.

"What if he makes bail, though? He could be out tonight and just come back. He knows where we are now."

I grin and shake my head. "The club has friends in high places. We were the victims here. We did everything right. He ain't getting out. I don't think a single judge in the county's gonna grant that fucker bail."

I tell her what we learned about the fire up in Valdosta, Georgia. The woman who hired Clive right after Violet dumped him. Offered him a cut of the insurance money if he'd make sure her house burned down.

Greedy little fuck was happy to put his business on the line for a little green. Too bad that bitch didn't tell him she planned to have her husband doped up on sleeping pills so he slept through the fire. Murder charges, fraud, stalking, arson… "I think you can sleep soundly from now on."

Violet laces her fingers through mine and kisses the back of my hand. "I'm so sorry I brought this to your door," she says. "Shadow, how can I ever thank the club? How can I ever repay you for this?"

I pull my hand away and swat her on the ass. "That fucker came to my house," I tell her. "He threatened me, my brothers, you, on club property. This is club business now. No matter how it became our business, we handled it. We take care of our own."

I leave that out there—our own—because, yeah, I'm including her in that. Whether she's mine for a weekend, a week, or something else, while she's under my roof and in my bed, her business is my business.

"It's handled," I tell her. "Now, let's go eat."

FOURTEEN
VIOLET

DINNER IS LIVELY TONIGHT, and to my relief, no one talks about Clive and what happened. Maybe it's part of some unspoken code here. I don't know.

The only way I can stop my hands from shaking and myself from feeling sick is to repeat in my head over and over that I'm safe for now. I had no idea Clive could be capable of really hurting anyone—let alone tracking me down and showing up with a baseball bat studded with nails. Who does that?

I must be staring into space because Jackie shouts over the conversations at the table. "Hey, nerd girl! You wanna pass that salad you spent so much time on?"

I reach for the salad bowl and send it down the table. Tonight, most of the guys are sitting on the couches, drinking and watching college sports. They're eating together with plates on their laps, and just the women are at the table.

It hits me that this is my last meal here. The last time I can look over and see Cammy laughing her butt off. The last time Stella will grab my sleeve to whisper some hilarious detail about a running joke that I'm too new to understand. This is the last time I will follow Shadow's massive arms and shoulders with my eyes as he jokes around with his biker brothers.

"So, what's next, librarian? Where's home when you're not riding out a storm at the compound?" Stella's question is innocent enough, but it brings the reality of the situation back in a rush.

I give her the simplest answer, swallowing down a mouthful of salad, my throat suddenly very dry. "I'm hoping the condo I'm renting is ready."

She gets dragged into some conversation by Penny. I finish my dinner in silence, just listening and watching the women chat. There are curses and laughter, shouts, and even smoke as someone lights up something that definitely isn't a cigarette.

I feel someone looking at me, and I glance up to meet Shadow's intense stare.

He's frowning, and that expression only deepens when he sees me looking back at him. Is he ready for me to go? To get out of his hair and stop freeloading? I haven't eaten or drunk that much, and they've all been really generous about feeding me, but I wonder if I should offer to pay for my food or something. There is still so much about this place and these people I don't fully understand.

As much as this place shocked and terrified me at first, one thing I do believe is that it's a home. There are people who care about one another here. Meals and shared experiences, games and love. Lust, I correct myself. Lust.

What Shadow and I have sure as heck can't be anything more than that. But these people share a certain kind of love with one another. And I feel fortunate to have been included in it for as long as I have.

When we're done eating, I clear the table with Penny and one of the prospects, Jizzy.

"You all right?" he asks me. "After today?" He looks nervous. He either doesn't think he should be talking to me, or he doesn't want to bring up what happened.

I smile at the kid. "Thanks for asking. And don't worry. I told Shadow I forced you to let me outside."

"Shadow'll get over it. What matters is that you're safe. I kept you inside when it mattered."

He wanders off toward the kitchen, his arms full of dirty dishes. I follow him and am rolling up my sleeves to start loading up the dishwasher with Stella when Shadow appears in the kitchen. He doesn't say anything. Just leans in the doorway and watches me. I look at him sadly, until Stella nudges my hip.

"Go on," she says. "We got this."

"I don't mind—" I try to argue. I'm happy to help. After all they've done for me, it's the least I can do, but Stella points.

"Go," she says. "You cooked. No need to clean up too. Cammy's just trying to get out of her turn."

"Shut up, bitch." Cammy is suddenly at my elbow, giving Stella a smirk before turning to me and holding out her hands. "Now, give me that plate, and go fuck your man."

I flush hard. My man. I don't know how I'm supposed to respond to that, so I don't. I just hand Cammy the soapy plate, give Stella a sad smile, and walk to Shadow.

He doesn't say anything, just turns, and I follow him back down the corridor toward his bedroom. Once we're in his room, he shuts the door. The lights are off, and he slams my body against the closed door, locking me into place with an arm positioned above me.

"Violet James," he breathes.

"Johnny Butcher," I say.

We don't say anything else. He lowers his mouth to mine and snakes a hand under my hair, pulling my face toward his. His lips tease mine, kissing lightly, slowly.

It's like he's imprinting the memory of how I feel on his brain. I think that's what he's doing because I'm doing it too.

I run my hands along the sides of his neck. I stroke the stubble on his throat, cup his chin, and hold his bearded jaw close to my face. I savor the taste of him, the mellow sweetness that will always remind me of whiskey. I memorize the way his tongue probes my mouth, tasting, tangling, dancing with mine.

The kisses grow more intense, and I feel Shadow's erection as he presses his hips against mine. I don't know how many times I have had sex with this man, but tonight, I want to make love to him.

I have to leave this place soon. Nothing is holding me back now. The roads, my condo, Clive. I can make every excuse in the world, but what matters is that Shadow's and my time has come to an end.

This is goodbye, and I want to make it count. I try to ignore the sting of tears that burn through my nose and behind my eyes. This is stupid. I'm still here, and this is a fling. Fun, right? This is what people my age do. We meet people, we connect. Story over. Chapter complete.

I've never been a casual person, but what future is there for me and a man like Shadow? I fumble with the zipper on his pants.

"Will you tell me about your tattoos?" I ask, my lips just inches from his. "I want to know all your stories."

If he's feeling anything about my question, he doesn't reveal it.

"One last game?" he asks. "I don't have any whiskey."

I laugh in spite of my sadness. "No drinks," I tell him. I want to be sharp tomorrow. When I have to make the tough decision and walk away. "Just questions and answers tonight."

We move to the bed.

He gently takes off my top and pants, then unfastens my bra.

I feel cold, but I ignore the chill in the air, and after he unzips his jeans, I tug them down over his hips. I memorize the hairs on his legs, the muscles of his thighs. I kneel on the floor and kiss the tiny birthmark under his belly button.

Then we climb into bed. We hold each other for a few minutes, and I run my fingers along his right arm. "Start here," I ask him. "Tell me everything."

We talk for what feels like hours. He tells me about the shitty tattoos he got when he was in high school and let one of his buddies who wanted to be a tattoo artist work on him. He has some cover-ups and some faded older work, but the gorgeous ink on his right shoulder and arm is what I'll never forget.

His right shoulder has a skull etched in only black, the detail of the bones and shadows so intricate that it's hard to look away from. The skull is what you'd notice if you only saw him in a sleeveless shirt, but along his triceps and over his shoulder are a flowing cloak and a scythe.

"The Grim Reaper?" I ask.

He nods. "King of Shadows."

I rest my head on his chest and trace the lines of the skull with my fingers. "Are you a Shakespeare fan?"

Shadow snorts. "Sweetheart, I coasted through high school and never looked back. I don't think I've ever even watched anything by Shakespeare, let alone read it."

My hair spills out across his chest. "There is a fairy king in *A Midsummer Night's Dream*," I explain. "He is a contradictory guy. He's a bit of a matchmaker in the story, and it all works out in the end, but he toys with people's hearts," I say. Shadow's heart beats hard under my fingers, and I breathe in the scent of his skin. "At one point, he's referred to as the King of Shadows. Obscure literary reference, I know. Nerd girl," I explain, grinning.

"You're that and more," he says quietly.

He rolls onto his side to face me. We hold hands facing each other, and Shadow kisses my forehead, my eyes, my nose. I lift my lips to him, and the kisses are soft again, exploring. I feel the press of his thick erection bob against my skin, and I sigh.

"I'm gonna miss this." I reach my hand between us and wrap my fingers around his shaft. I fondle the underside of his penis, the silver barbell threaded through the skin. "And this," I say, stroking the silver balls on either side with my fingers.

He groans and flops over onto his back. I kneel over him and kiss the head of his penis, then lick long, wet strokes up the underside. I wrap my lips around just the tip and suck lightly, using my tongue to lap at the base of his head.

He relaxes into my efforts. I suck him into my mouth, using my hand to add pressure to the shaft and stroke my way up and down his erection while my mouth forms a tight seal over his head.

"Fuck, Violet." He grabs my hair and helps me set the pace, moving my head up and down gently.

I suck him hard, wanting to finish him in my mouth. I want to feel him inside me. I want one more night of his mouth on me, his perfect body fitted to mine. But first, I want to please him. Give him the one thing we haven't shared yet.

When he stills his hands in my hair and murmurs, "Sweetheart, stop," I don't. I look up at him, my lips still wrapped around his cock.

He groans deep in his chest at the sight, and I smile, pulling my mouth from him only long enough to say, "Come in my mouth, Shadow. I want you to."

He shakes his head. "I want to fuck you."

"Later," I promise. "First, I want this."

I suck him all the way into my mouth and use both hands, one to circle his shaft and the other to gently cup his balls. I lift the weight of his sack and stroke the tender seam just underneath. He bucks hard and gasps, working his hips so his cock goes even deeper into my mouth.

I have to make an effort to stifle the impulse to gag, but I quickly recover. My mouth floods with saliva, and I use it to slick my tongue all over the head of his cock. I jerk him off with one hand while I cup his balls and suck him deep. The whole world fades to darkness as I slam my eyes shut and focus on his pleasure. I want to feel the moment when he loses control, when he chases that bliss to the edge and then dives, dives, dives.

"Violet…baby…sweet…fuck…"

He pants and curses, dropping f-bombs, his hands splayed out beside him on the bed. I love it. Love that I can bring this to him. Give him this intensity. I want to remember it, how this feels, him losing control and giving everything he is over to me.

I don't ever remember giving someone oral sex before

coming close to this. My mouth is wet, drooling with the size of him, my lips and jaw tightening with exhaustion, and yet, I suck and bob my head, lost to a frenzy of my own making. I want to pull the arousal from his body, force it into my mouth, and taste it. I want to drink him down.

I feel both dirty and excited, my body thrumming with life and need. I have to ignore the throb between my legs because there is no way I'm moving my hands to touch myself. I'll take care of myself later. Right now, I'm one with Shadow, part of the moment and pleasure and pain that makes this *us*.

Then, I feel it. His body tightens and his breathing changes.

I don't stop.

I double down on the movements—sucking, licking, squeezing, jerking—and he roars, bellows like the shadow king he is, as he climaxes in my mouth. I don't want to choke, don't want to gag, but I've never swallowed anyone before. I feel like a goddess. I did this for him. I made him feel so good, he's literally exploding inside my mouth. I have to hold back a smile as he thrusts and spurts until, finally, my mouth is so full, I need to lift my head or I'll spit his semen all over his belly.

I pull my mouth away and swallow fast. I breathe in deep through my nose and wipe my mouth, but Shadow pulls me on top of him and kisses me, his tongue against mine. The fact that he wants to taste himself on me is more than I can handle. I whimper and wriggle my hips against him.

He doesn't say anything, just kisses me, tastes me as his heart rate slows. After what feels like ten minutes but is probably only two, he growls at me. "On your back."

I do as he asks, lying down and settling the pillows behind my head.

"I'm not gonna stop until you come at least five times," he says. "So, how do you wanna do this?"

I moan in anticipation and close my eyes. "I don't want to think," I tell him. "Just take me, Shadow. Take me however you want me."

He lowers himself between my legs and plunges his tongue deep inside me. No ceremony, no shyness, I grab his head and hold it firmly against me. He licks me from the tip of my clit to deep in my core, scratching my lips with the soft hairs of his beard. It's delicious, erotic, tickling, and perfect all at the same time. I can't believe how fast I'm coming, but I've been primed and ready since I took him in my mouth. I come fast and hard against his mouth, wetting his chin with my juices.

He licks his lips, then reaches past for me a condom. He slides it on in record time, and then—somehow already hard again—he enters me fully in one long, deep thrust. He holds his weight up and fucks me hard—a desperate, needy bang that has the mattress smashing against the wall behind us. I don't care.

He could open the bedroom door and scream my name for all I care. Shadow is mine, and all of this, for now, is mine for the taking.

We have sex so many times, Shadow runs out of condoms. It must be a sign. He offers to go out to the GTO for more, but I don't think either one of us is going to be able to walk tomorrow. I must have burned thousands of calories in his bed, and I'm sweaty, sticky, and exhausted when I finally snuggle up behind him, my face against his bare shoulder, and fall asleep.

I wake in the early morning. Shadow is snoring lightly, his back to me. My face is still resting against him, my arm tucked under his.

I can't believe I slept like this all night, but somehow, with Shadow, time and fears and insomnia and tossing and turning are foreign concepts. With him, all I feel is comfort.

As quietly as I can, I pull my arm from under his and tiptoe into the bathroom. I shower and use the toilet, brush my teeth, and collect my toiletries. His vanity looks bare without my stuff beside his.

I pull on the same clothes I wore yesterday and towel-dry my hair. I have to laugh when I look in the bathroom trash. I don't even want to know how many condoms we used the last couple of days. I counted at least four last night alone. If there's any consolation in my leaving like this, maybe it's that he won't be able to sleep with anyone else right away. At least not until he shops for more.

I shake my head and stare at myself in the bathroom mirror. It's stupid to even think this way. Shadow has more condoms in the GTO, and I'm sure every guy here has his own supply. If Shadow wants another woman once I'm gone, I can't let myself cry over it.

I'm not his.

I never was.

Never could be.

I try to remind myself of that when I tiptoe past his sleeping form and pick up my bag. I turn to look back at him, and it happens. I let my eyes burn a second before I swipe the tears away, and then I turn very quietly and twist the knob.

"What the fuck are you doing?" Shadow is out of bed, his hand on my arm, before I can even open the door.

He's naked, and it takes all my resolve not to tackle him, climb back into bed, and go back to sleep. To forget there is a world outside this compound that I have to get back to.

"I didn't want to say goodbye," I say, my voice breaking.

"So, don't," he says. His voice is low, and I can't make out what he's feeling.

Then it hits me.

I want to stay.

"Do you want to put on some pants?" I ask, taking in every inch of his naked body. I laugh to try to cover my emotions, but his face is an unreadable mask.

"No," he says. "Sit."

I sit on the couch beside him, and God love him, he plops his bare behind right down next to me. This might be the only time I've seen him naked when he wasn't erect. I know the feeling. My heart feels like it's dropped from my chest to the soles of my feet. I can't even look him in the eye.

"Should I pay the club for the food or the shelter?" I ask. "The drinks, even. We pretty much polished off a whole bottle of whiskey."

He grunts. "No."

I lace my fingers together and look down at my hands. "I don't know how to thank you, Shadow. You took me in when I was terrified. When I had no place to go. Then you made me feel not just safe, but welcome. And Clive..."

I meet his eyes helplessly. "How can I thank you enough? I can't ever repay all this."

He doesn't say anything, just stares at me. My heart

plummets even further, probably lower than the bottom of my feet now.

I just wish he'd tell me how he feels. What he wants. Does he want me to stay? Does he want more?

"You have my number in your phone, right?" I ask weakly.

He nods. "And you have mine. Anytime you need an orgasm, a drink, anything, you know how to reach me."

I don't need orgasms and drinks. What I think I need is him. I don't say that, though. I'm an unemployed librarian, and he's a biker. A badass. An ex-con. He's a lot of things. But what he's not is mine. No matter how I wish he were.

"Will you walk me out?" I ask.

He looks at me as if he's fighting back words. I wish he'd say them. I want to know how he feels, what he needs. But he just gets up and slips on a pair of sweats. He slides his feet into motorcycle boots and doesn't bother putting on a shirt.

"Now?" he asks. "You're going now?"

I consider his question. If I don't leave soon, I'm going to lose it. I won't be able to hold myself together, and I do not need him seeing the tears. I'm more than just a damsel in distress, but that's all he's ever seen of me.

I've gotta hold my head high, say my goodbye, and do this thing.

Keep it casual.

I can fall apart later.

He yanks open the bedroom door and storms through the compound. He ignores the looks we're getting from the few people awake. Jackie opens one eye from where she's passed out on the couch and gives me a weak wave before going back to sleep. I scan the room for Stella or

Cammy, but I don't see them. I wonder if they are asleep with any of the bikers. I wish I could be here later to ask.

But I grip my bag tighter until I feel Shadow's hand take the larger bag from me. I let him, appreciating that, as weak and tired as I am, he's carrying some of the weight.

"You want coffee?" he asks, as if the idea just occurred to him.

I consider it, but then my stomach roils at the thought of it. I just want to go. Need to make this goodbye short and as sweet as it can be. It's going to hurt. And even contemplating bombing my stomach with acid makes me feel vaguely nauseous.

"No, thanks," I say.

We leave the compound through the side door and head back to the lot where my car has been completely put back together. It looks like they may have even cleaned it after searching it for the tracker. I don't bother thanking Shadow again. I'm starting to sound like a broken record. And maybe I'll text him later. Something light, after I've shed my tears and filed this experience away in the memories category.

I pop the trunk, and he tosses my big bag inside. I set my overnight bag in the footwell of the front passenger side and then close the doors. I keep my keys in my hands so I don't accidentally lock myself out of my car. While I have a suspicion that someone in the compound could break in to my car, I've relied on their charity long enough.

It's time to step out and stand on my own two feet. If Clive is in jail with no hope of getting out, he won't be calling. He won't find me. He can't get to me. So, I am, for the first time in a long, long time, truly free.

It's time to find a new path. The road is wide open

ahead of me. And all I need to do is get behind the wheel and drive.

I look down at my hands again, then pull the driver's side door open. I move to climb in, but Shadow catches me with one hand and pulls me to him.

I rest my head against his chest and wrap my arms around his waist. He lifts my chin and leans down to kiss me. "Violet James," he whispers.

"Johnny Butcher," I say back. "My Shadow."

I pull away as the tears burn the corners of my eyes. Before any of them falls, I climb behind the wheel, turn the key in the ignition, and put the car into drive. I pull slowly through the lot, past the now-clean aisles.

The prospects must have been busy while Shadow and I were…uh, also busy. Stacks of yard debris and trash are in the corners of the lot, but the path out is perfectly clear.

Shadow doesn't move, standing in place where I left him like a statue. Like a shadow—unmoving unless his person moves. Maybe that's a sign from the universe too. I'm not his person.

If I were, he'd have followed me.

Stopped me.

But he didn't, and I drive away.

FIFTEEN
SHADOW

FOUR WEEKS LATER...

I roll into the parking lot of the Shady Lane Motel. The last time I was here was the afternoon after Violet left. Malcolm didn't have the money he owed the club ready, and I may have taken out my frustration on Malcolm's face. To be fair, I would have done that either way. He had extra days to pull the cash together, and in the end, he had it. He just didn't want to pay it back.

They never do.

I yank open the door after parking my bike in the completely empty lot. Business ain't booming, but unless my beating last month meant nothing to Malcolm, he'll have what I'm here to collect.

But Malcolm ain't the one at the counter when I walk through the door. An older woman, maybe in her mid-fifties, with hair dyed an obnoxious shade of purple-red and a cigarette between her lips, waves at me with five long, painted fingernails.

"Hey there, hon," she says, plucking the cigarette from

her mouth and setting it in an ashtray right there on the counter. "You looking for a place to stay?"

She's looking me over like I'm an afternoon snack. Normally, a woman's appreciation would have me turning on the charm. Not today. Not here. Definitely not now.

"I'm looking for Malcolm," I say curtly. "He around?"

She shakes her head. "I'm filling in. I'm his cousin Dana. You wanna leave a message?"

I lean my elbows on the counter. "He's expecting me, Dana. I'll wait."

She leans her elbows on the counter so our faces are so close, I can smell the stench of cigarettes on her breath. "Baby, must have been some kind of mistake. Malcolm ain't here."

I turn away, cursing under my breath. This is the one time it would be damn convenient to give my clients my number. I want to call him. I want him to know I'm after him. He got extra time out of us and half the normal rate of interest last month. And he still tried to default on his debt.

"Call him," I say quietly. I turn to face Dana. "Call your cousin and put him on speaker."

She crosses her arms over her chest and gives me a smirk. "Baby, you're hot, but you can't waltz in here, snap your tattooed little fingers, and have everybody around here asking how high to jump."

I'm across the lobby in the blink of an eye. "Dana, I'm not the kind of man you want to fuck with. Not today. Not any day. Have you seen your cousin's face? Does he still have a black eye and a busted lip?"

She suddenly grows serious, as if she's doing the math in her head. *Yeah, bitch. I'm the one who rearranged your cousin's face.*

"Get him on the phone now." I wait, glaring at her while she fumbles her cell phone in her hand. A thin line of smoke rises from the burning cigarette beside her.

Malcolm must answer on the first ring. "It's me," Dana says, glaring at me. "There's some guy with a real shit attitude here to see you. He says you're expecting him."

I curl my hands into fists, my blood boiling over. I have had to be hard on women in the past, but I try to make a policy of not doing business with anyone I am not willing to *work* with—no matter what the job requires.

Malcolm says something I can't hear, and I slam my fist on the counter. "Put him on goddamn speaker," I tell her.

She does as I ask, though, and drops her phone on the counter.

"Tell him I'm sick, literally shitting up my guts, Dana. I'm not fucking around. I'm—"

I pick up her phone and talk right into the speaker. "Listen up, you fucking maggot," I tell him. "I'm the one not fucking around. I don't care if you have to wear an adult diaper or come to this shitbag motel with a load of your own crap in your pants. If you're not here tomorrow with what you owe me and double interest, I won't be alone. And you won't need to worry about shitting yourself when I'm done with you. There are worse things waiting for you if you don't show your face, Malcolm."

"Turn off the cameras," I tell her.

She doesn't move, but I hear Malcolm through the speakerphone. "Do it, Dana."

She frowns at me, those glossy lips going thin.

"Don't panic, Dana. I'm not here to hurt you, but I have to do this."

Dana gives me a puzzled look as I walk to the front glass door. I lift my foot and kick with all my strength, sending my boot through the plate glass. It shatters into pebbles but doesn't fall to the floor. Safety glass. I guess that's a good thing.

I turn and point at Dana. "I'll be back tomorrow," I promise, then I pull the door open and walk through it. When I slam it closed behind me, then the glass crumbles, falling to the floor like a million marbles.

When I get back to the compound, I'm on fire. Fury burns through my body, sparking in my limbs and making me so furious I want to fight something else. I go to the back lot, where we have a shed with gym equipment. I work out hard, punching the bag, doing pull-ups, and lifting weights until I'm dripping with sweat and spent.

I storm back through the compound and head to the bar.

"You need a water or something stronger?" Stella leans forward, putting on a show.

I look away. "Water," I bark.

She hands me two bottles, and I twist the cap off one and take a long drink. I'm only slightly cooler, but she doesn't deserve to be on the shit end of my wrath. "Thanks, Stel."

I'm getting up off the stool with both waters in hand when she stops me dead. "Talked to Violet?"

I freeze, but I don't answer.

"I didn't get her number before she left," Stella says, her voice practiced and careful.

I turn to face her, but Stella turns away, wiping the counter clean and chattering on as if this isn't the first time in a month that anyone has brought up Violet James.

"I just thought, you know, when you talk to her next that you could tell her the girls say hi. She never really liked calling us bitches, so I'm sure she'd say something PG-rated like girls or ladies. She was sweet like that, don't you think?"

She's not looking at me, and I can't decide whether to storm away or break something else. Since I can't do either without looking like a pussy, I drop back onto the stool.

"I haven't talked to her."

"Oh." Stella's pouring on the fake surprise a little thick, but I let her.

I actually like having someone mention Violet to me. It's a relief to get her out of my head where she's lived constantly for the last month.

"You know, Shadow, you could do that. Text or call her. Just check in on how she is." Stella cocks her chin at me. "Sometimes it's nice to reach out when someone's on your mind. Assure yourself that they're doing okay. It doesn't always have to mean anything or go anywhere."

I don't say anything, just glare off into the distance.

"Or you know," she continues, "you could invite her over for a drink or dinner. Take her out, even. Maybe the phone call will lead someplace. I don't think you'll know unless you try. God knows I'd call her if I had her number. I think about her all the time. Don't you?"

I surprise myself when I admit it. "I can't get her out of my head. Not for one goddamn minute. My room smells like her. My books remind me of her nerd shit. I hate everyone and everything that isn't her."

Stella covers her mouth with her hand, but I can tell she's laughing behind her fingers. "I miss her too," she says. "And who knows. Maybe she's as miserable without you as you are without her."

I hold up my hands, the knuckles scarred and marked with bruises. "Our lives aren't exactly compatible, Stel. I don't really walk the straight and narrow, and she's…"

"Nerd girl," Stella supplies. "I know." She leans back against the bar and sighs. "Shadow, you know people change. I'm not saying you're ever gonna stop all this." She waves her hand around, motioning toward the shelves of alcohol bottles, the dart board on the wall, or the massive TV. "But a lot of guys find old ladies. They manage."

"Shades of gray don't work," I tell her, shaking my head. "In this world, you're either good or you're bad. You're powerful or you're weak."

"Shadow, I can smell a line of bull like that a mile away, and you're sitting in sniffing distance." She shakes her head. "Black-and-white is for checkerboards and floor tiles. Real life, real people, aren't like that. Love isn't like that."

I snort when she says the L-word. "It ain't like that."

"Okay. Maybe you're not head over heels for this woman. Maybe you'd just be a little bit happier if you could see her once in a while. Fuck her brains out on the GTO and take her home at the end of the night."

She gives me a look. "Life is hard, Shadow. The people around here know that better than anybody. But that doesn't mean we don't deserve a little happiness. A little fun. You had something with Violet. I think you owe it to yourself to at least see how she's doing."

She turns around, opens the fridge, and grabs two beers. She pops the tops off and hands one to me. We clink the bottles at the neck in a toast and drink. "If you won't text her," Stella adds, "I will. I wouldn't mind having another set of hands cooking some nights. Jackie's fucking trash in the kitchen."

I shake my head, the first smile I think I've felt all month on my face. "Thanks, Stel." I take the beer and the bottles of water back to my room. I've just turned on the shower when there's a knock at my door.

I flip the water off and open the door to Phantom. "You're back," he says. No other explanations are needed.

I nod. "I'm going back tomorrow. He had the runs and had a woman, some cousin, running the lobby."

Phantom thinks for a minute. "Malcolm's abusing our patience."

"He is," I say. "But I made sure I left a little something to remind him of that."

Phantom studies my face but says nothing. "Ranger called while you were out. That fuckwad with the baseball bat's pled out. He's going away for fifteen. He's waived extradition, so he'll be transported up to Georgia to serve out his sentence. That ain't public knowledge yet, but I thought you'd want to know."

"Thanks."

Phantom looks like he wants to say more. I wonder if he knows about the door at Shady Lane. I know him well enough to know that he wouldn't think I did nearly enough. If it were up to Phantom, we'd be at Malcolm's bathroom door right now.

He heads out, and I close the door behind him. I turn the shower back on, but before I get in, I fire off a text.

> Me: Got some news today. Your ex is
> going away for a long time. 15 years up in
> GA. Thought you'd want to know.

I debate saying more or calling her. Even just to hear

her voice on her voice mail, but I can't. Whatever Stella says, whatever romantic fucking notions anyone has, this shit can't work. I click send, drop my phone onto the bed, and go rub one out in the shower.

When I get out a half hour later, I'm unsatisfied and starving. I dress fast and grab my phone. I have two new messages.

> Violet: Wow, hey. That's good. Thank you so much for telling me. How are you? Been okay?

And then, finally.

> Violet: Maybe I'll give you a call in a day or two. I've been really, really sick. I'm just about to drag myself to the doctor. X

I grab the phone and fire a message back.

> Me: Sick, how? Are you alone? Send me your address in case you need something, and text me when you're home safe.

She sends me her address and another X, but then she doesn't say anything more.

I pace the floors furiously. If she's sick enough to go to the doctor, maybe she shouldn't be alone. Maybe she'll get light-headed or dizzy. I pack up an overnight bag before I can even stop myself. I want to be ready. If she needs groceries or soup.

I run out to the kitchen, where Cammy and Penny are baking cookies.

"We got any soup?" I ask.

The women trade confused looks. "You mean like a can, Shadow? What are you looking for?"

"Soup, goddammit. What's hard to understand about soup?" I throw open the pantry, my heart thumping in my chest. I can't cook. I don't know anything about soup or tea or ginger ale, but I think about everything I crave when I'm sick.

Problem is, I'm almost never sick. And I don't know what Violet likes. "Can you just send Stella in here?"

Penny gives me a look, and Cammy heads out to the bar. I'm scouring the shelves, grabbing anything that looks like sick-people food.

"Shadow?" Stella speaks to me like I'm a toddler holding a bomb. "What are you doing with those potato chips?"

I look around to make sure we're alone, then I lean close. "I texted Violet like you told me to, and she's sick. I don't know what she needs. What does she need if she's sick?"

"Not those." Stella grabs my arm. "Let's take your truck. We'll hit the grocery store, and we'll get her everything she could need. You drop me off back here and take it to her. Sound like a plan?"

I nod, then head out toward the lot like my ass is on fire. I check my phone every five minutes, but there's no word from Violet. Maybe she went to urgent care or some shit. Maybe there's a line, or she needs to go to the pharmacy. I'm going to shop for supplies with Stella, and then, if I haven't heard back from Violet, I'm going straight to the address she sent me.

SIXTEEN
VIOLET

THE NEWS ISN'T GOOD. I mean, it *is* good, depending on your perspective. I can't exactly be happy at the moment, though. After puking my way through the last two weeks, I finally realized that I hadn't had a period since before the hurricane. Since before Shadow. I took a test. And it came back positive.

Pregnancy math is weird. I had my last period at the beginning of the month of August when I was offered the job in Tampa. I remember because I was so crampy and miserable, I actually joked with my sister that getting the job offer was a little apology from the universe for how bad I felt.

My period should have come around the first of September, but it didn't.

It's now the first week of October, so that means—using pregnancy math—I'm nine weeks along. The only time I've had sex with anyone over the last six months was with Shadow. That means there's no doubt in my mind who the father is, and the doctor's appointment I had today confirmed it.

Dr. Sally puts her hand on mine as we talk in her office after she gives me the results. I have a lot I need to do quickly, like start prenatal vitamins, but they are going to put me on a special diet to help treat the intense morning sickness. I've lost eight pounds in the last week alone, and I'm feeling more and more terrified about the damage that can do to me and my baby. I need to be resting and eating, not puking and losing precious nutrients before they even get into my system.

"Violet," Dr. Sally says, her voice gentle. "Now is the time to call on your family, your friends, the baby's father. If you can take time off work, get extra rest, you might make it through the worst of this in just a few more weeks. If not," she says, "we'll consider more aggressive treatments."

I don't disagree. I want to stay off medications if I can possibly manage it. Too bad time off and rest are things I definitely cannot afford right now.

"I'm thinking of moving to Chicago," I tell her. "My younger sister is in college there, and I'll have a bit more support. For now, the job I found is full time. I'm still in the probationary period, so I can't take time off. I have to work ninety consecutive days before they pay for my health insurance. I've only been there three weeks."

"We have wellness programs we can refer you to if your health care becomes compromised," the doctor tells me. "And if you decide to relocate, you'll want to reach out to some OB-GYN practices to find a doctor before you move. Now isn't the best time for a major change, but it will be harder the longer you wait. For now, the best thing you can do for yourself and for your little one is to take good care. Taking care of yourself is taking care of your little bean."

We schedule my next appointment, and I run to the pharmacy in the lobby of the medical plaza to stock up on prenatal vitamins before I leave. I'll have to order groceries or something when I get home. I feel so weak and so woozy, it takes all my focus to make it back to my condo safely.

As soon as I walk through the door, I have to rush into my bathroom to be sick. It's the worst possible feeling in the world, but I try to be brave.

"I'm doing this for you, little bean." I'm sitting on the bathroom floor of my third-floor condo. The cold tile seeps through my jeans, and I rest my head on my knees, tears burning my eyes. I should tell my sister. Should call my parents. I've known that I am pregnant for the last month. But until I got in to see the doctor, had it confirmed, I spent all the energy I had on dragging myself to work and convincing myself that I can do this—even if it means I'm doing this alone.

I can't believe I'm pregnant. At my age, of course it was always a possibility. I have never even had a pregnancy scare before. Have always used condoms. Even with Clive.

My stomach roils just thinking about him. Can you imagine if I'd gotten pregnant by a man who would stalk me? Who would abuse my trust?

I guess if I was going to get pregnant by any guy, a gorgeous man I had a three-night stand with isn't as bad as it could be.

I know I have options. I can give the baby up. I can terminate. I can raise it with my sister in Chicago or move home to my parents. The funny thing is that, right now, I don't want to share this news with anyone.

Who knows if things will turn out okay? Waiting until I'm past the twelve-week mark doesn't mean that nothing can go wrong. I've been spending every night reading forums and chat threads online about women in their first trimester.

Of course I would read everything I possibly could about pregnancy, but somehow reading about something that's happening to me, inside me, makes it much more real. I can't let myself think about it too long, though. Because thinking about being pregnant means thinking about the father of my child.

Thankfully, I'm too nauseous to have too many coherent thoughts. I close my eyes and let the cool tile ease the heat that seems to radiate from inside me. Thank goodness my condo was newly renovated when I was finally able to move in. I don't have to worry about other people's funk on the floors as I lie there, alone, trying not to heave up my insides.

I don't know how long I spend on the bathroom floor before I pull myself up, brush my teeth, wash my face, and wander out to the living room. The bag of prenatal vitamins and my purse are on the floor by the door where I dropped them when I ran in here to puke.

I work from home full time for a small nonprofit. I'm the research manager for the development arm, which is a lot of words to say I manage the database of donors and grants that our contract grant managers and our fundraisers rely on to bring in donations. The pay is crap, but the hours are great.

I text my boss that my doctor's appointment went great—you know, for my bad allergy flare-up—and feel a tremendous amount of guilt. At some point, I'm going to have to let them know that I'm pregnant, but three weeks after they hired me seems a little too soon, even for a rule-follower like me.

I fire up my laptop and go to the kitchen to make some tea. Since I need to take the vitamins with food—assuming I'll ever be able to keep food down again—I put the pill bottles on the counter next to my potted plants. A nice reminder to do the small things—sunlight, water, and space—to keep myself alive and healthy.

The kettle whistles, and I steep some ginger tea while sticking a lemon wedge right into my mouth, sucking on the bitter pulp to hopefully ease my misery. Nope. Doesn't work. Within ten minutes, I feel the lemon juice coming right back up, and I have to run to make it to the bathroom.

This time, the lemon juice burns my throat, and I'm just done. Done. It's already getting dark out, and any work I didn't get done today will have to wait until I'm not puking my guts up. I grab a towel from the bar, lie down on my side with my cheek on the cool tile, and cry.

When I wake up, it's completely dark, and someone is pounding on my door. I grab the towel and pick myself up off the floor, wondering who on earth would be knocking at this time of day.

I peer through the peephole and see nothing but a massive leather vest.

A leather vest.

It's him.

It's Shadow.

I flip the dead bolt and open the door with shaking hands.

I see him, and everything inside me crumples. No, scratch that. My knees actually give out. I tumble to the floor, still holding the towel in my hands that I used in the bathroom for my floor nap.

"Violet, what the fuck." He rushes inside, slamming the door behind him.

"I'm okay," I croak out, but even I don't believe me.

He has two big market bags in his hands, and I have to laugh at the colorful floral designs printed on them.

"What is... What are you... Oh no. Can you help me up? Hurry, Shadow. I need to—"

Yeah, I don't make it. Lying right on the floor of my living room, while the sexiest man and the father of my baby, whom I haven't seen or heard from for the last month, is kneeling beside me, I heave right into the towel I was holding.

"Jesus Christ," he mutters, but he doesn't sound disgusted. He holds the long locks of my hair away from my face and puts a hand on my back. "Sweetheart, what's going on?"

I hold up a finger, grateful for a second that he's probably held back the hair of a puking woman many, many times in his life. This can't be that big of a deal, so I'm gonna do my best to treat it that way too.

"It's just food poisoning," I gasp between heaves. "You can't catch it. I'll be okay." I try waving him away, but he just comes closer. I smell the familiar scent of him, and something deep inside my chest tightens.

God, I missed him. I missed this. I cannot believe he is here.

He slides his hands under my knees and picks me up in his arms. "Bedroom or bathroom?"

I can't even hold up my own head. As soon as I feel his heat beneath me, I literally sag against him. "I have a bucket in my bedroom, and I've been sleeping on the floor of the bathroom, so your choice. They're all the same to me now."

I'm so weak. I can't hide it. Can't even pretend. I just let myself be weak in his arms. I close my eyes and thank my lucky stars he's here.

He walks toward the back of the condo, noting where the bathroom is, but opting instead to take me to my bed.

"I made tea in the kitchen," I say weakly. "You can drink it. I don't know if I have much else in the house."

"I'm not drinking your damn tea, but I think you should," he says. He sets me on the bed and holds my face in his hands. "How long have you been like this?"

I change the subject. "Can't talk. Can I lie down? Why are you here?"

He smooths the hair back from my face and tucks the covers over me. He sits on the edge of the bed and studies me. "I brought you sick-person food."

I smile weakly. "Sick-person food sounds good. What's up with those bags? I didn't figure you were the van Gogh flowers type. But I guess we never really made it to a supermarket, did we?"

The corner of his mouth ticks up, and he shakes his head. "Stella. They're hers. She says hi, by the way. The girls miss you."

That gets me. That really, really gets me. A sob chokes its way up my throat, and tears sting my eyes. "I miss them too," I whisper. "I'm so, so tired, Shadow. I've been so sick…"

"I know, sweetheart. I'm going to take care of you." He strokes my head.

"Mmm-hmm," I mumble, knowing that he's here and that I'm not alone.

I won't tell him about the baby. Not now. I need time to process this news for myself. I need time to figure out why he came. What he wants. If this is the last time I'll ever see him—or if maybe he missed me too.

I remember how much it hurt leaving him that last day at the compound. It seemed irrational at the time—missing someone I'd only known three days—but seeing him here now, it all comes back to me. It's like no time has even passed. I fell in love with Shadow. And even if it makes no sense and can't be real, can't last, being with him was the happiest I've ever been. The best time I've ever had. And the only true home I've ever felt as an adult.

For tonight, at least, I need that from him. And with everything that's going to be ahead of me, it doesn't even feel selfish to take it.

He turns off the lights, kicks off his boots, and sits beside me on the bed, stroking my hair until I fall into a blissful, peaceful sleep.

SEVENTEEN
SHADOW

THE SECOND VIOLET FALLS ASLEEP, I'm out of bed. I close her door quietly behind me and head back to the living room. I turn on all the lights, lock the doors, and take the groceries to the kitchen. Her place is cute, generic and clean in a "flip it and rent it" kind of way, but she's added a lot of character. I feel like I'm getting to know her in a different way through her things.

Her kitchen is decorated in a strawberries-and-baby-blue color scheme, and by God, she leans into the theme. The teakettle on the stove is sky blue. The oven mitts and dish towels have strawberries on them. She has potted plants everywhere—like, crazy-plant-lady everywhere. I recognize a few fresh herbs because they have those little chalkboard signs with the names written on them: thyme, sage, basil, and mint.

I unpack Stella's groceries and send her a text.

Me: She's sick. Puking up her guts, but nothing coming out. Soup okay?

I get a dozen sad-face emojis back and then a thumbs-up.

> Stella: Make it plain. Nothing in it for now. Just broth. Have her sip it slowly, a cup at a time. See if she can keep it down. Then you can add crackers or rice. Add a little salt to the soup, and if you think she can handle the electrolyte drink, serve that too. Maybe room temperature. Cold might actually be hard on her tummy.

This is the longest fucking text message I have ever read in my life. I swear to fuck, I thought there was like a character limit on that shit. But I read it twice, making sure I get every piece of advice.

I thumbs-up it because I'm exhausted from reading it and don't have the energy to reply. But then I think the better of it and text back.

> Me: Thanks, Stel.

That was a huge freaking mistake, though, because she replies again. It's just to ask me to check in later and let her know how Violet is, but I'm done reading and communicating.

Now's the time for action. I go through every cabinet and cupboard and put away everything I bought. I find the pots and pans and go on the hunt for the washing machine because it grosses me out to have that towel just lying around.

I find the washer and spend way too long reading the instructions. We have commercial machines in the compound—big things almost like what we had in prison, but this is so high-tech, all sensor-operated and shit, it takes me like twenty minutes before I feel confident where to put the damn detergent. But I manage to start a load of laundry and am relieved that the machine seems quiet enough it won't wake Violet.

I take a small blue pan that matches the décor in the rest of the kitchen and put it on the stovetop. Dumping in a can of plain old chicken broth with a dash of salt from a strawberry-shaped shaker, I start the burner, then remember she said she'd put a tea someplace. I see it on the counter by the plants where some paperwork and a brown paper bag are just sitting out.

I hesitate before looking at the papers, but I figure if this is the shit from the doctor, it can help me to take care of her if I know what the doctor told her. I scan the details.

Violet James, thirty-two years old. Dr. Sally Yamaguchi, OB-GYN.

My heart stops in my chest. Why would Violet go to an OB-GYN? My mind leaps to the worst-case scenario. She looked thinner than I remember, and she's been vomiting. Could she have some lady problem? Cancer? An STI?

I've been fine since we were together, but it's been a bit since I've seen her, so who knows. My eyes tear down the paper, braced for words like tumor or mass, but what I see shocks me even more.

Patient presents with hyperemesis gravidarum...

I grab my phone and punch in the term. What the actual fuck is that?

And then my heart plummets into my shoes.

Hyperemesis gravidarum... Excessive nausea and vomiting during pregnancy.

Pregnancy.

Violet is pregnant?

I scan the rest of the report.

Gestational age estimate nine weeks.

Follow-up by telehealth in two weeks.

I grab the brown paper bag and pull out the bottle. Prenatal vitamins.

Holy fucking shit.

I drop down onto a strawberry-shaped chair cushion on a bright-blue-painted kitchen chair, but then I startle when I hear the soup boiling.

"Fuck." I jump up, turn the burner off, and let the soup cool since Stella said not to give her anything too hot or too cold.

I do the math in my head. If Violet is nine weeks pregnant, and we were together just over four weeks ago... Was she pregnant when she met me? Is the baby even mine? I rack my brain, remembering what she said when we were together. The time we fucked without a condom for just a minute before I came all over her tits. She'd said she was about to get her period. That means she shouldn't have been fertile. I suppose she could have been pregnant then, but...

I pick up the phone.

"Stel, I need help."

I explain the situation to her.

"So, does that mean the baby's mine?"

"Oh, Shadow." Stella sounds so happy, I am already braced for her to tell me it is mine. But I listen anyway. "Pregnancy math makes no sense, and yeah, it's possible that if she was with someone in the week or two before she met you, then you could have a paternity question going on. But the math works for it to be yours, based on what you've told me. Did she tell you you're the father?"

"She's asleep," I tell her. "We haven't talked. She puked and passed out."

Stella and I talk for a couple more minutes, and I swear her to total secrecy. I don't need anybody knowing about this before I know what Violet's intentions are. For all I know, she won't want to carry it. Won't want to keep it. I'm gonna keep my cool until she's well enough to talk.

I make a second call. Phantom doesn't pick up, and I don't leave a voice message. He calls me back a minute later.

"Sorry, was on the shitter," he says. "I don't take my phone in the can."

"Didn't need to know that, but thanks for calling back." I tell him I have a family emergency and I'll be out of pocket for a couple days, won't be coming home. "I may not have a chance to get much work done," I say.

I know I don't have to explain. Phantom runs a tight club. He knows who owes us money, when it's due, and who's assigned to collect.

"What do you want me to do? Give him more time, or send somebody in?"

"Your call," I tell him. I like to let my prez make the decisions. "But we gave him an inch last month, and this month, he's taking a mile."

"Noted. Maybe I'll go myself. If Malcolm thinks he was shitting himself today…"

I laugh. "Thanks, brother."

"Take care of family. You need anything, you call." He hangs up without saying goodbye, and I walk over to test the temperature of Violet's soup. It's still hot, so I fold back up the doctor's notes and put the prenatal vitamins back in the bag where I found them.

If Violet feels strong enough to get up, maybe she won't automatically assume I saw them. I'll give her time to tell me the news herself. I need some time to process it too.

———

"Another sip." I hold the spoon out to Violet.

She opens her mouth, and I feed her the broth. "I can't believe how good this is. What did you put in this?"

"Salt," I laugh. "Good old-fashioned salt. Although you got some fancy shit in that strawberry shaker. At first, I thought it was sugar because it's pink."

She swallows, closing her eyes and humming as the plain, tepid broth goes down. "Himalayan salt," she explains. "So delicious."

I lit a few candles in her bedroom and brought in clean towels so she'd have a supply in case the soup came back up, but she's managed to tolerate it so far.

I hold out the mug of ginger tea. "I'm gonna order a sandwich," I tell her. "I didn't know how long I'd be here, so I didn't shop for me. I'll eat in the kitchen so the smell doesn't bother you. Unless..." I lift my brows. "You think you're up for solid food?"

She covers her mouth and shakes her head. "Not yet. Let's not tempt fate. The fact that you got this much into me is a miracle. Today was a rough day." She falls silent, and I sit beside her on the bed.

"I'm sorry I wasn't here sooner. Sounds like you've been in some kinda way for a while now." I give her a little opening. A chance to spill what she knows about the baby, but she looks away.

"Shadow, this isn't how I wanted things to go. As much as I wanted to see you again..."

I hold up a hand. "Well, I'm here now. Let's make the

most of the time we have." I get up and collect the dishes. "I'll bring water and more tea when I come back. You want anything? Some of that sports drink?"

She shakes her head. "I'll let the soup settle. Thank you."

I turn to leave her room but stop at what she says next.

"I missed you every day. Every single day."

I don't know how to respond to that. I firm my lips and head into the kitchen. I put the dishes in the dishwasher and pull up an app on my phone. I order a sandwich and then sink down on a damn berry cushion to wait for the delivery.

I need to face the giant fucking elephant in the room at some point. She missed me. Missed me every day. I sure as hell missed her every day. I missed her so much that some nights, I'd lie in bed and my chest would ache. I'd remember her smell and the way I slept like a goddamn corpse with her beside me. I feel like I haven't had a decent night's sleep since she left. And I asked her to stay, but she didn't. Not that I blame her. I don't know what a man like me could offer a woman like her.

I'm a criminal. Lawless, through and through. I live by a code, but that doesn't mean I'm not a single wrong step away from a one-way ticket back behind bars. I have the money and the power to buy sheriffs, cops, judges today— but I'm almost forty. How's it gonna be when I'm sixty and can't kick ass like I can today?

I have never been a guy who thought he'd live to see the age of thirty, let alone be planning to turn fifty or even sixty. But meeting Violet changed me. I don't think I could change enough to deserve her, though. My phone chirps when the food is here, and since I don't know the access code to let the driver in, I run to Violet's room to ask for her keys.

When I enter the room, she's rubbing her belly through the blanket, staring blankly down at her hand.

"Hey."

At the sound of my voice, her eyes snap up and she smiles. "I was congratulating my stomach on a job well done. Soup's still where I left it."

Something inside me goes feral in that moment. She wasn't talking to any damn soup. She was talking to the baby. *Our baby.*

"Good, sweetheart. Rest and I'll be back."

She gives me a smile as her eyes slowly close.

I eat standing up at her kitchen counter, dropping Stella a text.

> Me: Soup worked. Keeping it down so far.
> Good call on the salt.

She texts me back a massive row of emojis and likes the text. Stella's good people. I don't know a ton about her, but I'll have to do something nice for her—detail her car or something—when I'm back at the compound.

A few days and maybe Violet will spill it. Tell me about the baby and what she plans to do. What she wants. Until then, I'm gonna do my best not to get attached. I don't do relationships, but that was before I met Violet James.

EIGHTEEN
VIOLET

SHADOW IS THE VOMIT WHISPERER. As disgusting as it is, my morning sickness has dropped to really manageable levels by the end of the third day. I tried to convince Shadow that he didn't have to stay and nurse me back to health, but he insisted. And since I wasn't ready to tell him that the condition I have won't go away in just a couple of days, it seemed easier to accept his help. God knows my body has needed it.

Shadow isn't a bad cook for a guy who can't cook. He's made me soup, rice, plain noodles, crackers, and fruit, which I guess isn't cooking, but it's the closest he's come, so I'm saying it counts. And if I didn't have to prepare it, it sure feels like being cooked for.

Since Shadow came on the day my doctor confirmed the pregnancy, I haven't been able to talk to anyone about it—not my sister or my parents. And, of course, not Shadow.

Since I'm new at my job, I've been working during the day, taking breaks to get sick or shower. And then at night, we cuddle in bed and watch movies. It's shocking to me how comfortable it is just being with Shadow. He's a human body pillow I wrap myself around every night. We haven't had sex or even kissed—maybe because he's not sure that I don't have some kind of flu or bug. And I have been puking every chance I get, so I can't say I expect him to pounce on me like he did during the storm. But a few days without any sex has given us something I wasn't sure we'd ever have—a relationship.

We can talk about anything—well, except the baby I'm carrying. We've talked about politics, religion, our families. It's amazing how much time is freed up to understand each other when we're not banging our brains out. I miss that, of course, but it's hard to imagine moving around that much. Just thinking about it makes my stomach churn.

Today was a fairly stressful day at my job. Shadow washed the sheets and bedding while I took two video calls. I had to go off-camera once to heave into a trash bin, but then I made it through the second meeting relatively unscathed.

So unscathed, in fact, I get a little overconfident. When Shadow tells me he is going to order burgers for dinner, I ask him to get me one.

"You sure about that?" He eyes me suspiciously. "You looked green after plain dry toast at lunch. You're ready to go in for a burger?"

"Plain," I tell him. "No fries, nothing on it. I think some protein could do me good."

Shadow has been adding chicken to my soups, but just the idea of a burger makes my mouth water.

"I can handle it," I assure him.

When the burgers arrive, I find out way too soon that I cannot, in fact, handle it.

"Nope. Nope, nope, nope." I cover my mouth with my hand and turn to run for the bathroom.

Shadow follows close behind, stopping me with a hand on my shoulder. "Sweetheart, stop." His voice is raw with compassion, and the ache in his tone brings a tear to my eyes. He's so caring and considerate.

"You don't have to—" I huff, feeling a wave of sour bile rise in my throat. The tears flow then. "I'm so sick of being sick," I tell him. I don't care if I cry and get snot on his shoulder. I don't want to go through this alone. I want to lean on him.

And he absolutely lets me. He picks me up and carries me into the bathroom, setting me down on the edge of the bathtub. I get sick—there's no stopping it at this point—but now I'm crying, too. Shadow stays with me, holds my hair back, and flushes the toilet for me when there's nothing left I can lose.

I wipe my nose and shiver. "I feel so gross. Throwing up is literally torture. I feel just yucky." I start brushing my teeth.

"Come on." He turns on the bathwater and pours in a splash of bubble bath from a bottle I keep on the shelf. While the tub fills, he strips off my clothes, gently kissing my hands and shoulders, neck and head.

When I'm naked, I step carefully into the bath, him holding my hand every second. "Shadow, your burger's going to be ice-cold. Go eat."

To my surprise, he pulls off his shirt and unzips his jeans. God, I've missed his body. He looks exactly the way I remember him—his arms thick, muscular, and dusted with dark brown hair. His Shadow King tattoo, his dense thighs, stubbled neck. He is beautiful. Perfect. A man of so many contradictions. I peek at his piercing, smiling a little bit and giving it a wave.

"Missed you, little guy," I say. Then I look up at Shadow, who climbs in behind me. "Do you have a nickname for your piercing? Do you call it, like, little Shadow or Mini-Me or something?"

He arches one dark brow at me. "No."

Once he's in the tub, I settle between his legs and lay my head back against his chest. "You have given up three days to take care of me. It's starting to become a pattern."

He cups warm water in his hands and pours it over the back of my hair, then uses his wet hands to massage my shoulders and the back of my neck. "A habit," he says quietly. "You're becoming a habit I don't think I can kick."

His words gut me.

"Shadow, you don't strike me as the relationship type," I say.

He stiffens, and his hands still on my shoulders. But then he keeps kneading, moving his warm, rough palms over my tight, tense muscles. "Never have been before. You're right about that."

"Would I be any different?" I ask. "Would you want a relationship with someone like me?"

"Not someone like you," he says. "You. Only you."

"I didn't think you wanted that when I left after the storm," I say, admitting the truth. "I wanted that, though. I wanted you."

He's quiet, and he stops stroking my hair, wrapping his arms around me and holding me tight to his chest. "I didn't know what to say. I thought I made my feelings clear. Maybe I needed more time to get clarity on what I felt for myself."

"What does that mean?" I ask.

"Still figuring that part out, sweetheart."

The answer is simple, but it feels honest. I can't help but ask him about his family, tiptoeing close to the idea of *our* family without giving too much away.

"Shadow, do you have any grandparents?" I ask. "Did you ever have a close relationship with them?"

We've talked a bit about our families, but not grandparents.

He sighs. "Tried to. Gramps on my dad's side was a real bastard. It's a miracle my pop wasn't a total son of a bitch. And Gram, well, she was more of the sending cards for special occasion type of lady. That's my dad's parents. My mom's mother—Grandma Betty—was a living, breathing saint. I loved that woman, and she worshipped me. Sewed all my clothes growing up."

I remember that now. Shadow's father died when he was only ten. His mom was a teen mom, so she was only twenty-five when she became a widow and a single mother. His grandmother passed two years ago.

"Been thinking about reaching out to my ma," he says softly. "She never really got over my going to prison. Can't say I blame her. I haven't exactly been the angelic little boy she wanted."

"Where does your mother live?" I ask, savoring the stillness in my body. Something about the water and Shadow's heat have me relaxed and easy. I feel good—if I can tempt fate by using that word.

"She's local," he says, a slight Florida twang in his voice.

I smile at it. Ever since going away to college in the Midwest, I've loved the Florida accent. It's subtle and only comes out in certain vowels, but it always sounds like home.

"Wow, Shadow," I say. "So, you haven't spoken with your mother in how long?"

His arms go slack around me, and I feel like he might get up and out of the tub. Did I push too far? I must not have, because he settles back against the porcelain, which is doing a heroic job holding the weight of both of us. He sighs, though, a long, ragged sound that breaks my heart into pieces.

"I try to be a good son," he says defensively, almost like he's arguing with himself. "I send her cards and flowers. I..." He hesitates as if he's not sure he wants to share this next thing. I run my fingers along the tops of his immersed thighs, trying to quietly reassure him that I want to know this about him. I want him to tell me. "I pay for a grocery service that brings her food every month."

"Is your mom alone?" I ask.

"Nah. Mom is married to a really decent guy. Straight arrow. He treats her well, holds down a good job. They've got a little place not far from here."

I'm confused. "If your mom is married and doing okay, why do you buy her groceries?"

He sniffs and runs a wet hand through my hair. "I don't know. I don't need to. It's just something I do. It started a few years back, before she met Gary. Ma was texting all the time, inviting me to dinner. I was working on some shit for the club and just never got around to going over. Ma said something once about buying all the stuff I love to make a homemade meal for me, and it fucking gutted me, like she was putting in all this effort every week to have stuff on hand just in case I made it. And I never did. So, I started buying groceries for her. I didn't want to feel like she was wasting her time and money on me."

I twist a bit, the wet ends of my hair covered in bubbles, and try to look up at him. He looks wrecked. He's a smart man. He knows he could make one meal a month with his mother. He could, couldn't he? The club can't have him so busy that he has no time for his mother, can it?

I cup his bearded cheek with a sad smile, then turn away, resting my back against his chest and closing my eyes. That just proves my point. How can a man who can't even make time for his mother be a father? This could never work. He would never, ever be able to do this.

I don't know what I'm going to do with this information.

I manage to blow-dry my hair without puking, and God bless him, Shadow makes us both a light dinner of chicken and rice. We eat quietly on my couch, the television playing an old movie in the background. But neither one of us speaks. He's beside me, our thighs touching, and it's nice.

And that's all it can be.

I'm overcome with sadness then. Will I end up like Shadow's mom? Raising a child who never comes to see me? Marrying a safe, stable man someday who will always stand in the shadow of the man I never got over? Because having Shadow right here and not being able to have him is killing me.

I jump up from the couch and run into the kitchen before the tears start.

"Violet, you sick?" Shadow follows me into the kitchen, where I'm standing over the sink.

"No," I say. When I face him, it's like everything hits me at once. I see him standing here in my kitchen. He's so huge and muscled, his heavy, dark tattoos a stark contrast to my cottagecore décor.

He doesn't fit. We don't fit.

I don't know why I even let myself hope for more.

I try to brighten my voice. "No, I'm just..." The tears come fast and hot. "I'm sorry. You don't have to stay. You've done so much for me, taken such good care of me —for the second time now. You need to get back to your real life. What really matters. I don't want to slow you down anymore."

"Why would you say slow me down?" He's folding me against his chest and wiping my tears when he says, "This is my real life, Violet. Don't you know you're what matters to me right now?"

I hear the right now, and it doesn't make me feel any better.

"Thanks," I say, sniffling and pulling away. "But eventually, you have to go back to the compound. To whatever you do for work, or are you planning on staying here and making me chicken soup forever?"

"You want forever?" His face darkens, and he stares at me as though I slapped him. "Is that what this is really about, Violet?"

I shake my head. "I can't do this."

I try to walk out of the kitchen, but I don't know where to go. If I run to my bedroom, will he follow me? I don't think I have the strength to watch him leave. To see us separated again, this next time for who knows how long.

I pinch the bridge of my nose and try to calm down. I know I'm exhausted, emotional, not to mention hormonal. But I have to know what this is once and for all. I can't spend the next nine months or nine years wondering what could have been.

"I didn't want to leave you after the storm," I say quietly. "I wanted you to want me to stay."

"I did," he says quickly. "I said—"

"You said I could come back whenever I needed an orgasm," I remind him, but there is no cruelty in my voice. I lift my arms helplessly. "I can't help it if I want great orgasms and the man who gives them to me. I want all of you, Shadow. I wanted all of you. And I knew that would never be possible. Even if you did feel the same way, how would we make it work? I'm a librarian, and I am truly not judging, but I don't know if I want to know what you really do for the club."

He listens to me, his face completely devoid of expression. I can't tell if he's furious, hurt, or bored.

"It makes no sense, and we hardly know each other, but I know enough to know I want it all. I wanted you, Shadow. And you're back now, but how long will it be until you have to leave? Until I can't be your top priority, and then..." I don't want to say this. I don't want to throw back in his face that I don't want to be like his mom. Someone he sends groceries to so he doesn't have to feel the pain and guilt of not being there.

I don't have to say it, though. Shadow closes his eyes and huffs a soul-weary sigh. "Is that why you haven't told me about the baby?"

My heart gallops in my chest. I am too shocked to deny it. "How did you know about that? How did you—"

He points toward my potted plants. "The first night I got here, your doctor's notes and the prenatal vitamins were right there on the counter." He lowers his eyes. "You probably didn't think I'd notice that you hid them away somewhere while I was showering the next morning. I did, Violet. I fucking notice everything."

He doesn't come closer to me, but now, he stares me in the eye. "I notice because I care, Violet. This isn't food poisoning. You're pale and exhausted. You're weak and trying to hide what's going on from everyone. At first, I wasn't sure if it was because you didn't know what you were gonna do about the situation. But now, I think it's because you weren't sure what you were gonna do about me."

Shame floods my entire being like an illness. I feel terrible—stupid, even. He's a smart man. Of course, he would put two and two together.

"It's yours," I say quietly, just in case there is any doubt. "I'm sorry. But it is."

Shadow stands there looking partly stricken, partly shocked.

"But look, I don't need anything from you. I don't need child support, you don't need to be involved. I have a really supportive family. I haven't even had time to tell them yet, but when I do, my sister is going to want me to move to Chicago, and I know my parents will pressure me to bring their grandbaby back to Atlanta. I have support. I'll be okay. I'll send you pictures and emails if you want updates."

At that, he does move closer, his green eyes sparking with something dark and angry. "You'll send me pictures?" He rakes a shaking hand through his hair. "Ever since I set eyes on you, I've wanted nothing but you. To protect you, to keep you safe. To take care of you. What the fuck makes you think I wouldn't do the same for my kid?"

I shake my head. "Shadow, we've been through this. You took care of me because I needed you to. But life isn't a tropical storm. I don't need you to protect me. I love when you do, and I will forever—and I mean *forever*—be grateful that you freed me from Clive." I wrap my arms around myself and shiver. "Can you imagine if I had your baby and Clive was out there walking free?"

I can't think of it. The very idea makes me sick. What he would have done to me or to the baby. The danger I would have felt being on the receiving end of that man's fury. And the terrifying reality of what happens to women just like me every day who don't have a Shadow to drive the real darkness away.

"I mean it," I say. "I'll never be able to repay you for all you've done, but you're finished now. It's okay. I'll be okay."

"Fuck that." Shadow shakes his head. "I won't be okay. I was never okay. I haven't been okay since you walked away from me almost a month ago." He starts pacing circles in the kitchen, nearly tripping on my berry-shaped kitchen rug.

I have to hold back the giggles that want to overtake me. This is ridiculous. Insane, really. This could never work. He literally does not fit in my life. And what would I do? Bring the baby to the biker club? The compound has smoking, drugs, booze, sex. I shake my head. It can't work.

"Violet." Shadow stops his frantic pacing, smooths the rug with his foot, and then stands on it, so far from me I can't smell him or touch him. I am glad for that. I don't think I could think clearly or resist holding him if he moved any closer. "I'm in love with you. I don't give a shit if this doesn't make sense. I want you. I want you with me every day."

I shake my head. It's what I want too. It's what I've dreamed of hearing. But it's too late. "You'll resent me," I say. "If you stay with me just for the baby, you'll resent me. And our child. And then we'll all be miserable."

Then he comes close to me, holds my arms gently in his hands. "Look at me, please, Violet. Because if you don't, I'm gonna fucking blow. I can't take how this feels."

I look into his face, and his eyes are shining, his formerly unreadable face now a mask of agony.

"I can't lose you. I want to make a life with you. I want to make a family with you." He moves his hands from my arms to the sides of my face, and his touch is so light, it's like he's afraid he's going to break me. Or that I could break him. "I want this. Maybe not the strawberries everywhere, but I want our version of this."

I laugh, a few tears running down my face. "Having a relationship is hard work, Shadow. God knows I tried with Clive, and that went all to shit."

"I'm not that fucking asshat." He flares his nostrils and glares at me. "For fuck's sake, Violet. Is that what you think of me?"

"No, no, of course I don't. But Shadow, I've never, ever had anything like what I've had with you. I can't stand the thought of being away from you for five minutes. If I lose you, it will destroy me. I can't let anything come between me and this baby, if I have it. Not even my feelings for you."

"That's not gonna happen," he growls.

"You can promise me forever?" I ask. The question is quiet and sincere. Not accusing. "How will that work, Shadow? There's no room in the compound for a crib. I can't park a stroller in the garage next to the GTO."

Now, I'm sobbing. The memories of what we had feel so stolen, so fleeting. Like the past we shared is a closed chapter and we're wasting our strength trying to pry that book open and find the page where we left off.

He holds me close to him, and I let myself cry against his chest. He breathes into my hair, and I feel the hum of his breaths, the patter of his heartbeat.

I carry a part of this man inside me, a life that is as much him as it is me.

Someday, will I see the curve of his brow on my little baby's face? When I teach my child to play in the sun, will I think of him every time I see a shadow? I don't know how people do these things. Raise families. Love and lose. I feel so unprepared. All I know is what's in my heart, and none of what I feel makes any sense.

"Violet, nobody can promise anybody forever," he says. "My parents were high school sweethearts. They had me. They got married. They did everything right." He whistles low. "One small decision, one wrong turn, and anything can happen. My parents didn't get forever, but that doesn't mean they didn't try. All that matters is that both of us are willing to try."

"Are you?" I ask. "Are you willing to try because I am pregnant? Would you even be here if I weren't?"

He looks at me like I just said the world's stupidest thing, but his voice isn't mocking. It's patient. "Sweetheart, I didn't know you were pregnant when I came. And for all I knew, you didn't plan to keep it. I stayed for you. I'm here for you. If I try because I love you, then what the fuck does it matter if I try for you and our baby?"

When he says *our baby*, he looks like he's going to lose it.

"Ever since I saw that report, I've wanted to hold you tight. Tell you everything that's in my fucking brain. I'm not that guy, Violet. I can't be flowery and poetic. I fucking want you. It's that simple. I want to be in your bed and in your kitchen—" He kicks a toe at the strawberry rug. "Minus the knickknacks. I want to try. The baby just speeds up the timeline."

"So where does that leave the club?" I ask.

He shakes his head. "What do you mean?"

"If you choose me, doesn't that mean you have to quit being a member?"

NINETEEN
SHADOW

MY ANSWER IS AN IMMEDIATE, "NO."

I hold on to Violet like I can't bear to let her go, and I can't. Her skin, her hair, the scent of her. Those things are what my body craves, but knowing that she's carrying our child, *my* child. It's like a drug. I don't want to leave her side.

"I am a club member through and through. It's in my blood. My brothers are my family. They will always be a part of me, and I will always be a member of the club."

"How, then?" she asks. "Do any of the other guys have kids or even wives?"

When she says wives, a massive shit-eating grin covers my face. I can do this. I can make this woman my wife.

"Fuck yeah, they do," I tell her. "Phantom has two teenage girls. Blade's a single dad. We don't have a good track record as far as marriages go, but somebody's gotta be the first. I'd put my money on us."

"I don't want you to marry me out of obligation," she says, her face smashed against my chest.

I hold her head and don't say anything. I have to

choose my words carefully, and I'm an asshole. Feelings have never been my strong suit.

"Violet, I don't do anything I don't want to. I don't obligate myself to anyone, not even the club. Having honor and loyalty are different from being compelled." I finally breathe into her hair. "When I do ask you to marry me, and I will do that someday, you'll know it's because it's what I want more than I want to breathe the fucking air."

She's crying again, and I don't know if it's hormones or happiness or misery, and I'm not gonna ask. I just hold her and let her.

"Shadow," she finally whispers. "I want to try."

I pick her up in my arms and carry her to her bedroom. "Then we're fucking going to give it our all. You hear me? We're gonna try."

I set her on the bed and kneel between her legs. I hold her hands and kiss each fingertip. "Sweetheart, it won't be easy, but I can be in the club and be your man too."

"You're mine," she says softly, fluttering her eyes closed. "And I'm yours. It's hard to believe that just a month ago, we were strangers."

"We got to know each other pretty well, pretty fast," I agree. "I wouldn't have it any other way." I stand up and gesture toward the bed. "Why don't you lie down? I'll turn off the TV, and we can go to bed."

"Do we have to go to sleep?" She looks at me, a seductive grin curling her full lips into a delectable smirk. "I haven't been sick in a few hours, so…" She waggles her eyebrows.

"You think you can?" My mind races. I've had my cock on lockdown since I walked through that door and picked her up off the floor. But I know exactly how fast I can wake it up, if she's feeling up to it. "We can stop if—"

"Let's try to be fast enough that I don't have time to feel sick, 'kay? Make me feel good, Shadow. Help me forget how shitty the last month has been without you."

I don't know if this means that Violet has accepted that the club is as much a part of me as she is, as our baby is. But now is not the time for worrying. My woman is pulling off her clothes, and my hard-on is throbbing.

"I don't have condoms," she says, sounding apologetic. "You're the only person I've been with in ages, so I just haven't kept any around."

"The good news is I don't think we need them anymore." I leave my jeans and shirt in a heap on the floor and practically dive into her bed like it's a swimming pool.

Violet laughs, and I climb under the blankets with her, for the first time in days able to look at her body and let mine fully respond.

She's okay.

She's not sick.

She wants this.

She wants me.

"You'll let me know if we need to stop?" I ask.

She shrugs. "Worst-case, I'll put my head over the side and puke on the floor."

I shake my head. "You're a nut, Violet James."

"You're amazing, Johnny Butcher." She reaches for my beard and strokes the hairs, trailing a finger along my lower lip. "I dreamed of you every night. I'm falling in love with you, Shadow. Is that stupid?"

I chuckle. "Probably. But if that's the case, then I'm stupid too."

I reach for her hair and weave my fingers through the

strands, wrapping them around my hand and tugging lightly. "What do you want, baby?" I ask her. "How do you wanna come?"

"Every way," she sighs.

I kiss her for the first time since we said goodbye a month ago. My lips graze hers lightly, but overcome with need, I can't hold back. I devour her mouth, plunging my tongue inside. She moans low in her throat and kisses me back while scrambling to straddle me.

I sit on the bed with my back to the headboard and kiss her while she angles her body on top of mine. We kiss, and I cup her breasts, wondering briefly about how much this wicked, sexy body is going to change over the next few months.

The idea of fucking my woman, *my* woman, while she's carrying my child sends my dick into overdrive. I'm hard and throbbing, desperate for release with just a few kisses.

Fuck, I've missed her. I've missed her more than I knew, more than I could accept. It's like a craving you learn to tolerate until finally you get to have that thing— that precious thing that comes from outside you and yet somehow makes you feel more like yourself than you do without it.

"I love you, Violet," I pant against her mouth. "I love you."

"Show me," she says. "Say it as much as you want, but don't forget to show me." She lifts herself up a little and feeds me one of her nipples. "I love you too. Now, please, for the love of God, fuck me."

I willingly do, drawing her thick, hard nipple all the way into my mouth. I swirl the tip of my tongue against her peak and feel her throw her head back as the pleasure courses through her.

"So good," she whimpers. "Harder, babe. Harder."

I obey her demand, clamp her nip between my teeth, and lightly bite down.

She squeals but leans into me, pressing her chest to my face. "More," she begs. "Oh my God, that feels so good. It's even more sensitive. I can't..."

She's panting and sighing, moaning and tearing her fingers through my hair.

"Good, baby. Good." I mumble against her breast, the tender skin so, so soft where my hands cup her. I grip her tits together and spread my attention between both nipples, scraping with my beard and licking, sucking until a mottled flush climbs across her chest.

"It hurts," she pants. "I want you so bad, it's like my body aches for you."

"Is this too much?"

"No." She opens her green eyes wide and stares at me. "Don't you dare stop. I need more, Shadow. Give me everything."

She doesn't have to ask me twice. I release her breasts and reach between her legs to stroke her wet pussy.

"Suck your juices off me," I tell her, waiting for her to open her mouth for me.

I slide my fingers between her lips, being careful not to go too hard so I don't gag her. She's had enough of that for a lifetime. She tentatively flicks her tongue against my fingers, slowly tasting her own juices on my skin.

"You see why I can't get enough, baby? This is why I love making you wet. You're like fucking candy."

I kiss her, tasting the flavor of her essence on her tongue, and my cock starts to weep.

"Ride me," I tell her. "I'm gonna fuck you senseless, but I need you on top now."

She moves quickly, centering herself above my cock. She gasps as my erection fills her, inching her way down slow and steady. When I'm fully seated, she reaches behind me and grabs the headboard. Then she starts to work those hips, rocking forward and back, making greedy little circles as my cock tickles her walls.

"Fuck me," I tell her. "Ride me, sweetheart. Fuck me hard."

Her eyes are clenched shut, her lips parted, and little moans slip out with every breath she takes. She is stunning, my woman, her dark hair splayed over her shoulders, her full tits jiggling with every roll of her hips.

I stare at her, watching transfixed as she chases her climax, riding and fucking, rolling and gasping, using the headboard for leverage to drive her body into mine.

I grip her hips, help her pick up speed as she jerks back and forth, the sensual rolling becoming a frantic, greedy itch only my body can scratch. She howls, tosses her head back, begs me for more. More of me, more of this. All of me.

While she's riding and fucking, I pinch her nipples between my fingertips and roll those tender peaks until she's screaming my name, whimpering that she's gonna come.

"Come for me, sweetheart." I encourage her, lifting my hips in time with hers, driving my cock as deep into her as I can with her on top.

She shudders and nearly slows down, but then she chases it harder, pounding me so forcefully, the headboard bangs the wall in a steady, rhythmic beat.

"Don't stop," I demand. "Don't you dare stop." I urge

her on, thanking my angels that with her on top like this, I can control myself a little more. I'd never forgive myself if I blew my load and cut her pleasure short.

She releases the headboard and claws my shoulders, leaning her chest into my face and clinging to me. "Baby," she cries out, "baby, baby, uhhhhh..."

And then, she's falling, spiraling over that edge, her mouth open, her sweet breath in my hair, her tits crushed against my face.

I hold her, feel every powerful shake as she rides that climax, a climax that seems to go on and on and on.

When she finally stills, she licks her dry lips and looks at me. "I don't know if that was the pregnancy or just missing you, but that was intense."

"You okay?" I ask. That was a lot of movement and a lot of shaking for a woman who's spent the last couple of days unable to keep down even water when the morning sickness is at its worst.

She is breathless, trembling. This is how I first bonded with her. Her skin against mine, our sweat, our passion. Questions, answers. Laughter, tears. Blood and fear. I never want to spend another day without this woman, and I need her to know that.

"I'm amazing," she says, sounding clear and happy.

"I want this every day," I tell her. "Not just the fucking, but I'll take as much of this body as you'll give me. I want this. Being together. Being there for each other. Sickness, health. Fear, pain. I'm in this, Violet. I'm in this with you."

Her lips part and she licks them. "I believe you. And I want the same thing. All of us." She pats her belly. "It doesn't feel real yet since all I feel is sick." She cocks her head and gives me a sideways smile as she thinks about it. "And maybe a little more sensitive, which I'll take—thank you very much, hormones. But I want all of what we can be. No matter how hard it gets. I want to try with you, Shadow. Every day in every way."

We kiss again, but this time, it's without tongues, without desperate hunger that only the other person can satisfy. This kiss is a promise. A vow we make to each other. To the tiny little soul inside her that only happened because of what we share, who we are, and who we will become together.

She breaks the kiss. "Your turn," she reminds me. "Let's do this while my body is cooperating." She covers her mouth and makes a fake gagging sound. "You just said in sickness and in health. I've got the sickness part *down*."

She rolls onto her stomach and holds her ass high in the air. "This," she says. "I have had a thousand fantasies about this since I left the compound."

I'm more than happy to make that fantasy a reality. She's still wet when I fist my cock and slide it against her pussy lips, but I want to coax another climax out of her. And since I can go in bare, I want to savor as much as she can take.

I rub the head of my cock along her wet seam, making sure to hit her clit with each stroke. She wiggles her ass, and I clamp my fingers against her plush cheeks. "I wanna smack this ass so bad," I grit. "I don't want to hurt you, though."

"I'll tell you if I need you to stop, Shadow. Spank me, baby."

So, I do, palming her ass before I lift my hand and bring it down against her skin. She immediately cries out in pleasure, her pleas for more causing my cock to weep precome. My eyes roll back in my head, and I use her hips for leverage, letting my cock slide between those wet lips until I'm as deep as I can go.

She pushes her ass back against me, making little banging movements in time with my thrusts.

"Shadow, you feel..." Her words are muffled by her arms, but I get the gist. "You feel..." She moans with pleasure, rocking and rolling as I power my body into hers. The tightness of her, the slick smack of my thighs against hers. This is like nothing I've had before because Violet is nothing like anyone I've known before.

"You too, sweetheart," I say, grinding deeper and harder with each thrust. I'm a slave to the power of my desire for her, arousal driving me forward with a force greater than gravity.

My jaw starts to lock up, I'm grinding my teeth so hard trying to make this last, but without a barrier between us, this just feels too damned good. I release on a moan, bellowing into the silent room, not giving a fuck who hears us. She won't be here for long anyway. Neighbors be damned.

As I'm blowing my load inside her, she starts to quiver, to shudder against me, and suddenly, I feel her walls tighten.

"Fuck," I hiss as a second climax rocks her body.

I hold her hips, rocketing into her, and then collapse on the bed, spent and sweaty and satisfied—for now.

She's panting, a light mist of perspiration on her breasts. "I think we found a cure for morning sickness," she says.

"Definitely prefer this. I'll frickin' puke if I have to eat any more soup."

"Let's try for real food again tonight." She yawns and cuddles up beside me. "Maybe not straight for tacos and pizza, but I can try to cook us a burger. Maybe if it's less greasy and delicious, I'll manage it."

I mumble against her hair, but I can't form any words. I'm too...something.

Happy.

At peace.

I'm holding the woman I love, a baby I put inside her growing in her belly.

There's nothing more to say.

This is it.

The start of our future.

I close my eyes and drift into the deepest, most peaceful sleep of my life.

The next morning, we wake up still naked, somehow rested after multiple rounds of fucking and sleeping that kept us at it all night.

Whether sex can cure her morning sickness or she's just getting better with time, it doesn't matter.

We have a big weekend ahead of us, so at the first sign of the sun, I quietly climb out of bed and head into the kitchen.

I'm standing naked on that strawberry kitchen rug, making Violet tea while I wait for my coffee to brew. I'm so lost in thought, I don't hear her come down the hallway.

Violet's hair is messy, and she's wearing the T-shirt I threw on the floor last night.

"You feelin' okay?" I head over to her, a mug of ginger tea in my hand.

She takes it gratefully and lifts up on her toes to give me a kiss. "Yeah," she says. "I slept great. I feel great."

"Good," I tell her. "We've got a big day today."

It's Saturday, so my plan is to get Violet moved in with me, at least as a start.

"When's your lease up?" I ask. "You here a year?"

That would complicate things some, but I figure if I make a visit to the landlord and offer to buy out the lease, they might let her out.

She blows on the steaming mug of tea, sits on a strawberry pillow at the table, and shakes her head. "I'm month-to-month. When the condo wasn't ready when it was promised to me, I told the landlord that I would have to find another place to go. They offered me all kinds of incentives to stay, but I told them the only way I'd move in was if they let me go month-to-month. I pay a little bit more, but I only need to give them thirty days' notice to leave. I can be out of here pretty quick. Why?"

She cocks her head at me, and I explain. "I've got some shit to do today, but I want you with me. I'm not going to leave you alone every morning and every night through this. You're sick, I wanna know. I wanna be there."

She nods slowly. "I want that too. Do you want to stay here? I will get rid of the strawberry rug."

I chuckle. "Nah. No point in you paying rent. I want you to be able to quit that job if you want to. Find a better one if you like. But there's no reason for you to put up with puking on Zoom if you don't have to."

She rests her face in her hands. "The things we do for our kids."

Kids. Plural. I can see a day when our life is filled with little ones. We'll see how we do with the one already on the way.

I grab my phone and send a few texts, then I kiss

Violet's head. "I'm hitting the shower. How soon till you can be ready?"

"Ready for what?" she asks.

I cup her bare breast through the thin fabric of my shirt. "Sweetheart, I told you. I'm taking you home."

Two hours later, we pull Violet's sedan down a gravel access road. "Where are we?" she asks.

I drive for about five minutes down a path that winds through dense trees. Thankfully, the area was relatively untouched by the tropical storm. Any damage that was done has long been cleaned up. But if we do have another storm, we'll always have shelter at the compound.

Once the trees clear, I steer her car down a long driveway that leads to a garage. A sleek black car is parked out front.

"I normally don't keep her here, but if you'll be here most of the time, she'll be safe. I have a one-car garage that fits her and the bike, but I'm going to look into adding a carport so we at least have a shelter for your car. I'll leave my truck at the compound, so I'll always have wheels."

Violet turns to me, looking adorable in the passenger seat of her own car. She's sucking on a ginger candy, and I smell its spicy sweetness as she asks, "Is this your place?"

I get out of the car, go around to the passenger side, open the door for her, and take her hand as she steps out.

"Yeah," I tell her. "Now, *our* home."

I lead her past the GTO, which she pats hello and greets with a little giggle. Instead of walking her to the front door, I lead her through the grass around back.

When she sees it, she gasps. "Oh, Shadow. Oh my God."

That's the same reaction I have every time I'm here.

The house I bought about six years ago is right on the

shore of a fairly clear, shallow river. Houses have been built for miles in either direction, but the dense trees and small boat slips that most of us have afford a lot of privacy. The river itself isn't very deep, so we don't get the show boaters and water skiers. Mostly, older guys fish off their small private piers, and the younger crowd swims, catches frogs, or kayaks quietly down the ten-mile stretch that leads from the spring where it starts to the Gulf of Mexico.

"She's spring-fed, so the water tends to be too clear for gators, but we'll get the occasional one out here. I'll teach you what to look for and how to protect yourself."

The water is surprisingly clear, and even though the day is overcast, Violet walks to the shore, kicks off her shoes, and puts her bare toes in the water.

"You're kidding me," she says, turning to face me. "This is yours? I thought you lived in the compound."

"I stay there a lot, and I don't have a ton of storage here, so I keep the books and shit that I don't use that often in my room at the compound. But I can sleep here every night and keep my room. Perks of being a VP. That plaque on the door means it's mine for as long as I hold the office."

"So, you'll stay here with me?" she asks, her voice sounding hopeful. "And then what, just go to the compound when they need you?"

"The Club is my job, Violet. I'll go every morning like other guys go to work. But I'll be home for dinner most nights. If I can't, you can come to me, with or without the baby."

I don't tell her that I don't know how well the Club will handle having a baby at the compound, but the other guys have their kids around, playing video games or doing homework. "It's not an orgy twenty-four seven in there," I tell her. "And I'm sure it'll be good for some of those shitheads to see another side of life."

The club is the only family most of us have. It's what binds us, bonds us, and that's never going to go away. I can't imagine not combining the sides of my life—my blood and my brothers.

Violet wraps her arms around my waist and squeezes tight. "Baby, this is incredible. I can't believe I get to wake up every morning and look at this." She looks over her shoulder and then cups my chin. "I won the lotto of life."

I grin. "Jizzy and a bunch of the others are bringing my truck to your condo this afternoon. Let's get you moved in sooner rather than later."

She cuddles herself against my chest but then leans back and frowns a little. "I assume you've got a bathroom in there? Because I think I…"

We hold hands and run for the back door.

My place is swarming with bikers by sunset. Stella and Violet are hugging out back, watching the sun disappear into the river. I can hear Stella's excited voice even through the glass of the sunroom.

Thankfully, my neighbors live far enough apart, I doubt the noise will travel that far or be that loud. I shake my head at the irony.

Weeks ago, I was watching these shitheads snort coke off Jackie and Penny. Now, Penny is shooting orders at the prospects as they move the last of Violet's sparse belongings into the house.

"What are we doing with this?" Penny asks, holding up a box that is marked *Strawberry Shit*.

I shake my head. "Kitchen. Get rid of my generic shit. Bin it, for all I care. Set hers up so it feels like home."

Penny cocks her head at me and reaches out to punch me gently on the shoulder. "Of all the assholes to pick up an old lady, I can't say I pegged you to be the first to fall." She nods in approval. "I like nerd girl. I think I'm gonna like nerd baby even more."

She walks past me, carefully balancing the kitchen items, and I say a silent goodbye to my décor. It's fine. It's just stuff. And with a baby around, we're gonna have to cram a lot more stuff into this place.

Phantom walks up to me and sighs. "All right, then," he says.

I almost laugh. "What's that supposed to mean?"

He groans. "I got two fucking daughters, Shadow. Everything's gonna change for you."

My mood darkens a bit. "You think I can't handle it?"

His intense dark eyes stare at me, and he looks taken aback, like I told him his mother stinks. "Fuck no," he says. "I was about to tell you the best days of your life are ahead."

He's quiet for a minute, then he yells for the brothers to clear the fuck out. He extends his hand to me, and I take his. We clap backs in a half hug, and Phantom holds me close for a second. "You ever need light duty," he says, "you say the word."

I know what he means. I don't know how many assholes like Malcolm I'm gonna wanna shake down while I have a baby at home. Phantom balances our business with his personal life well, so I hear the invitation he's extending.

"I'm good," I tell him simply. "That changes, and you'll be the first to know."

We release each other, and I thank the rest of my brothers for their help. I sent Cammy and Jackie ahead with a bunch of cash to buy everybody pizza and booze on me.

The party of the year is at the compound tonight, but I won't be there to take part in it. I'll be here, at home, right where I'm meant to be.

Stella hears the bikes and truck fire up and comes in through the sunroom to join me in the kitchen. She throws herself at me and gives me a tight, hard hug. "That's all I've got," she says, then releases me with a huge smile. "Never mind. I wasn't going to give you a big speech and tell you how proud of you I am and how I believe in you. But it's all true. This is good, Shadow. Good for you, good for Violet. I'm so, so happy for you."

I hug her back hard and then give her a gentle shove away. "Now, get," I tell her. "I gave Jackie money for drinks, and you're gonna be pouring all night."

Stella gives Violet another hug goodbye, squealing that she'll see her next week.

Once we're alone, Violet and I collapse on my couch. I have all the lights off and a couple candles lit, the ones that crackle like there's firewood inside. She rests her head against my shoulder and sighs.

"It's been how many hours since I barfed?" she asks. "Maybe happiness suits me."

I kiss the top of her head. "Suits me too."

We sit in silence, the crackle of the candle wicks and our breathing the only sounds. It's peaceful. It's home.

"Can you believe we only met like a month ago?" she asks. "How the heck are we gonna tell my parents how we met?"

I shake my head. "That's on you, sweetheart. I don't

know how you explain I brought you back to a place you thought was a sex dungeon to ride out a hurricane, and then I rode you until the hurricane passed."

"Let's agree to never say the words sex dungeon in front of my parents."

"Deal."

I throw my arm over the back of the couch. "What are we going to do with the second bed?" I ask her. "You like yours? After you sleep in mine, you can decide which one you like better."

"Can we have both?" she asks. "I'd put mine out in the sunroom. I want to wake up to that view every single morning."

I don't have any window coverings out there, so sleeping in the sunroom would most definitely give the locals a show.

"I want to fuck you in every room in this house," I tell her. "But I'm not sure how much sleep we'd get in the sunroom. Sunrise, no blinds..."

She snuggles closer to me, then lifts her face for a kiss. "How soon till we can start?" she asks.

I lift my brows at her. "Start..."

"Fucking," she whispers. "If we plan to cover every room..."

I stand from the couch, take her hand, and blow out the candles. "Let's start upstairs," I say.

TWENTY
VIOLET

ONE YEAR LATER...

The doorbell rings, and I pad through the house in my bare feet to answer it. I open the door to a huge bouquet of balloons and a teddy bear.

"*Ivy?*" I scream, knowing there is no one in the world who could be behind this wall of happiness except my sister.

"Violet." Ivy hands the bouquet of balloons to my dad, who is standing behind her.

Ivy launches herself into my arms and squeezes tight. "Okay, I love you, congratulations, and all that shit. Now, where is my nephew?"

I motion behind me. "Shadow is feeding him. Go on in."

I hug my parents hard and thank them for everything they are about to do. I start giving them instructions before we're even in the house.

"Baby." My mom strokes my hair and smiles. "It's your wedding day, and you don't exactly look like you're ready.

Let's get you dressed. We'll have plenty of time to go over the instructions before you leave. Now, where's Johnny?"

My parents adore Shadow. Like, adore him as much as I do. I never realized how much my father loves cars and talking mechanics with someone. As a guy who never had any sons, he's formed a really close bond with Shadow. They don't like to call him by his biker name, but it's not that they disapprove.

Ivy loves it and won't call him anything but Shadow. She's even gotten into the hierarchy of the club.

She graduated college in May and has been renting a place in Tampa to be close to her nephew. Mom and Dad traveled down once a month while I was pregnant, but they are talking about moving to Florida to be closer now that little Johnny is here.

I'm just about to close the door when I see another car pull into the drive, and the occupants are out of the car before the dust has even settled.

I step out onto the gravel in my bare feet and open my arms. "Daphne. Gary."

Shadow's mom walks on low heels across the drive to meet me. As soon as we're in hugging distance, we grab each other and hold on.

When I went into labor two weeks late, Daphne was the only one who could get here fast enough to drive me to the hospital. Shadow was about an hour south of Tampa, working on something for the club, but his mom was able to make it in ten minutes. Gary drove us to the hospital, while Daphne sat in the back seat, holding my hand and video calling my mom so she could see me before her first grandson arrived.

"Hi, gorgeous." Daphne hugs me close. She is a

stunning woman, in fantastic shape, and looks more like a Hollywood actress than the mother of a full-grown man. Shadow stopped buying his mom groceries after we told them I was pregnant. Instead, he and I go over every other week to have dinner with his mom and her husband, Gary. "Is your mom here yet?"

My mom and Daphne have become as close as sisters. Since Daphne and Gary live just up the road on the same river as this house, I see them almost every day. Daphne will stop by after work to check in on me, give me time to shower or nap while Shadow is off with the club. She makes a special effort to include my mom in every visit.

It's all weirdly working out way differently—and way better—than I'd ever imagined.

Daphne and Gary hustle off to find Mom and the baby, and I'm barely able to close the door before the first van, with the club members and their women, arrives.

"Party bus." Jackie is the first off the van, and I shake my head. She looks lovely in her plain black dress, even though we told everyone to just wear jeans or casual clothes.

We got married last summer before little Johnny was born, in a courthouse ceremony with just our parents, Ivy, and Phantom. This is a vow exchange, a small commitment ceremony that our friends insisted we have. Since I was enormous and still miserable with morning sickness—which did not end just because I was happy, having great sex, and no longer in the first trimester—Shadow and I didn't take a babymoon. Now that little Johnny is three months old and I've pumped enough to feed him through the weekend, my parents and Ivy are going to stay here and care for the baby for two nights while Shadow and I go stay at a local resort for some pool time, massages, and uninterrupted sleep.

Well, our sleep will probably be pretty darned interrupted. Since I am clear to have sex again, I'm thrilled to have a couple of nursing-free hours to sleep with my husband—in every possible way.

The bikers file out of the van and take their places in the folding chairs that are set up in the sunroom. Stella comes over to me, her eyes wide. "What the hell, bitch. You're not even close to ready."

I smile, totally unworried. Stella picked out a dress and shoes, which are lying on my bed upstairs. I'm showered, so all I need to do is change my nursing bra to something more suited to the strapless design, and I'll be good to go.

"I'm fine," I tell her. But she grabs my hand and drags me through the house, calling Ivy's name.

My little sister meets us as we're headed up the stairs.

"Your sister needs hair and makeup. Let's go."

My sister follows Stella, and I just shrug, not really caring if I have hair and makeup. Today is a party. A chance for everyone to get together, for the families of our blood and our hearts to come together. To spend time with little Johnny. And to celebrate with us. Whether I have lipstick on or baby spit-up on my shoulder, it's going to be an amazing day.

An hour later, the prospect known as Jizzy—his real name is Dylan, and now I can never not think of him as Dylan—knocks on my bedroom door.

"Photographer's here!" he yells. "You wanna let her in?"

I whirl on Stella. "Who hired a photographer?" I ask. "We agreed we were just going to let our families take pictures with their phones."

"It's your wedding present from the club bunnies," Stella explains. "You should have pictures to capture the first day of the rest of your life."

I smile, warmed by their generosity. "I think the first day of the rest of my life was the day I met all of you," I say.

"That was a great day," she says, giving me a hug. She opens the door and barks orders at the photographer, a cute young woman who takes her work very seriously. She poses me, my dress, and calls up the parents for some pre-ceremony pictures.

Finally, we're ready.

I kiss Daphne and my mom, and I hug Ivy and Stella. Then they all head down the stairs while I take a moment in the room I share with Shadow. I look in the mirror.

So much has changed about my life. A year ago, I was terrified, alone, on the run from a man I didn't even realize was stalking me. I had high hopes for the future, but a detour on my path derailed every single plan I had. I could not be more grateful for storms, for unexpected journeys, and for the destination I never even knew I wanted to reach.

As I walk down the stairs of the home I share with my husband and son, I feel every eye in the sunroom on me. Music is playing from a small portable speaker, and my dad is waiting at the foot of the stairs to walk me down the short aisle through the folding chairs that leads to Shadow.

Holding my dad's arm, I hear the click of the photographer's camera, and I smile without even having to try.

I'm so, so happy.

I have everything I could have ever wanted—and so much more.

I stop when I reach Shadow, who is standing with Johnny in his arms. Phantom, who arranged for the minister to come to the house for this ceremony, stands apart from the folding chairs, looking over at the bikers, the women, and the river.

I frown when I see the baby. "What happened to his tuxedo T-shirt?" I ask Shadow.

Shadow shakes his head. "Spit-up. A big one." He leans close to me and whispers in my ear. "Don't yell at me for this. The onesie is a gift from the club."

Shadow holds our son to show me he's wearing a white onesie with a motorcycle printed on the front. The text on it reads, *I'm proof a bike isn't the only thing my daddy rides.*

I groan and cover my face with my hands, careful not to smear the makeup Ivy insisted on putting on me, but then I laugh. And I laugh so hard, tears leak out of my eyes, and a little milk seeps from my nipples. Perfect. Real. Honest. I couldn't imagine it any other way.

I kiss my baby's cheek, and he scratches at my face with a soft, chubby hand. He's so gentle and sweet, and he's very much at ease with his father, our parents—everyone at this point. I hope he always stays so mellow and happy. Smiling is a new thing, but he does it often. And I feel like he's doing it now.

Shadow juggles Johnny in one arm and takes my hand with the other. "You look beautiful, sweetheart," he whispers, loud enough that I'm sure the minister hears him. "I can't wait to smear that makeup and mess that hair."

I laugh and rest my head on his shoulder. "Same," I tell him. "Now, let's get married and have a party."

As the sun sets over the river, it casts a beautiful golden

glow over the sunroom. Shadow and I exchange simple vows, and my sister reads a poem she picked out just for the occasion. As a librarian, I approve of the choice, but it's Shadow who seems incredibly moved by her words. I notice him wipe a tear from the corner of his eye when she finishes.

After we exchange I dos, my mother takes baby Johnny, and everyone snacks at the buffet we had catered. The van to take the bikers back heads out around seven. Mom, Dad, and Ivy have changed into pajamas and are playing with Johnny while Daphne and Gary remind them to call if they need backup.

Shadow lugs our overnight bags down the stairs and takes them out to the car. I kiss everybody goodbye and try not to cry saying goodbye to my baby for the first time since he was born.

"I'll be thirty-five minutes away," I tell Mom. "I can come home any time for any reason."

"I know, honey. I raised two girls who turned out pretty amazing. I promise I'll be smart enough to call if I think he needs his mama." She kisses me goodbye and then gives Shadow a huge hug, patting him on his broad back.

We leave after a few more rounds of kisses to our son's cheeks, and then I head for the new carport where my car is parked.

"Sweetheart, this way." Shadow cocks his head toward the garage.

I follow him inside, where he's got the GTO loaded up with our bags.

"No way," I tell him. "We're driving this?"

He pulls me close and leans me over the hood for a long, passionate kiss. "I thought if you had any second thoughts about leaving our son, we could shut the garage door, get dirty, and then go right back inside."

I laugh, kissing him back. "If you want to scar me for life, then yes, please have sex with me on the hood of your classic car with my parents on the other side of this wall."

But when he cups my ass and pulls me close, I half reconsider our plan.

"Do we still have condoms in the glove box?" I tease as we get in the car.

"Yeah, but I'm gonna toss 'em." He fires up the ignition. "I wanna fill you with as many babies as you can handle."

I hold up a finger. "Let's get through a few more months with the one we have before we work on any more, okay?"

"I love you, Violet Butcher," he says.

"I love you too, Johnny Butcher. So, so much."

We met in a storm, when the world was dark and terrifying and I couldn't find my way through.

Now, the future is spread out in front of us like an open road. No matter what lies ahead, I know I won't ever be scared again.

I won't be alone or lost.

Even if there is no sunshine, there will never be a darkness too great that I can't find my way through.

Not as long as I have my Shadow.

Thank you for reading Shadow's Protection and beginning the ride with Hurricane Heat MC. I hope you're ready for more because Phantom's story is about to make you **swoon.**

>> *Are you ready for Phantom?*
Visit ***menofinked.com/phantom***
to learn more and get your copy

Or turn the page to read the first chapter...

PHANTOM'S HEALING
CHAPTER 1

"Cameras are for show." Our point man for this deal, a guy I know only by the name Elliott, discreetly angles his chin toward the security equipment mounted above us. "System's not connected."

I shake the man's hand and search his eyes. "Right. We checked that out before we agreed to meet here."

He doesn't need to know how much intel we've done on this operation. He just needs to know that we have. This ain't our first rodeo, but it is our first moving this amount of product for this particular client. We don't normally meet, but for a job this big, I demanded an in-person location on a busy Saturday when the recycling center would be open with lots of foot traffic.

I'm supervising this gig. Viper, our enforcer, and Hawk, our road captain, are handling it with me while Savage is parked in a strategic position in case anything goes down.

None of us are wearing our club leathers or anything that could make us easy to identify later. Viper and Hawk look like they're dressed up for Halloween in soccer dad outfits. They won't exactly blend, but with their golf shirts, sunglasses, and baseball caps, they'd be tough to pick out of a lineup. That's all that matters.

Despite the summer heat, I'm in a long-sleeved button-down shirt that covers my tattoos, black jeans, and dark glasses that I only remove when I look Elliott in the eye. Elliott and I nod at each other, the CEOs of our respective organizations, so to speak. Then our guys get to work.

Savage and I walk back to our bikes and climb on, but we don't leave. We watch, taking everything in.

This job means a shitload of cash for the club. And when a job pays that good, there's always a reason. My guys are on high alert for any sign of cops, feds, or even the competition. We're not the only ones in town who want to be on the receiving end of a paycheck that's going to be this big.

Even still, not one of us wants anything to go down that could land us in lockup. Or, in my case, back in.

It was one thing going away when my daughters were little. They didn't understand why Mommy and Daddy didn't live together or why sometimes Daddy had to go away for months—even years—at a time. It was normal for them, and they just lived it, spending Father's Day visiting me across a table with more supervision and cameras than a reality TV set.

But they're teenagers now. They know what it means if Daddy gets arrested. Convicted. *Sentenced.*

I don't give a fuck what happens to me. Sometimes in this life, the juice is worth the risk of the squeeze.

But the older my girls get, the more I realize that nothing is more important than being here for them. And I don't just mean alive—I mean not behind bars and being free.

I've got a bigger plan in mind, and while this deal is probably the worst possible way to go about it, the money we make is money I need if I want to get my girls for good this time.

Taking care of Shayla, though, has proven a longer and harder job than taking her out would have been. But I'm not that man. I don't hurt women or children—not unless they come for me and mine and ignore a clear first warning.

I give nobody second chances.

One of the reasons I'm here today at all is so I can take care of Shayla and my girls the legal way. The right way. And there's no chance I'm letting that plan go to shit. No matter what.

A sudden buzzing breaks through my focus on the handoff taking place in front of me. When I'm on a job, no one gets through to me on my cell phone.

Nobody except my daughters.

I don't bother to check the first buzz of a text alert. I've got a special tone set up so I always know, day or night, if Holly or Daisy is trying to reach me.

But the first buzz is followed by a second. And then the damned phone starts ringing.

I swipe the lock screen and almost dismiss the messages until I catch a look at the text. I glare down into my phone, trying to make sense of what I'm reading.

"You got business?" Savage lifts his chin at me. "Take it. I think we're cool here."

I nod at Savage, my eyes never leaving the quiet transaction happening ahead. When they look about done, I scan the text from the unknown number.

> Holly: Dad, I'm borrowing a phone
> because I don't want Mom to know I
> messaged you. Daisy and I are in trouble.
> You've gotta come now.

Like a volcano bubbling before it bursts, my guts are churning before the blood turns to ice in my veins. Whatever the fuck is happening, I need to get to my daughters, and I need to get to them *now*.

I listen to the voice mail, which is incredibly hard to hear because Holly is whispering from some place that's noisy as fuck. She leaves an address and says to get there as soon as we can, or to call this number when I see the message.

"You got this?" I shoot Savage a look.

He nods slowly toward Hawk and Viper, who are discreetly putting bags of aluminum cans inside the covered bed of a pickup truck instead of dropping them here. A couple of those bags will have cans filled with a product my guys have been hired to move. The rest are just normal, nothing to see here, empty cans gathered up for recycling. The only difference is we're taking them out of the recycling facility when we leave.

"Looks like they're about done." Savage nods.

I make eye contact with Elliott, who's playing point on this deal, so I make my presence and authority known. I may be leaving, but I'm far from uninvolved.

Then I fire up my bike. "Any problems, you handle it any way you want." I glare at Savage, and he grins.

"Wouldn't have it any other way."

I know he'll handle this shit. He's been by my side, at my back, or even in front of me, taking heat since he patched in to this club.

Savage is ex-military and has the most time in legit life out of everyone in the entire club. He is the one I trust to run into trouble first and not to look for a way to save his own ass. He's got more than just the drive and the loyalty. He's got training, guts, and passion.

"I'm out," I say before peeling out. If my kids are in trouble, no amount of money or danger will keep me from getting to them.

I head for the address my daughter sent, trying my best to keep myself from blowing every light and running every stop sign. Holly gave me no clue what kind of trouble they are in, but this isn't the first time my kids have used someone else's phone to reach me.

To say the situation with my ex-wife is complicated would be putting it mildly. The power could be cut at the house. She might have left the kids alone with no dinner while she's off with her latest fuckboy. Or there could be something more twisted that my brain couldn't even dream up. Shayla wasn't always the person she is now. Fuck, maybe she always was and I just didn't see it... didn't want to.

All I know is, the sooner I get my girls away from her, the better.

I race into the small parking lot at the address Holly sent me and drive toward the only building with lights still on. It's not even dinnertime, but it's Saturday, so most of the businesses are dark. I head for the glass door and yank with such force I'm surprised I don't pull the thing off its hinges.

I storm into the place and immediately see my girls. My vision goes red, and I blindly run toward them.

"Come here." I open my arms, and they both jump up and run toward me. They tackle me in a bear hug, and I close them in tight, relieved as fuck that no matter what trouble they are in, they are alive. They don't look hurt. They're okay.

As soon as the hug ends, the adrenaline kicks in. The girls both start talking over each other, but I'm scanning the premises for threats.

"Dad, we're so sorry—"

"Dad, Mom wanted us to—"

I hold up my hand and take in the scene. The first thing I see is a woman. A stunningly beautiful woman whose intense stare makes every inch of me take notice. She's got long, dark-brown hair curled and styled to perfection. But she doesn't look stiff or made-up. Her full lips are glossy, and she wears sparkly makeup around her big brown eyes.

I look around, but I don't see Shayla and, even more bizarre, the place looks calm. Holly and Daisy go back to sitting on a plush tan love seat covered in cream pillows. The woman is sitting in an armchair that looks fancier than anything I've ever owned. Her legs are crossed, and she's sipping tea.

I can tell from all the sinks and shampoo bowls that I'm in some kind of beauty shop, but there are so many plants and seats, this place looks more like a café or somebody's home. It's nice and all, but my blood pressure won't chill the fuck out until I know why I'm here.

"You said you were in trouble," I say, turning toward my girls. "What happened? Where is your mother?"

Holly and Daisy trade anxious looks. My elder

daughter is a lot more forgiving of her mom, and she just looks down at her hands. Daisy stands up and rushes back into my arms, her eyes filling with tears.

"Dad." Her words come spilling out so fast, her mouth pressed against my chest, that I almost can't understand her. "Mom brought us to this new salon for back-to-school styles and said we could get whatever we wanted. So, I got color, which is extra, because I've been doing the color myself at home—"

"Hold up." I reach for Daisy's shoulders and lean her back to study her face. There's no fucking way my kids would send an SOS because of a goddamn haircut. "You said you were in trouble."

"I think I can explain." The woman who's been noshing on lunch with my kids stands up and extends her hand. "I'm Poppy. This is my salon."

I look down at her hand skeptically, not sure if she's part of the problem or trying to help. I give her hand a quick shake, but I don't give her my name. She gives me an apologetic smile, and I notice tired-looking purple shadows under her eyes.

"Your wife—" she starts.

"*Ex*-wife," I correct.

She licks her lips and nods. "Ex-wife. Well, Shayla is new to the salon. She came in for services today with your girls and left without paying. I tried charging the card we put on file when she booked the appointment, but it was declined. I don't have any way of charging her for the services she got for herself and the girls today."

I must look confused because Holly stands up. "Dad, Mom left us here after her hair was done." She holds out her phone to me, and I read the group text she sent to both girls.

We're not paying that bill, so I want you to get the hell outta there and take an Uber home when you're done. I'll meet you there. Be chill about it. I don't need her calling the cops on us like that last place.

I nearly crush Holly's phone in my shaking hands, but I know how expensive the damn thing was. I bought it for her three months ago for her fifteenth birthday.

"Your mother tried to bail on the bill?" I look from Holly to Daisy. "She pulled that shit before?"

That's when the floodgates open. Daisy is in full meltdown. "Dad, yes, but it wasn't our fault. We didn't know. The owner of the last place called the cops on us and said if we didn't stay until Mom came back and paid, she'd press charges against all of us, including Holly and me. This wasn't our idea, Dad. We swear we didn't know."

Holly is deathly quiet, and when I look at her, she's too pale. "Dad, I tried to make sure she wasn't planning anything like that again. I asked her if she had the money this morning. But you know what she's like." Holly looks down at her feet and laces her fingers together so tightly, a knot even tighter forms in my gut.

Daisy points to the salon lady, still talking through tears. "Poppy has been so nice to us, Dad. She didn't threaten to call the cops. She didn't yell. She even bought us food because we've been here all day, and we were starving."

My kids, whom I pay everything for—child support and then some—were *starving* and had been dragged into some bullshit haircut scam?

"How much is the bill?" I ask, keeping my voice as calm as I can until I have all the facts.

"Let me get the total." Poppy gets up from her seat and

walks to the back of the salon, where I see a counter and a mounted tablet that doubles as a mini cash register.

Goddamn it.

This is the worst time to notice, but this woman is fucking gorgeous, and Shayla is proof that I don't have the best track record of finding the good ones.

As I watch her walk across the salon like she's strutting on a private runway, I can't stop my mind from imagining those long legs wrapped around my neck, all that hair sweaty and tossed across my pillows.

I tug on my beard and try to ignore the way my fingers itch to cup her full ass. She's tall, stacked, thick, and... *Fuck.*

I turn away from scoping out this woman and lower my voice to talk to the kids. "You're really all right? Other than being hungry and your mom running out on the bill, you're safe?"

Now that I'm with my girls and I know I'm going to fix whatever's got them in a panic, my blood pressure is dropping.

It's damn hard not to stare at Poppy's perfect ass in dark black jeans and the long waves of hair that almost reach her waist, but if there was ever a perfect distraction from a beautiful woman, it's my kids.

Holly nods and Daisy sniffles. "Dad, you don't know how bad she's gotten. Mom left us here and didn't care what happened. What if Poppy had called the cops? That last lady wanted to have us arrested, Dad. We're just kids. What would have happened to us?"

At my daughter's fear and pain, my vision goes dark with rage again. I've been locked up. Arrested. Searched and booked. Abused and neglected. There is nothing, and I mean nothing, on this green earth that I wouldn't do to protect my kids so they never know that kind of shame and powerlessness. I'm strong mentally and even more so physically, and God knows I've made a lot of bad choices —still do. Part of playing the game is paying the price, and I've paid dearly.

But this... Shayla setting up my daughters like this... Not once, but twice.

"When did this happen before?" I bark. I need to know. Not because it matters right now, but it matters in the long run to my plan. "Forget it. You can tell me later. Did your ma pay that other place?"

"She did, but that was the worst part," Holly says, her cheeks still looking too pale. "She had the money, Dad. She was just... I don't know. Trying to get away with something."

The dull echo of Poppy's heels on the floor pulls my attention back to her. My body ricochets from rage to lust as she offers me a device, her soft hand touching mine as she hands the tablet over. I grit my teeth and will myself not to act like a horny teenager, and I look down at the itemized bill. The total has so many zeros in it, I about shit myself.

"This is for haircuts?" I sputter. I'm not excusing Shayla's shit, but maybe she was the one getting scammed.

Poppy nods, the long curls of her hair bouncing. "Shayla had a full-head highlight, cut, and style. That service can start at three hundred for a senior stylist, and there is a slightly higher charge for long hair." She looks me over like she's trying to figure out if I'm going to fight her. "Then the girls..."

I do the math in my head, and I guess it all adds up. I've been getting haircuts for as long as I can remember from the bitches who hang out at the compound.

After prison, anybody with a gentle touch and a willingness to do the job was my only qualification. It must cost a pretty penny to keep these plants alive and lush couches looking so clean.

"Dad, these are totally normal prices. The other place was even more." Holly's at my elbow now. "And we really should tip."

Tip? Sweet baby Jesus, no wonder the women at the club are all too happy to drink our free beer and eat our food. They must be broke on haircuts. I know what I've been paying for the girls' essentials, but this shit?

I drew the line this past summer on fake nails because that's a money pit I'm not ready to fall into for kids too young to hold down their own jobs. I'm going to have to work a lot more gigs like the one we had today if my plan to have them full time is going to work.

I blow out a long breath and hand the tablet back to Poppy. Her face shadows like she expects me to bail on the bill, but I reach into my back pocket and peel off a wad of hundreds—enough to cover the bill and food.

"Here." I am about to hand her the money when I turn to Holly. "How much do I tip?"

She grins and stands beside me, lacing her too-thin arm around my waist. "Dad, she took really good care of us before all this. The food, letting us call you. At least what you'd tip in a restaurant. If you pay on the tablet, you can pick a percentage if that's easier."

It's not easier. I don't leave a digital trail until I absolutely have to. I peel off two more hundreds and hold them out to Poppy.

"No, really, it's okay. You don't have to do that," she says, holding her hands up in front of her. "I'm grateful you were willing to take care of the bill. It's not just the materials, it's the time."

I shake my head, not needing to hear the details, and hold out the cash until she takes it. "You took care of my girls when their own damn mother couldn't be trusted to." I pull out my phone. "Is this your number? You let them use your personal phone?"

She nods.

"You keep my number in your phone. You see my girls on the schedule again, you call me." I sigh. "I'll cover it. No questions asked."

I turn to the kids. "What are we going to tell your mother?"

Holly's face drains of the little color that's left, and Daisy puts her hands on her hips.

"I don't want to go home to her right now. I mean, she literally drove off like no one would dare to arrest two kids alone. What if they did?" Her brave anger starts to crumple, though, and she looks like she's going to cry again. "Don't make us go, Dad," she whimpers. "Can we stay with you tonight, please?"

I open my arms, and both girls slam against my chest. I kiss the tops of their heads and notice for the first time how beautiful their hair looks. I stroke a big blue curl that falls along the side of Daisy's face.

"You got that here?" I ask her.

She beams up at me and nods. "So much better than the at-home dye Mom lets me use."

I look past my daughters' heads and catch Poppy staring at us.

"You did good work. If anything could make my girls more beautiful, it's this." I kiss the kids again. "This is what we're going to do. I'm going to message your mom that you told me you were getting your hair done, so I stopped by to see it. I won't say anything about the bill. I'll just tell her you asked to come crash with me for the night."

I don't say that this will, no doubt, start World War whatever we're up to now. Every communication with Shayla is like an act of aggression, but there's no way I'm sending the kids back to her tonight. She drew first blood by abandoning them in the middle of a fucking scam. I pull out my phone and shoot off a text to the bitch.

"Girls, thank Poppy for taking good care of you. I rode up here on my bike, so Shadow's going to come meet us with a pickup."

The kids start to gather up their dirty plates and cups, but Poppy shoos them away. "It's okay," she tells them. "I have to clean the salon anyway."

"Go on and wait out front," I tell them. "Make sure Shadow can see you. I'm going to talk to Poppy for a minute."

The kids thank her, and I notice Holly leans in like she wants to hug Poppy, and Poppy nods, then holds the girl close.

"We're really so sorry about this," Holly says again, her voice tight. "I hope you know it was never our idea."

Poppy puts her hands on Holly's shoulders and lowers her head to meet Holly's eyes. "You did the right thing telling your dad," she says warmly. "And I know you didn't mean to hurt me. Adult things like this are complicated, but it's okay. Now, I want you to put this behind you and feel confident with your new hair. Okay? If you want to come back, you are always welcome in this salon."

Fuck. Her words hit me like a boot to the gut. She's

smart. I'm so goddamn happy she said that about the hair. The last thing I need is for the kids to feel guilty every time they look in the mirror, walking around with a visible fucking reminder of what their mom is. What she tried to do to them. *Dammit all to hell, Shayla.* Fuck that bitch and the bullshit she puts on these truly good girls.

Holly and Daisy head out front, their pep almost returned to normal levels. Once we're alone, I turn to Poppy.

"I didn't say thank you," I tell her in a low voice. "This is a debt I can't repay, you being here for my girls." I search her face. "But I've got to ask. With a bill that big, why didn't you call the cops?"

Now that we're alone, I look my fill. Poppy isn't just attractive and well put together. Sensuality oozes off her in waves, and I don't know if it's just that I haven't shot a load in a while or if it's her full tits, generous ass, and long hair, but I'm again imagining all the things I'd like to do with this woman in a place far more private than this waiting area.

She meets my eyes, her big, doe eyes matching my intensity. "As soon as your girls got the text from their mom, I could tell they were not involved. They were shocked and so upset. All they kept saying was their dad was the best and he would take care of everything," she says simply. "I'm a mom. There's nothing I wouldn't do to protect my son. I wanted to give you a chance to make it right, and you did."

"And if I hadn't?" I ask, flicking an eye to her hand, and notice no ring but a small tattoo etched on her ring finger. "Would you have called the cops or sent your husband after me?"

At my words, her gaze drops. "I, uh, don't have a

husband. I'm a single mom. And I don't know what I would have done. I'm just grateful you made this easy. So, I should be thanking you."

That's not something I'm used to hearing. I'm used to people thinking I'm a fuckup. That I always choose the hard way, always go too fast, too deep, too everything.

"It says a lot about you," I tell her. "Beautiful, smart, and caring."

She blushes at my compliments, and the pink staining her cheeks only makes her that much hotter.

"I'm sorry about all this. Shayla wasn't always such a bitch," I tell her, shaking my head. "Maybe it's partly my fault. God knows I wasn't always the easiest man to be married to. I'm kind of a handful."

A smirk covers my face almost despite myself. I don't tell her that the work I do is far from legal. I just don't profit off the backs of innocent people. The men I deal with know exactly what game we're playing.

"I believe you are a handful." Poppy's words are breathy, with a hint of something more. The electric current in her voice travels through my body like I've stuck my finger in a socket.

We fall silent, the tension in the room thick and sensual as smoke. Then Holly knocks on the glass door, breaking the moment.

We both look up and see a pickup idling.

"That's my ride," I tell her, turning to leave. "Remember what I said. I'll cover their bill. No questions asked."

I don't know how soon they'll need to come back, but it won't be soon enough. Seeing this woman be so sweet to my girls moves something in me, something I've kept locked down hard deep inside. I turn away from it, from her, and head toward the door.

"You didn't tell me your name," she calls after me. "Or should I just put 'Holly and Daisy's dad' in my contacts?"

I stop at the door and look her over from head to toe, then back at her stunning face. "Phantom," I tell her. "You can call me Phantom." I'm about to leave when I turn back. "I'll be seeing you, Poppy."

She looks flustered, and I give her a grin before heading out to the lot, slapping Shadow on the shoulder, and handing him the keys to my bike. Then I get into the truck with my kids.

As we pull away, I look through the glass window of the salon. I see Poppy at the door, just watching. Before the warmth pooling in my gut makes me do something stupid, I look over my shoulder, back up the truck, and pull away.

>> Visit *menofinked.com/phantom*
to learn more and get your copy

A SEXY MOTORCYCLE ROMANCE SERIES!
It's time to visit the OPEN ROAD.

Book 1 - Broken Sparrow (Morris)
Book 2 - Broken Dove (Leo)
Book 3 - Broken Wings (Crow)
Book 4 - Broken Arrow (Arrow)
Book 5 - Broken Hearts (Eagle)

Also available in discreet paperbacks

Learn more by visiting
menofinked.com/open-road-series

BECOME A MEMBER OF THE FAMILY...

Want a place to talk romance books, meet other bookworms, and all things Men of Inked? Join Chelle Bliss Books on Facebook to get sneak peeks, exclusive news, and special giveaways.

Want to be the first to hear about the next Men of Inked book or everything Chelle Bliss? Join my newsletter by visiting _menofinked.com/inked-news_ or scan the QR code below.

LOVE AUDIOBOOKS?

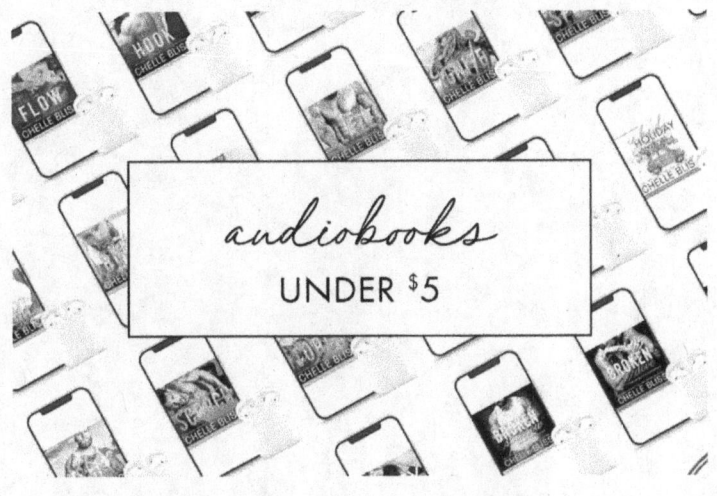

All audiobooks are only $4.99!

♥ Men of Inked Reader Guide ♥

*Visit **menofinked.com/guide** to grab the extensive Chelle Bliss Reading Guide, which includes a family tree, printable guide, and information about the Gallo family saga.*

ABOUT THE AUTHOR

I'm a full-time writer, time-waster extraordinaire, social media addict, coffee fiend, and ex-history teacher. *To learn more about my books, please visit menofinked.com.*

Want to stay up-to-date on the newest Men of Inked release and more? Tap here to join my newsletter or visit *menofinked.com/inked-news*

Join over 10,000 readers on Facebook in Chelle Bliss Books private reader group and talk books and all things reading. Tap here to become part of the family or visit at *facebook.com/groups/blisshangout*

Tap here to see the Gallo Family Tree or visit *menofinked.com/gallo-family-tree*

Where to Follow Me:

facebook.com/authorchellebliss1
instagram.com/authorchellebliss
bookbub.com/authors/chelle-bliss
goodreads.com/chellebliss
amazon.com/author/chellebliss
tiktok.com/@chelleblissauthor
pinterest.com/chellebliss10